The Dark Side of Sweet Dreams

Can another dimension help human beings to change their foreseen annihilation, or is reality an irreversible fate?

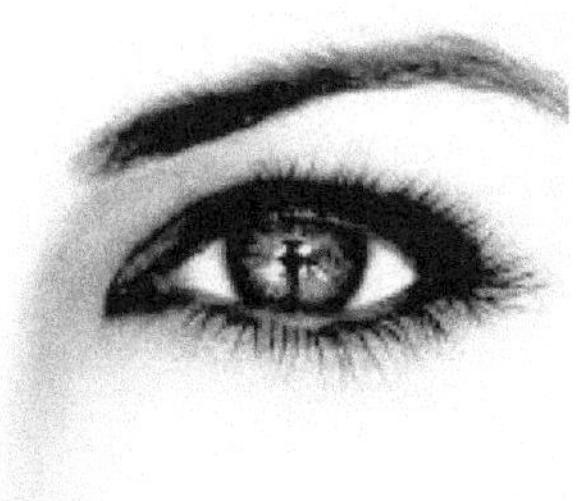

J.S. Alves

Dare to dream out of the darkness.

First Printing, 2017

Revised Edition

ISBN 978-0994967800

Published by Ideas Lighthouse
Ontario - Canada

www.ideaslighthouse.com

Cover design by Luiz Chanoski

CHAPTER 1 – Hello Earth

Feeling something moving over her legs, Clara instinctively stretched her bare arm to reach the lamp switch on the nightstand, turning on the lights. Slithering over the sheets a rattlesnake abruptly stops, lifts its head and coil its body. It opens its mouth while rattling, suggesting an imminent strike. Clara prompt pushed her body against the headboard in a vain attempt to get as far away as possible. She tried to scream, but no sound came out of her mouth.

The snake snuck forward, getting closer to her face while flickering its tongue as if it was whispering something. The reptile then moved back a little bit and exposed its fangs, readying itself to bite.

Clara woke up panting, finding herself sitting on her bed, and relieved to realize that there was no snake over the sheets. The sunshine filling her bedroom reassured her that it was morning already.

"Oh, thank God it was only a dream," she sighed while rubbing her eyes. As she prepared to get up, she heard a rattling sound, and screeched, jumping to the opposite side. Leaning over her arms, she cautiously looked down beside her bed, to realize that the rattle was coming from inside a bowl of cereal she was snacking on the night before. Such noise was caused by the vibration of her cell phone against the grains. She quickly grabbed the phone and picked up the incoming call.

"Hi, Asha… oh, ok. I need to get dressed, come in," Clara said, walking up to the window and waving to Asha who was by the front gate. Asha was her American friend and was in Chile for a student exchange program.

"So, are you ready for ten-hours hiking?" asked Clara after opening the door and giving Asha a kiss on the cheek.

"I'm very ready!"

"Ok, give me a few minutes to change my clothes," Clara replied, as she headed back to her room, followed by Asha. She took off her pajamas and quickly put on her faded Capri jeans, a white t-shirt, and black tennis shoes.

"So, have you talked to your friend from the observatory? Can we tent inside the premises overnight?" Asha asked while tying up her hair in front of the mirror.

"Yes, we can, but we need to wait for the station to close. They have free tours on Saturdays, and they have to work until ten o'clock," Clara answered, and came by Asha's side to apply sun protection lipstick.

"That's fine, at least we can have a safe sleep."

"Oh yeah, and I need a good sleep because last night I had a freaking nightmare," Clara replied.

"You do look tired, what kind of nightmare?"

"Snake, I dreamt about a snake. Anyway, I'm glad it was just a dream. Let's go," Clara said, grabbing her backpack and heading towards the door.

"Yikes, I hate snakes," Asha replied, wrinkling her nose and shaking her head while following Clara.

"I can't stand snakes, and it was in my bed, a disgusting rattlesnake. I was so terrified that I got paralyzed. Oh, I don't even like to remember," Clara said, putting her right hand on her forehead. She had no idea that her dream was actually a premonition about something supernatural coming to her life.

"Let's change the subject then. How long we need to walk until we reach the foot of the hill we are challenging?"

"About two hours," Clara answered, and they started to walk down the road.

The walk under the scorching sun of Chilean summer was a challenge, particularly for Asha, unfamiliar with hot weather. They arrived at the observatory a little bit before closing time, and Asha decided to joy the last free tour, while Clara chose to stay outside the building.

Exhausted, Clara sat on a small flat rock and looked at Santiago city lights, twenty-five miles away. *Why did I dream with a disgusting snake? It can't be something pleasant,* she ruminated, recalling the dream from the night before.

The wondering moment was interrupted by a car filled with rowdy people arriving at the station entrance. *They are a little bit late, the visiting hours are almost over,* she thought while looking at her smartphone clock. Asha was still inside the building, so Clara had no choice but to wait. She looked down the hill and saw the lights of a couple of cars making their way up to the observatory.

"What the heck, these people should know that the station is about to close in one minute. Why are they coming at this time?" She asked herself.

Later on, Asha came out and sat beside Clara

"A bunch of drunk guys came in looking for trouble, so I decided to end my tour. By the way, I met your friend, he was guiding the tour, and he's hot," Asha said laughing and elbowing Clara.

"Yeah, I know, but he's just a friend. Why these people came at this hour? The station was about to close," Clara asked moodily.

Asha pulled a smartphone from her pants pocket, typed something, and then gave it to Clara.

"This is the reason," Asha said, pointing to the screen "those guys who just arrived were told that the media is flooded with news of an outer space radio signal. They got some coordinates from the internet and came to the station to use the telescope, to look at the area where the signal is coming from. Of course, they won't be able to see anything, but you know humans, we need to believe in something, and at this moment something is coming from outer space," Asha said pointing to the sky.

"Here it says that the signal comes in precise intervals. Let's listen to the audio file," Clara said while scrolling the screen up and down, and then clicking on a file.

"That's interesting," Clara said, listening to the recording over and over, "It sounds like those laser gun shots in slow motion. How do they know it's coming from outer space?"

"Apparently, it was confirmed by some reputable international space agencies," Asha answered.

They waited for fifty minutes until everybody left. Once Clara's friend closed the station gate, they were able to set up their tents and headed for an expected night of sleep. The next day would take another ten hours to get back home, and that was the end of Clara's weekend. On Monday another normal week was waiting for her, and on Friday, she was turning twenty-four.

#

"Today, the United States, along with the European Union, would like to confirm some news vastly reported by the media around the world," said the NASA administrator. The silence in the press briefing room was palpable.

"After careful research, we are pleased to confirm a signal coming from an alien civilization outside the solar system."

The audience remained silent and without a single sign of excitement.

"The space agencies involved in this research have confirmed that the radio signal is clear, coded, and it isn't generated by known natural sources, which suggests that, whoever is sending it, has the same level of technology we have, or even higher. We will take a few minutes to answer just a couple of questions. Further and detailed information will be available on the NASA website," said the speaker, feeling the apathy coming from the audience.

"First question… Mr. Smyth," said the NASA administrator, after watching some people raising their hands and pointing her finger toward a journalist sitting in the first row.

"Mrs. Lumber, we are aware that the signal is coming in multi-frequencies. Have we decoded the message carried by the signal?"

"You are right, the information comes in multi-frequencies, which suggests that it was purposely built to reach intelligent alien life, but we haven't decoded the signal yet, and we are reaching out to the scientific community for contributions," She then moved her arm to point to another journalist in the fourth row for the next question.

"Have we located where exactly it is coming from, like a planet for instance?" asked another journalist.

"I can confirm that it is coming from an area near a star in the Sagittarius constellation. Next question, you," said the administrator, pointing at a journalist wearing a floral shirt, "You look ready for summer, so am I," the audience laughed a bit.

"Will we try to contact them?"

"We need to decode the signal before taking further actions, we can't take for granted that it's a welcome message. After that, we need to check if NASA has the resources, and technology to take other steps, like contact, or even reach the source."

"Why did NASA take so long to inform the public? This signal has been around for a while already. We, American journalists, feel embarrassed by deploying news issued by foreign agencies," said the same reporter.

"We need to provide credible information, and without following the protocols, we could have jeopardized the good reputation we have. You know that speculation can quickly provide fuel for conspiracy theories."

"But how did the eastern agencies get reliable information way before us?" asked another journalist.

"As I said, we need to follow the protocols. We are also open for contributions to decode the message, which might contain significant information for the scientific community. I'm sorry, but we are out of time. I'll close the question period now, and we will keep you posted, have a good day," said the administrator, and left the room through the curtains right behind the pulpit.

#

Clara wasn't excited about her upcoming twenty-fourth birthday. She finished college two years ago but hadn't made new friends since then.

Living with her dad, since her mom died six years ago, had been a boring routine, and she was aware he was trying his best. His life consisted of work, a glass of wine here and there, and weekly visits to his mother, who was living with his sister Maria, two blocks down the street. His hair turned gray, and he was marked by an ever-present sadness since his wife passed away. She died in an accident when the arm of a mining excavator struck her head while she working underground

Clara's light-brown, straight hair, and light-green eyes, were in harmony with her smooth, tanned, skin. And, although her five-foot-five height was common for Chilean women, she dreams of being taller and having long, curly hair, way below the shoulders.

Living in the suburbs of Santiago, Chile, was not easy. She spent almost four hours a day between subway and buses, to get to her job at a college. The financial commitment to cover her student loan, cell phone, and food, on the top of the transportation costs, was draining her resources. What made her feel even worse, was the occurrence of people taking their own lives, using the subway tracks. It seemed that all her emotions became more intense after she saw a person jumping on the train tracks in front of her, while she was waiting for the train. The scene was gruesome, and she couldn't erase the picture of the train striking the woman. It conjured up an image of her mother being hit by the arm of the excavator.

Complaints aside, she was aware that the quality of life in her country was not as bad as it could be. Having foreign friends on her social media, she was mindful of the fact that some were in a worse situation. Many of her friends did not have a chance to go to university, most were unemployed, and had no prospects for the future. Although she liked her country, she was committed to moving to the United States, after finishing to pay her college loan. Her aunt, who lived in Miami, Florida, was her ticket to fulfill her dream.

It was her birthday, and it seemed like any other day, except that she got some phone calls from her best friends. Dad wasn't the type of a guy who enjoyed celebrations, yet he left a cute card, along with a one-hundred-dollar bill under her coffee mug before heading to work that morning. The gesture brought tears to her eyes because the money was a sign that he was surrendering of Clara's idea to pursue her dreams. It was a huge sacrifice, for him, to see her moving away after losing his wife.

Work on Friday ran as usual, until the end of the night, when some of her co-workers invited her to go out with them. They usually went out on Fridays, and she often opted out, as she liked to get up early on Saturdays, to go hiking in the mountains around Santiago.

"Hey, Clara, what's up? Where's the party at tonight?" Carlos, one of her co-workers, asked.

"I'm fine, but no party for tonight, I'm going home," she said smiling.

"What? No way. Come on, it's your birthday! This happens just once a year," Carlos replied.

"I can't, the subway only runs until midnight, and it's ten thirty already, so it isn't going to work," she tried once more.

"Hey, I can give you a ride. There, problem solved." Carlos said with a grin, "Also, some students from the business course are going as well. It's gonna be fun, come on!" he insisted.

"Ok, let me call my dad," she said, grabbing her cell phone.

"Hi, dad. Listen, I was thinking about going out with some friends to celebrate my birthday, but I'm concerned about getting in late, and waking you up… well Carlos, one of my friends, says he can give me a ride… no, we don't know where are we going yet, but I can call you later and let you know. Ok, bye dad," she said, hanging up the phone.

"Ok, let's go. Where are we going?" Clara asked.

"Yes! It's gonna to be quite a celebration. Let's go to this place on Vitacura. They have a terrace, and it's gonna be perfect for the hot night ahead," someone from the group suggested. Everybody agreed, heading off to their cars.

When they arrived, the place was crowded, and they had to wait twenty minutes to get a table for seven. They started with a round of beer. Clara was not used to alcohol, yet she agreed to have a glass and took occasional sips.

"Guys, did you hear that Americans detected intelligent life on another planet? It's gonna be awesome, and I can't help thinking about these aliens coming, and bringing some order to this shit. This planet is a mess," said Carlos.

"Bro, it gives me chills. I can imagine myself travelling in a spaceship," one of the women said.

"I don't think they are coming to rescue us from the mess we have created. I don't even believe that our generation will be able to see aliens. What do you think, Clara?" asked Rodrigo, a guy seated beside her.

"I dream about communicating with them one day, but right now I have other priorities. My head is in the clouds, but my feet are on the ground."

"Wow, she's a philosopher. I like that," Carlos said with a wink, "well, let's keep our feet on the ground and beer on the table. Waiter, one more beer!" Carlos yelled toward the bar.

Drink after drink, the four men, and the other two women were becoming louder and louder. Clara gave up her beer, having barely touched it, besides, she hated the taste of warm beer. As she pushed it away, she suggested that they should call it a night.

"Come on, the night is just beginning," Carlos said in a slurred voice.

"I'm sorry, I need to get up early tomorrow," she said firmly.

Rodrigo took Clara's side and said, "Yeah guys, I think we should go, besides I need to get up early as well, it's late for me," he said, looking at his watch, "I can't stay longer, but I can give Clara a ride home so you guys can stay longer if you wish," he added.

Carlos pointed to the others while counting "one, two, three, four… five, yes, I can fit everybody in my car so we will stay longer."

"Ok, thank you guys," Clara said while standing and waving to the group, "Bye everyone thanks for the night."

"Bye Clara, happy birthday," a co-worker yelled, watching them depart and adding afterward, "What a loser. She didn't even drink her beer."

"What a waste," Carlos said, "Wait, did they pay for the beer?"

"No worries," one of the women said, "Rodrigo left money with me, so I'll pay their share."

Clara felt relieved after leaving the bar, and she was about to get into Rodrigo's car when she freaked out, "Oh my God, I forgot to pay for my share."

"Don't worry, I took care of it already," Rodrigo said while starting the engine.

"I'm sorry, I'll pay you back," Clara said, now inside the car.

"Oh, don't worry, I'm pretty sure it was less than a million-dollar bill, and that I can handle it. Where do you live?" Rodrigo asked.

"Oh, take eastbound, I'll give you directions when we get closer."

"So, do you have to wake up early as well?" Rodrigo asked.

"Well, I don't have to, but I want to. I go hiking every Saturday, sometimes even for the entire weekend."

"Really? Wow, that's a commitment."

"It's not a burden. I love it, and I wouldn't trade the view from sitting on the top of a mountain for a glass of beer. Contemplating nature is my drug. I get a natural high," she said with a smile.

"Wow, is that good?"

"It is for me, and it's usually peaceful, except..."

"Except?" Rodrigo asked, impatient about the hesitation in her voice.

"Well, once I was camping with some friends. It was late-night, and I decided to climb a little hill near the campsite, just to have a better look at the city. Right behind the hill, a kind of dim light appeared in front of me. It was the size of a small car and stopped about ten feet away. It stayed for a few seconds, and then it moved around me, like if it was scanning. After completing a full circle, it went away fast, disappearing. That freaked me out, and I went downhill as quick as a flash," she said and giggled.

They were about to get on a ramp to access the freeway when they had to stop at a police checkpoint. The stop was a standard procedure during the weekends, so police could check for those driving under the influence.

"Your driver's license please," the cop said to Rodrigo, "have you guys being drinking?"

"Less than a glass of beer," Rodrigo answered, looking into the police officer's eyes.

"Who is the woman?"

"She's my fiancé."

"Ok, you can go," the officer said, handing back Rodrigo's document. They were released, but couldn't move because there was a car in front of them, still to be released.

"Hey, I am officially your fiancé, and I didn't even know it," Clara asked, making fun of Rodrigo for what he had said.

Rodrigo looked at her, and moved his head for a kiss, slightly holding her head, but she put her hand between them, stopping him.

"Hey, hold on!" she said, puzzled.

"Well, let me say that if we are engaged, there is no problem with us kissing each other," Rodrigo said smiling.

"Well, we aren't engaged, not even dating," Clara argued.

Rodrigo was silent for a minute.

"I'm sorry, I just took for granted you wanted to... it won't happen again," He said and drank some water from a bottle grabbed between the seats.

Clara was about to say something, but the traffic started to move again. Rodrigo drove for about six hundred feet but had to stop again, because of a traffic jam by the end of the ramp.

"Not again, what now?" He complained when, without warning, the ground started to shake violently. The power lines on the street poles began releasing massive sparks, while the cars in front of them were moving up and down as though they were on waves.

In front of them, a man got out of his vehicle and squatted down while holding onto his car door. He was frantically looking in all directions, as though trying to protect himself from imminent hazards. One electric pole came down and fell on the car in front of them, jolting the man three feet away, motionless on the ground. Then all the surrounding lights went out.

Clara had never seen a quake like this before, and she was scared to death. Glass shattering, Masonry falling from buildings, and car alarms going off just increased the panic. From the car lights in front of them, they could see the vehicles moving up and down to a rhythm that never seemed to end.

After what was only fifteen seconds, the shake appeared to fade. People got out of their cars, as another shake started. This time, it was far more violent, and even trees nearby were knocked down. After another fifteen seconds, the second shake stopped, but some small aftershocks continued, giving the sense that another quake was just about to happen.

Except for a few lights coming from some cars along the road, it was pitch dark. Dust filled the air while explosions caused by gas leak sounded all around. They could see the shadows of people passing by the headlights of cars, as they tried to escape the chaos. From the darkness, they could hear people crying, screaming as if in pain, while other voices called out for calmness.

Clara reached for her phone, to find that it wasn't working. She wasn't surprised though, because she was aware that communication in these events was almost impossible.

"Let's get out of here," Rodrigo said, opening the door. In front of them, they could see black smoke coming from the entrance of the tunnel, illuminated by the headlights of cars.

Rodrigo grabbed a shirt from the car trunk and a flashlight from the emergency kit. He ripped apart the t-shirt, soaked it with water, and handed it to Clara.

"Put it on your nose to breath, don't inhale the smoke."

He then grabbed her by the arm, to walk through the dark along the road, just in the opposite direction of the tunnel.

After walking back for about six hundred feet, using the same ramp they used to access the freeway, they reached the street they were on before entering the highway. The same police officers they had chatted with before, were now trying to help some wounded people, but the darkness was impeding their efforts.

"We need to find some water and a safe place to spend the night. There is nothing we can do right now," said Clara.

"I agree, we could put ourselves in danger wandering around in this darkness. The streets have some cracks that can easily hurt us so badly that we will be stuck here."

They started to walk with their flashlight pointing to the ground. At some point, Rodrigo directed the light to the other side of the street and stopped. They saw what used to be a convenience store next to a gas station, and people were streaming out of it through a shattered glass door.

"Follow me!" Rodrigo said to Clara. They made their way inside the store and spotted some people rummaging through the shelves, grabbing food and water, and it was exactly what they were looking for. Rodrigo and Clara managed to get some bottles of water, and stuffed some chocolate bars into their pockets. They knew looting wasn't legal, but they were aware it was necessary for them to survive.

They made their way out of the store, and after walking for another one hundred and fifty feet or so, they came to a fallen tree, finding in the branches a level of calm, and then sat, contemplative. There were no buildings around them, so they decided to stay put and make their next move for after the sunrise.

It was impossible to sleep; the ground was still rumbling with aftershocks and fire could be seen billowing out of some buildings in the distance. Barking dogs, car alarms, and the voices of people surrounded them, were increasing their discomfort. They could hear explosions in the distance, and the sirens of ambulances and fire trucks sporadically pierced through the air. A scream and some gunshots rang out further off.

"It sounds like hell," Rodrigo whispered in the dark. Clara shared fear in his shaky voice.

It was eight o'clock in the morning when they could finally see the havoc around them. Dense gray smoke filled the air, turning the place something surreal. A lot of buildings were intact, but many showed visible cracks, while others lay destroyed in pieces on the ground. People were frantically digging through the rubble, trying to rescue those trapped under the debris. Occasionally muffled voices called out, adding more stress to the frantic atmosphere.

People were passing by Clara and Rodrigo, apparently trying to get home, some stopped to ask for water. Those staying put were residents, unable to access their homes. Some were laying on the ground while others were examining the damaged buildings, dazed expressions on every face. The air was choked with irritating smoke, and dust covered everything.

Rodrigo and Clara started to move again. They knew they could be mugged for the food and water they carried so the sooner they got home, the better.

"Let's go this way. It's eastbound, and that's the direction of my house," Clara said, pointing to her right.

"Listen, Sara, I live in the opposite direction, but not far away. I think we should go to my place. I need to check on my parents and see if they are ok," Rodrigo said, avoiding eye contact.

"Oh no, no way, I have to reach my dad. I can't leave him guessing where I might be or even if I'm alive. I don't even know if he's hurt. I need to get home, and by the way, my name is Clara!" she replied angrily, still trying to make eye contact with him.

"I get it… I'm sorry, I'm not thinking straight, and I need to see my parents," Rodrigo said, shaking his head. He suddenly turned westbound, walking away from Clara.

"Wait! Are you crazy? We need to stay together," Clara yelled, surprised by his attitude.

"Sorry, Clara," Rodrigo said, turning to her, "I think you've been watching too many Hollywood movies. No, we don't need to stay together. We need to survive. We aren't in a fairy tale, this is real life. Good luck," he said, turning his back to Clara and making his way westbound.

Clara was speechless, watching Rodrigo walking way through the rubble. Suddenly, the sounds around her seemed to grow dim. *Water*, she thought, *I need water*. She grabbed a bottle from inside her shirt, gulping it down, sat on the ground and ate a chocolate bar, which helped re-orient her. She regretted not having something to eat the night before. Clara realized that she was probably breathing in smoke, so she opened the last bottle and again moistened her "mask" to help minimize the toxic effects. After a few minutes, she noticed her energy coming back. Her mind was clearing up, and Clara realized that she was probably better off without Rodrigo's company anyway. She stood up and walked eastbound.

Weakly, she walked for about six hours in the heat of the day, witnessing people looting stores, while police and soldiers tried to bring order to the chaos. Some buildings were still on fire, and many people called her for help, although, there was nothing she could do for them. By 3 o'clock she was barely able to keep herself standing, and decided to rest. Sitting on a fallen fence, everything faded away.

A strange tickling sensation slowly filled her consciousness. *Was I asleep?* Clara startled awake, yet she couldn't move right away. It seemed like her right arm was numb. She managed to open her eyes, but at first, could only see light shadows that slowly evolved into blurry images.

Sensing close to her, she heard a voice, "She's waking." Suddenly, Clara felt two hands grabbing her left arm, to roll her over, and she found herself flat on her back. Someone placed something like a pillow beneath her head, and she felt a deep ache inside as if something was burning, keeping her immobilized. After what seemed like five minutes, she managed to move her arm free. Clara saw a chubby woman in her fifties, dressed as a nun with another person beside her.

"Are you feeling ok, honey?" the woman asked in a gentle voice while making some signs to the other person, who nodded and left them.

"Yes… actually, no. Everything hurts, where am I?"

"Well," said the woman, receiving a cup brought by her companion and handing it on to Clara, "first try to take some sips of this tea, slowly please," she said to Clara, who moved to sit up. She took the cup of tea and drank it entirely, and the woman then handed Clara a bottle of water.

"Take it, it's yours, we found it under your shirt," still thirsty, Clara grabbed it and again drank the entire bottle.

"You've been in this place since yesterday afternoon," the woman said. "I think you sat on that fallen fence over there," pointing to a distance about thirty feet away, "you must have touched a high-voltage power line that came down during the earthquake. I was here and turned when I heard a sparking noise and saw you lying down on the fence. At first, I was scared, but by the grace of God, some firefighters were working nearby shutting down the lines, so they came to check you over for first aid. Your vital signs were fine, so they left you here with me, and headed off to help other people."

"Oh, this is a church," Clara noticed, looking at the small old brick building in front of her. There were many other people nearby, some sleeping, some moaning, others just chatting.

"Yes, as you can see, this is a church. People have spent the last two nights outside, in the yard, because everybody is scared to go inside. I slept inside, God knows when He is supposed to call me home, so I'm not scared," the nun confided in her with a kind smile.

"Where am I?" Clara asked "Which part of the city?"

"You are in Florida neighbourhood, honey. Not the American State, which is probably better off than we are here," She chuckled to herself.

"Florida?" murmured Clara, "So I'm not far from home!" she said with excitement.

"I don't know, honey. I don't know where you live," the nun replied, just as she heard someone calling her name and she excused herself.

"I'm close to home," Clara murmured and stood up. Her legs were responsive, yet a little shaky. Her entire body was aching, probably because she had been sleeping on the ground for so long. There was a long bruise on the palm of her right hand, which she surmised, was probably caused by the fallen power line. Clara opened her mouth to ask someone for directions when something vibrated near her thorax. *The phone!* She thought and search for it in the pockets of her jacket.

"Hello?"

"Clara? Clara, my daughter, are you ok?" her dad asked anxiously, his voice full of emotion.

"Yes dad, it's me. I'm ok, I just..." Clara's relief was interrupted by two beeps. The connection dropped, and she realized the battery was dead.

She tried to turn on the phone but no success, so she walked inside the church looking frantically for the nun.

"I need a cell phone. I was just talking to my dad when my phone died. I need a phone, please!" she begged the nun, eyes watering.

"Listen, honey. I'm not aware that anybody here is carrying a cell phone, and if someone does have one, it's probably not working. Please just calm down. At least you know your dad is ok. You can make your way home as soon as it's safe to do so," the nun suggested calmly.

But Clara was no longer listening to the sister. She called to someone nearby for directions and then ran toward home. After about a half block, panting and dizziness forced her to reduce her pace to a reasonable walk. She was tired and feeling disoriented when she finally caught sight of her local subway station. Abandoning all concerns, with renewed hope, and ran as fast as she could to reach her home.

About three hundred feet from home, she could see her father in front of their house. She ran toward him, and they hugged, tears streaming down their faces.

"Clara, where have you been?" her dad asked, holding her face between his hands.

"It's a long story dad, but I'm fine. Nothing much happened to me. I mean, compared to others," her voice trailed off as she remembered all she had seen. I'm alive because, it's not my time yet, thank God!"

"Yes, yes, thank God!" he agreed, kissing her forehead. "Come, it's almost dark, and there is a curfew in place," Clara's father said, and both got inside the house.

Clara found aunt Maria inside the home, but not grandma. Her dad reached out to her again, telling her that grandma had died, not directly from the earthquake, yet from a heart attack.

"Oh no," Clara said sorrowfully, as she clung to her dad and aunt.

"We buried her this morning in a public grave. The morgues have been overwhelmed, and there was no room for regular funeral services. The army has stepped in to help and even provided a simple requiem," her dad said and, downcast, choke back tears.

"But I'm so relieved you made it back, I feel alive again. Although we don't have electricity, running water and the food is running low, I have something for us," her dad said, lifting from the floor a cardboard box with some holes in it and a live chicken inside.

"I'll cook it for tonight," he said and headed to the kitchen with the box in his arms.

Clara went to her bedroom to take a shower and change her dirty clothes before dinner.

During the meal, Clara told her dad Maria and, all she'd been through since she had gone out with her co-workers to celebrate her birthdate.

"Wow, you are lucky that you were delayed at a checkpoint right before that tunnel. We heard that it partially collapsed and many people were trapped and died due to smoke inhalation or carbon monoxide poisoning. Even though you were struck by a power line, and survived that as well. Someone rescued, and took care of you," aunt Maria mused out loud.

"Yes… it is something like a miracle, isn't it?" Clara agreed, stopping for a moment and idling. She stared absentmindedly into space while holding her knife and fork. Amid all traumas and her single-minded race to get home, Clara hadn't had a chance to really consider all the events she endured and how many times cheated death.

They finished the meal and frugally divided the leftovers into portions to be eaten in the coming days.

CHAPTER 2 – The American Dream

IT TOOK TWO WEEKS, after the earthquake, for essential cell phone communication to be partially restored. A local mobile company executive announced, in a national television broadcast, that all mobile systems were down, and it would take months to have the service fully operational. This information puzzled Clara, as she had talked to her dad on her cell a day after the earthquake.

It took a month until an emergency traffic flow was placed throughout the city, and people were slowly returning to their routines. The earthquake was so devastating that it prompted other nations to offer aid. Although the power of the shock was extremely high, the preparedness of the city minimized the initial number of casualties. The biggest current problem was how the city would manage to care for a large number of people left homeless. Long-term housing was needed, as the public shelters were only a temporary solution. To help with the situation, the United States agreed to release permanent visas for Chileans who had relatives legally living in the US. The only condition was that families could prove that they have enough funds to support their immigrant relatives for a year and that they passed the security check.

The news came to Clara through a text message from her Aunt Mirna living in Miami:

Hi dear! It seems like your dreams will come true sooner than you expected.

What do you mean Auntie?

Haven't you listened to the news? Check the internet about the United States resolution for Chile.

What news Auntie? We don't have internet or landlines. It's going to take a while to get technology back.

Oh, I'm very sorry my dear. I didn't realize it. Well, our government will supply permanent visas for Chileans with relatives in America. Pack your belongings.

What? Are you kidding me? I don't believe you!

Have I ever lied to you, hon?

I don't know what to say.

Clara burst out of the house, to find her dad fixing the fence, and she told him the news.

"Dad, we are going to the United States!" Clara said, euphoric, holding the cell phone with both hands.

"What?" he said, frowning and laying down his hands, sweat dripped down his face, so he wiped it with his sleeve.

"Look!" Clara said, showing her dad the phone screen.

He just stared at her phone for a long minute before nodding his head. "Well, you better answer your Aunt," her father said, a smile poking at the corner of his mouth.

Hi… you there? her aunt texted.

Hi, yeah, I was telling the news to dad.

Ok, we are checking the process to get all of you guys here, but we still need to find a solution for transportation. The airfares from Chile skyrocketed after the earthquake, it's cheaper to get a ticket to the moon, LOL.

Ok, keep me posted, Clara texted.

OK, TTYL.

#

Two months after receiving the news, Clara and her aunt Maria were on their way to Miami. The trip was only possible by ship because they didn't have enough money to buy air tickets for both. They decided to spend fifteen days on a vessel sanctioned by the United States to rescue Chileans leaving the country. Clara used the time to improve her English skills through conversations with crew members. It wasn't exactly an easy task due to the amount of slang they used, but she was for the opportunity anyway.

"It was a good option to travel by ship, despite the crappy weather, isn't it?" Clara shared with Maria, at the promenade, gazing stars in one of the rare luminous nights.

"Yes, sometimes I think this isn't real, and I'll wake up and realize that it was just a dream."

"A dream…" Clara whispered and paused for a minute, "It's funny that you said it because, since the earthquake, I can't remember all days of my life. It seems that I have lived just some moments," she shared, looking still into the dark of the sea.

"Oh, that's ok, I don't remember every single day of my life either."

"No, it's not about remembering everything. I don't remember a thing about two, three days ago for instance. It's like I'm just living fragments of my life," Clara said frowning while looking at Maria.

"Oh, it must be a minor side effect of your ordeal during the earthquake. You'll be fine," Maria said, looking at Clara, tapping her forearm, and turning her head to the skies, gently dismissing Clara's concerns, and a minute of silence came between them.

"I wonder how dad is doing. Aunt Mirna and I did everything possible to bring him with us."

"He will be fine," Maria said, keeping her eyes on the skies.

"Yes, I agree. Dad would be better off staying in Chile for now, especially because he opted to move to the company's lodging near the copper mine, and he will have an opportunity to make new friends over there," Clara said and looked at Maria, but she kept quiet.

After a long time of silence, Clara accepted the fact that there wouldn't be a meaningful conversation between them, so she excused herself from leaving, and made her way to the bed.

CHAPTER 3 – The Novus Mundus Planet

"AS INHABITANTS OF OUR PLANET, Novus Mundus, we have had the privilege of continuous growth for more than seven thousand years, and built a unique connection with Mother Nature," Hallan announced. He was pacing back and forth in front of his audience, always gesturing with his hands. He was finishing the Day Seven message, as he had been doing so for the last ten years.

As the spiritual leader of his community, Hallan was feeling the pressure to keep the attention of those present. When he started the service in this community, his audience had filled the room with three hundred seats, now it was reduced to merely fifty members.

The view of the landscape, provided by the semi-circle glass doors surrounding the dome-like white building, always inspired him as he delivered his message. The construction, suspended thirty feet above the ground, oversaw the lush trees that gave way to the horizon. While speaking, he enjoyed the fact that he could observe the sunshine hitting the top of the trees, and he could feel the hot air filled with the sweet scent of flowers wafting through the open windows. The audience, however, wasn't thrilled.

"We have faced challenges and many issues in the history of our planet, yet we were able to avoid initiatives that would quickly destroy the place we live," he said, stopping in the center of the first row of wooden chairs. His back was to the audience as he stood facing the horizon.

"Look at this majestic sight," he said, stretching his right arm towards a chain of mountains ten miles away from them. "I believe that without collective consciousness, we could never have achieved the quality of life and level of technology we now enjoy."

Turning to them, he continued, "Do you honestly think that isolated we would be smart enough to overcome systemic challenges? Would we have the power to succeed without the combined use of all our hearts and minds?" Hallan questioned the almost-comatose audience. He was met with silence.

He again started pace in front of the audience, "We now face a new challenge: we have discovered a new planet outside of our system that sustains life. And it looks remarkably like our own planet.

"Apparently, this new world, nicknamed 'Sick Planet,' is encountering significant challenges. It is accelerating toward the destruction of its physical layer at an unprecedented rate. It might even ignite in total self-destruction. How this will affect us, we have not quite determined. The extent of the fallout is unpredictable, even for our level of knowledge. The annihilation of life on that planet can damage organic waves, thus interrupting our current capacity to listen to the entire universe," Hallan stated in a monotone voice.

"Next month we will have an opportunity to vote on a new bill that will increase the power of our government to fight this threat. The problem is that just a few people participate in these meaningful decisions and we might be ended up with decisions that will affect our own privacy and security.

"Choosing not to participate can have a disastrous effect on our society." Hallan pumped his fist in the air to emphasize his point, yet their disinterest remained palpable.

"I've been concerned that the Novus Mundurians's individualist lifestyle is destroying our capacity to build relationships and keep an active community alive. This lifestyle will affect the very survival of our society," he stopped now, and slowly moved his eyes over the audience.

"Although we are wealthy people and understand the need to live as a community, we have isolated ourselves more and more. Yet, we weren't meant to live alone. If left alone, we die. Spiritually and socially, we need each other. Together, we need to participate actively in crucial decisions to build a better world. Please consider this," he paused again, surveying their faces, then abruptly finished the lecture with weakness in his voice," see you next Day Seven, have a good day."

Gavriel sat through hallan's message, his mother intently listening beside him, but he wasn't moved by the spirited plea. The name "Sick Planet" caught his attention only because sickness isn't something he was used to thinking about as a sustained condition in Novus Mundus. However, he still wasn't much interested in matters about other planets. Their problems were their own.

Gavriel was more concerned about his upcoming mandatory military camp on the micro planet Acqua. This would be Gavriel's first camp in another world. Acqua had an artificially developed structure, exclusively for environmental experiments and armed forces training.

He had heard from other Novus Mundus acquaintances, about the different animals, and landscapes built with genes imported from other planets. He listened, as well, that some species had been scanned in from alien worlds and developed with local genes. They were domesticated, and, after their mission, recruits were lucky permitted to bring home one of the animals.

Everything Gavriel had heard about Acqua's environment was exciting to him. He was looking forward to holding a weapon in his hands for the first time, and this thought filled him with a mixture of excitement and curiosity, but if he was honest with himself, it also made him feel a bit uneasy.

In his eight Novus Mundurian years, Gavriel already reached his adult height. His mom was always comparing his six-foot frame with his dad's height. She never noticed that he didn't like to be reminded of his absent father. His appearance resembled his mom Cillia, and his short curly brown hair and multicolour eyes identified him as a typical Novus Mundurian.

Gavriel had almost finished his mandatory education provided by the government. He hated attending classes in the Universal Consciousness Development studies or UCD, but it was part of his compulsory training over the ten years. Fortunately, he might be able to spend the two last years working for the government, if he worked hard enough to be accepted into its ranks.

"Hey, did you get anything from the message today?" Cillia asked, trying to start a conversation on the way home. Mom was always like that, fishing her information from him, even when the floating car was whizzing on an airway, one hundred feet above the ground, but Gavriel remained silent.

His mom, Cillia, was, for the most part, patient and lovely, though she was prone to being strict during the spiritual service lectures to ensure he was paying attention to the message.

He didn't understand why his mom took spiritual life so seriously. Everybody studied the basics in early education years, but only a few carried on their religious matters for the remainder of their lives. To make things worse, he felt embarrassed when colleagues from his school mocked him for attending services. If the subject ever surfaced during the virtual reality games he used to play with his friends, he would never hear the end of it. Despite all the technology and resources available, he would always complain about what he considered a boring life regardless of academic stress.

"C'mon, something… anything?" his mom tried again.

He wasn't interested in long chats but knew that his mom wouldn't stop questioning if he kept mute.

"I don't get this thing about helping a decadent civilization. Why bother with a planet that is probably dozens of light years from us? We live on one of the best planets in the universe. For many generations, we kept the values that made this world outstanding among others. Why, all of a sudden, do we need to help planets that are not committed to our values?"

"Yes, but don't forget that we might be affected if that planet collapses," his mom countered.

"Well, I don't know… honestly, I don't care."

He didn't want to engage in this conversation, so he chose to rechallenge his mom over the subject of spiritual services, something that always worked out.

"If it is vital to attend the spiritual services, why are there just a few people every time? How can just a few bodies, that look lifeless, make a difference in the world? Can't we use this time to do something else?"

"Listen, baby," she replied in a stern voice, "many people decide not to go to the spiritual services maybe because they don't need government bonuses to pay their bills, the way we need. Understood?" she said and gave him a cold look.

"Fine," he replied in a low voice, and the silence in the air was deafening.

"Grandma is in our home cooking!" Gavriel said after a few moments of silence.

"What do you mean, grandma is in our home? She is working on Zyon right now, and you know that" Cillia said, acknowledging that he was trying to get away from the conversation, and the rest of the trip was made in silence, just the way Gavriel liked.

When they arrived at home, suspended thirty feet above the ground, Cillia landed on the parking spot. One second after stepping out of the car she could smell the sweetness of jelimon pie, and coffee coming from inside the house.

"Mom?" she said out loud and ran toward the kitchen to find her mother removing a pie from the oven, placing it on the kitchen counter.

"Mom, what are you doing here?" Cillia hugged and shook her mom's shoulder in a mix of excitement and surprise.

"I decided to come from another planet just to bake for you," teased her mom in a soft-spoken voice. "I'm assigned to another project here on Novus Mundus, so I thought it was a good idea to drop in for a surprise." She smiled and headed toward Gavriel to give him a hug.

"What's happened to my little boy? He has grown up and grown a huge beard," Theena said, as she scratched a puff of hair under Gavriel's chin.

Gavriel was able to connect with his grandma once in a while, yet he noticed that she had aged a bit since the last time they had gotten together. Theena was four inches shorter than Cillia, and her straight black hair was carefully cut in an oval shape along with her face, to cover some signs of ageing. Her skinny body and sunken brown eyes betrayed her efforts at maintaining a young appearance. She definitely looked a bit older than her fifty-nine years old.

"Mom, when did you talk to Gavriel? When did you tell him that you were coming?" Cillia asked.

"I didn't tell him anything about it, what are you talking about?" Theena said, turning again to Cillia.

"But... he told me that you were here, in the kitchen, cooking," and both faced Gavriel, who was now picking a bit of jelimon pie.

"I don't know. I just knew it!" Gavriel said, licking the tips of his fingers and shrugging his shoulders.

Mom and daughter looked at each other and soon forgot the unusual occurrence as they began to catch up with one another.

"Well, I know you must be hungry, and the best thing to celebrate our reunion is a cup of coffee with jelimon pie," Theena said, as she looked for the cups and plates to set the table. Cillia helped her to set it all up, and in a few minutes, they were sitting at the table laughing and enjoying each other's company.

"Why is it so hot in here?" Theena asked, looking around in search of an answer.

"Yeah, this season seems worse than last year. The green cooling system isn't able to bring down these scorching temperatures. You must feel hotter because you are always inside a stable, controlled temperature, am I right?" said Cillia.

"Yes, you are right. I guess we'll have to get used to it."

"So, grandma, what's the news? What do you mean you were assigned to another project?" asked Gavriel.

"Well, I'm pretty sure you guys have heard about the new planet we have discovered. It isn't entirely new, as we had its existence cataloged in our scientific files a long time ago. In the past, we sent some plasma screeners toward that system. We dealt with the data available, and everything looked beautiful as the planet began its development. Besides, the celestial body was very distant from our local system, therefore not covered by our space program policies and so little concern or interest."

Theena stood and checked the stove, and went on, "the difference now is that we have detected, from organic waves, that the planet developed too quickly for our standards, and is reaching alarming levels of deterioration that might affect the integrity of our communication systems," she said, coming back to the table. She grabbed a bottle of a golden drink and poured it into a glass. She knew Cillia and Gavriel didn't like recreational beverages, so she didn't even bother to offer.

"Mom, aren't you drinking coffee?"

"After my happy hour," she said, showing her glass.

"How can this planet affect the integrity of our communication systems? If it is as far away from us as you just said, how can it possibly affect us?" Gavriel asked.

"Hallan explained everything in our spiritual service this morning, but someone was totally zoned out," Cillia said, leaning her head toward Gavriel.

"Well, you have probably heard in your UCD classes that the universe isn't just a mass of goods for us to consume and shining stars for our gazing. We are aware that planets containing organic life are living bodies, and they communicate with each other."

"Yes, but still, this one is really far from us," insisted Gavriel.

"I agree, although our universe is so united and sophisticated that we can easily compare it to our bodies in which everything is connected. And how can we read this the information in real time?" Theena asked, pointing her left index finger to Gavriel again.

"Because it's proven that organic waves work in multi-dimension and defy our known laws of time and space," he said, rummaging through the fruit basket on the table.

"Exactly! So, if something is wrong with your body, and you don't fix it, other parts can be damaged, or you might even be killed, like cancer that spreads to the entire body," Theena explained.

"Cancer?" repeated Gavriel, raising his eyebrows.

"It is an ancient disease that was eradicated through genetic modification, do your homework and research," Theena replied.

"But how do we know that the collapse of that celestial body can affect our communication," Gavriel asked, as he bit into a triangle-shaped yellow fruit the size of the palm of his hand.

"Because we have scientific studies showing that organic waves have been interrupted a few times in the distant past, but since we don't have quantum information on the variables involved at those times, we can't predict the outcomes now. The data structure is immensely complex," Theena said.

After many hours of chatting, Gavriel made his way to bed while mom and daughter continued their conversation on a more sensitive matter.

"So how has been your life without Jacob, your useless ex-husband?" asked Theena, looking in Cillia's eyes, seeing the tears that were forming. Still, the question was inevitable; Theena knew that eventually, her daughter would have to get over the collapse of her marriage.

Cillia turned her eyes toward the ceiling and froze for a while until a few tears rolled down her face.

"It's been ok during the days, but the nights have been awful. I was not expecting a life-long commitment from him, but leaving us during Gavriel's early years was tough." Her gaze turned to her mon, "Anyway, I found supportive people in our spiritual services and peace in my life in a way that I never had before," Cillia finished her answer, reaching out to hold her mom's hands as more tears rolled down her face. "What about your new husband, sorry, I forgot his name," she said, sheepishly wiping her tears away.

"It's Jardnn. Don't worry, I don't blame you. He's my sixth husband. Maybe it's time to settle, move to a northern resort and just enjoy life. But you know, all these professional commitments always bring some noise to my marriages, and I can't see myself staying put. Jardnn is ok; six days ago, he decided to visit his eldest daughter. He is working on Zyon, just on the other side of the planet from where I work. He will probably be joining me here on Novus Mundus after I finish my set of meetings on the central station," Theena yawned.

"I'm tired now, and I need a shower." Slowly she got up from her chair, and then remembered, "Oh, I almost forgot, what exactly did you say when you came into the house? You said something like Gavriel knowing about my arrival?"

"Oh, nothing mom, I think it was just a … miscommunication. You know that Gavriel comes up with some nonsense once in a while. Anyway, your room is always ready for you. Have a good night!" Cillia said, kissing her mom's cheek.

"Good night sweetie!"

In his bed, Gavriel was stargazing, something he used to do every night, as he looked up through the organic glass ceiling. The coming of his grandma, even if just for a little while, was a good break in Gavriel's routine. There were a few reasons: firstly, she would be an excellent excuse to skip the spiritual services; secondly, she was a highly-rated scientist who knew about almost everything when it came to universe exploration, Gavriel's favourite subject. She was also an excellent cook, which made a difference in the house because his mom was not really into cooking. *It's gonna be a lovely time*, he thought, before falling asleep.

It was morning, and the micro monolith blinds opened automatically, waking Gavriel gradually by allowing the warm sunshine and the fragrance of flowers to fill the room. He decided to shave to avoid grandma picking on him about the beard, and afterward, he went to the kitchen for breakfast.

"Where is grandma? Is she still sleeping?" he asked, looking around.

"Hey, I'm here. Where are your manners? What about a good morning before starting the conversation?" his mom said, standing by the coffee maker while holding a cup between her hands.

"Hi, good morning," he replied grumpily.

"Grandma left for her work already, but I'm here to keep you company, as usual. So, we need to bring grandma from another planet to have the honour of seeing you shaved, you look so cute," Cillia said, noticing his shaved face, and pinching his cheek with her hand.

"Oh, C'mon mom, don't start. I had a weird night already, and I don't need a yapoo awkward start my day," replied Gavriel moodily.

"Ok, let's be clear about our rules; you know that I don't like swearing in this house and strongly recommend you keep your mouth clean if you want company. Now, what happened in your sleep?" she asked, sipping her coffee.

"Well, first, it was scorching, what's going on with this weather?" he said, looking at the sun hitting the top of the trees outside, and some houses far away. The distant neighbour houses, built above the ground, gave the impression that the green forest had giant mushrooms scattered on the surface of the planet. "Second, I don't know exactly why, but I just had this disturbing dream, it seems like it was all night long. I just remember this guy in a dimly lit place, looking horrible. He had kind of rough, dark skin, and he was wearing a hat, and was staring at me the whole time."

"Wow, it must be something you ate last night or the excitement of having the grandma with us or both," Cillia said, now grabbing a piece of toast coming from a machine before sitting on a chair by the kitchen island.

"No, I'm sure it wasn't because of food, it was like surreal, yet real… I don't know. It was weird," Gavriel said, scratching his head.

"Well, have your breakfast now, the droid got some fresh fruit from the garden, it will make you feel better."

When Gavriel finished his breakfast, he quickly stood up and headed toward his floating car parked a few feet away from the kitchen entrance.

"Bye, Mom," he said as he left.

Still sitting, Cillia watched him flying away in his Suphcar. Sometimes she wondered if it had been a wise decision to get married at the age of eight. Her natural curly chocolate-brown hair framed her face and highlighted her bright multicolour eyes. She looked young for her sixteen years old, yet she knew she must look noticeably downcast whenever someone brought up the subject of marriage. She eventually had to get over it, although she desired to jump in time and take a shortcut through the healing of her pain. According to the government policies, this was her last year of leave of absence, and soon she would have no choice but to start working again, which might just be the distraction she needed to get through this season of her life.

#

On his way to UCD studies, the vision of the man from the dream was still tormenting Gavriel's mind. He was jolted from his thoughts by an incoming video request from Lennah.

"Shoot, Lennah, how could I forget my meeting?" he said to himself, remembering that they had planned to get together one hour ago to work on their alien relationship assignment.

"Lennah, I'm sorry, I totally forgot about our appointment, my grandma just came from…" he began but was interrupted by his classmate.

"Don't worry Gavriel, I know you didn't do it on purpose. Relax, just take your time and meet me at the Skywalker Cafe as we had planned."

"Oh, ok, see you there in about a half an hour," Gavriel said, hanging up the connection.

"Yikes, just another load on my day and the day has just begun," he thought. The issue wasn't about missing a meeting in itself. No, he had to admit, he hated being late for an appointment with Lennah because he knew that this delay would mean extra time working with her as per the UCD policies. He was pretty sure she was hitting on him so she could report their relationship as an accomplishment to the UCD evaluation body. Graduating from UCD with a built intimate relationship accomplishment, boosted the chance of getting employed by the government, which was the dream for most students graduating from UCD.

Except for the difference in age and a chubby look, Lennah resembled his grandma, Theena. Besides, they had been classmates for a long time, which wasn't an appeal for a relationship, he thought. He parked his car and made his way to the coffee shop.

"Hi, Gavriel! What a beautiful look," welcomed Lennah as he entered the dome-like building with live exotic animals filling the place. She was quite happy about his shaved face.

"Hi, Lennah. Sorry again, my grandma just came from Zyon, and I crashed out very late last night," he said while heading to a coffee machine and coming back with a mug of the steaming liquid in his hand.

"Cool! I'd like to meet your grandma. I've heard she's sweet and seems to be a smart cookie," Lennah said excitedly.

"Oh, sure. Why don't you come over tonight, so we can continue our research? That way we can get this assignment done faster," Gavriel said, masterminding a way to finish the job faster than he initially predicted.

"Deal, I'm in! What about your research, did you get anything new for our Novus Mundus presentation? I can't handle going over and over the same subject."

"I wish. Honestly, it seems like this is brainwashing, because we've been studying this shit for years. Anyway, I made a summary, and I swear I didn't plagiarize," Gavriel said, noticing Lennah's smirk face.

"I didn't say anything," she rebuked, raising her hands in defence.

"Ok, here we go." Gavriel started to read his research, finishing ten minutes later with "…and the discovery of Low and High-Density Artificial Gravity technology, allowed Novus Mundus's population to explore and develop the planet. The discovery of organic waves allowed Novus Mundus to understand some mysteries of our universe. Our challenge now is to fully decode the waves to use it in full communication. Today it is limited to just listening."

"Ok, that's easy. It'll be my part of the presentation," Lennah said.

"What do you mean, 'your part' of the presentation?" he asked, raising his voice while opening his arms. "I'm supposed to research, and you're expected to present, that's the deal."

"Not anymore. Have you received the message from our master? We're meant to share the presentation, the idea is to learn to express our thoughts," she said, avoiding his eyes.

"What?" He said, searching messages on his files. "What the yapoo! Why this last-minute change? I'm not prepared."

"I know, sorry! Don't blame me, master's orders, we'd better comply," she said, her lips pursed together while looking up.

He just covered his face with his hands and took a deep breath. "I hate these short notice changes."

"Calm down, we can handle it, don't worry."

"Then the next set of information is going to be my part? It's too much," he complained.

"Don't worry, I can present part of your speech. Just go."

Gavriel looked down at the projected text, hands on his head and elbows touching the table.

"Novus Mundus is famous in our galaxy for its vast fields dedicated to agriculture. It is the primary food supplier for two nearby planets. It receives light from two stars, and two-thirds of the globe's surface is covered by salt water, concentrated on the North Pole. I think I need ice cream, it's hot in here," he said, changing subjects abruptly.

"Don't push it, you are trying to buy time, move on," Lennah urged, motioning for him to hurry.

"Two planets are located near Novus Mundus: Zyon, at the distance of two travelling days, and Sion, at the distance of half a Novus Mundus-year," he stopped and looked at her.

"Seriously Gavriel," Lennah said, putting her hands on her hips.

"Lennah, this is unfair, because I'm doing all the hard work. You should present this last part." He looked at her, but she was purposely looking away.

"No, that's it, I'm done. I'm not planning to add a single word," Gavriel said, arms crossed.

"Are you telling me that you've finished? Don't forget that we might have a strike if we don't get the minimum score," She said.

"I'm done, end of discussion. Did you go to that alien music festival?" He asked, changing the subject right away.

"Yes," she said, and they kept talking for about one hour. Afterward, they headed to Gavriel's house in their own cars, which they linked together so they could continue their conversation.

Once they got home, the sounds of grandma busy in the kitchen left no doubt, in either of their minds, that supper would be delicious.

"Hi, grandma, this is Lennah, my classmate. Lennah, this is Theena," Gavriel said, introducing them.

"Hi, pleased to meet you, sweetheart," Theena said, winking at Gavriel while giving her a quick kiss on her lips.

"Hi Cillia," Lennah said, leaning toward Cillia and kissing her lips.

"How was your day?" Theena asked.

"It was okay, but it was sweltering hot," Gavriel replied.

"So, are you guys up for a drink while we prepare food? It will cool you down," Theena asked, taking a bottle from the table.

"What are you drinking?" wondered Lennah, curious about the glowing golden coloured drink.

"Oh, it's from Sion, a new liquid extracted from some local roots over there. It's a kind of sensation in all Novus Mundurian gatherings. You should try it, it's delicious!"

"Ok, just a little bit please," Lennah suggested.

"I'll pass, thanks," Gavriel answered.

"So, let's cook! Gavriel, can you cut the vegetables, please? Lennah you prepare a sauce using these ingredients here. Cillia, can you please make some juice? I'll finish the fish," Theena oriented them, and in a minute, everyone was at the big kitchen island doing their part, busy with conversation.

"I'm excited to hear about your work, Theena. Gavriel is always sharing your accomplishments with our class," Lennah said while mixing some spices.

"Oh, thanks for your interest. I have to say that it is like any other job. Still, I do like what I do. I work for the Alien Life Development Department, and I'm responsible for implementing the environmental policies for long life sustainability in alien planets" Theena said, her voice changed as she struggled to remove the skin from the fish.

"Wow, it sounds exciting?" Lennah slurred.

"Right now, our government is trying to introduce Low-Density Artificial Gravity on Zyon. This technology will improve the connection between peoples so that they can occupy their land wisely. You know, Zyon is half of the size of our planet and has four billion people, which is the double of our population," She said while tucking her hair behind her ear with the back of her hand.

"Of course, we are not doing this work for free, so we are asking them to trade the artificial gravity technology development for Zxylon, a purple mineral they have in abundance in their soil. Zxylon is vital for the batteries we use in our Suphcars," Theena said and paused to sip her drink

"Now here's something that might interest you. The government will hire some students for a permanent job to help with this project, and you both have skills and prerequisites to join the program. You should apply," Theena said.

"I'll pass, grandma, I prefer to dedicate my time to the New Discoveries area, there's more excitement over there."

"I'm interested," Lennah said to Theena. Turning to Gavriel, she asked, "Wouldn't you consider this job, at least for a while?"

"Nah, I don't think I'd like it, even for a short time," Gavriel said, prompting a noticeable drop in Lennah's shoulders.

"Good for you!" Theena said as she looked at Lennah. "I'm about to receive further information about my project here on Novus Mundus, and that may open an opportunity for you Gavriel," Theena finished.

"It's about the sick planet isn't? Everybody is talking about it," Gavriel said.

"Yes, everybody is talking about it, yet we don't have much information right now. What we know, so far, is that it has a size three and a half times smaller than Novus Mundus. Also, it's supported by a star that provides the same amount of light we receive from our two stars and proportionally has the same amount of surface water we have. We know something of its organic composition, and we have a fair idea about the level of technology present on that planet."

The meal took two hours, over which the conversation had switched to different types of food on each peer planet. The chat got a little more uncomfortable when Sion came up. Everyone was aware that conditions on this planet surface were becoming unlivable, and its population had to migrate to an underground structure, living and cultivating their food under strict light conditions. Star radiation contaminated almost the entire above ground surface, and Scientists said that the extinction of life on that planet is just a matter of time.

It was nearly ten o'clock when the sunset and everybody decided to call it a night, and Lennah headed home.

CHAPTER 4 – An Unpleasant Dream

"MOM," CILLIA HEARD SOMETHING like a voice in the distance.

"Mom, wake up!" Cillia realized it was Gavriel beside her bed.

"What… what's happened?" she asked, yawning.

"The guy, the guy again," Gavriel said, sweating, eyes staring at her.

"What? What guy?" Cillia asked, still sleepy.

"The guy from my dream last night, I had a dream about him again."

"Oh, your dream, so what's the problem?" She was barely awake and turned to her other side to get back to sleep.

"This was different, he was by my side in a Suphtrain, and he was talking to me," continued Gavriel. "He was asking me to talk to his daughter, and the odd thing is, it seemed like I knew his daughter."

"Hum, well sweetheart, I don't know what to say. Just give it some time, it will go away, ok?" Cillia said, surrendering to the fact that she wouldn't be able to go back to sleep.

"Ok," Gavriel acquiesced and turned back, with a mix of resignation and disappointment. It was morning already, so both just went to the kitchen for breakfast, and then headed for their own routine.

By the end of the day, Cillia, Theena, and Gavriel returned home, and got together at the kitchen, but Gavriel was afraid that spices used by his grandma, in the food, were the cause of his weird dreams, so he excused himself from the table and went to bed while mother and daughter remained at the table, talking.

He was surprised to find that morning came as a fresh day for him and went for his breakfast with a smile on his face.

"Good morning handsome, how was your night? Have you had another disturbing dream?" Mom asked.

"No, no dreams whatsoever, and I slept like a baby."

"Good, well, I have to rush today. Theena asked me to buy a fish from Zyon, she swears it tastes like heaven. Plus, Hallan from spiritual services wants to talk to me face-to-face so I won't be back before five o'clock, bye sweetheart!" she said, heading to her car.

"Bye mom, have a good day!"

This good luck could last more than twenty-four hours, Gavriel thought, but it seemed like destiny had another plan for his day. Soon after joining mega-airway, his Suphcar abruptly leaned on its left side, losing altitude, forcing many cars underneath to use the emergency exit way. The automatic emergency control drove him toward the trees, and he crash-landed three hundred feet away.

As usual, a couple of airway patrols arrived in minutes to check for injuries. The assessment was quick, and after passing through a health scan, Gavriel was released by the officer. His car was towed to an authorized repair shop. Sure enough, the unit had body damage and would take half a day to be repaired. Gavriel had the option to request a spare car for transportation, but the cost was not in his budget, so he called Lennah for a ride.

When they arrived at his home, Lennah was invited to stay for supper again, which she promptly accepted.

"I've heard someone needs to improve his driving skills, are you ok?" Cilia asked, acknowledging Gavriel's crash while placing some food on the table.

"Not this time, it's a faulty part," he replied.

"Well done then, and I'm glad you are well. Let's go for dinner, mom and I are hungry," Cillia said, and they all joined for the dinner.

"So, mom, what are the next steps for the Sick Planet? The government wants to increase our taxes for this project. Are we sending researchers over there?" Cillia asked during the meal.

"Well, I don't know about sending researchers yet, for now, we are just analyzing data. Our sensors detected a change in the planet's soil composition, probably due to the reaction with fresh human blood, and a rapid increase in the planet's surface temperature."

"Human blood-soil reaction?" Gavriel asked.

"We figured out that human blood contains a unique gene that, when combined with soil, generates a volatile organic chemical reaction which is detected by the planet itself. This response, in turn, generates a high signal over the organic waves. Our scientists believe that this marvellously engineered solution protects the integrity of the system because increases in those signals prompt countermeasures from the planet to stabilize the system."

"So, the human blood-soil reaction wave detected on the Sick Planet must be reflecting the shedding of blood from a lot of people, to have that strong of a signal in the organic waves!" Gavriel concluded.

"Bingo!" confirmed Theena, excited.

"What about the technology level…" asked Lennah, abruptly interrupted by Theena, who seemed intoxicated by the drink in her hand.

"And peaks suggest they are organized, and fighting for power," Theena completed, and then turned to Lennah, "what was your question sweetheart?"

"Yeah, you explained what happens with a fresh blood reaction, but what if the level of technology allows them to kill mass amounts of people without a blood-soil reaction, say for instance, like a thermal nuclear explosion?"

"Excellent question Lennah, and that's why we are concerned now. Our department of alien technology has detected thousands of thermal nuclear explosions on the planet, and that is a hint about the fast development of their technology.

"Well if they achieved nuclear technology and had some history of wars, they might destroy their own civilization," Gavriel said.

"Yes, and they might even destroy the entire planet if they are fighting for power," Theena finished.

"For now, we know for sure that the increase in its surface temperature is a body reaction to something threatening its system. It can be caused by a partial loss of mass stabilizer, that viscous black thing we have in our soil and can be used to produce fuel, or surface organic matter deterioration, or both."

"So, what are the next steps?" Gavriel asked.

"We have sent a second scanner to collect visual, and atomic data. We need to compare the information we have available. In my opinion, I doubt we can do anything in the short term, because it takes time, and time is against us in this situation. We are talking about 35 light years," said Theena looking slightly down to the table, and the conversation faded away.

It had been two hours since supper had started, and the conversation centred among mom, grandma and Lennah, so Gavriel decided to make his way to bed earlier than usual.

It was another bad night of sleep filled with weird dreams and unpleasant stomach aches, probably caused by the Zyon fish for supper. *I'm glad is Saturday, I wouldn't be able to go to school today*, he thought.

"What's happened? you look tired," Theena asked.

"Was it the dream again?" Mom asked.

"Yes, it was, it sucks."

"What dream?" Theena asked, peeling a fruit while showing a polite interest.

"Oh, nothing serious," he said. "I've just been having the same dream over and over again. It's been wrecking my sleep," He said, rubbing his face.

"Well, having four dreams on the same subject isn't something you can say is nothing serious. I think you should, at least, talk to someone with experience in this matter," Cillia interjected.

"C'mon Mom, where am I supposed to find a dream expert?" Gavriel replied sarcastically, "and, by the way, we are talking about three times, not four times as you said," Gavriel corrected while filling his cup.

"Just look to someone who is familiar with this subject, your face looks horrible when you have those dreams," Cillia said, in an attempt to help him.

"Hey guys, I think you both need a good cup of coffee." Theena intervened.

"Yes, you are right grandma," Gavriel said, sipping his coffee.

"As always," his grandma said with a smile.

"What's on your agenda for the weekend, grandma?"

"I'm going to the fresh market to buy some exotic ingredients for our supper tonight… hum, and maybe I'll visit some friends," Theena said, between sips of her coffee, "and of course, I almost forgot, I want to buy a hat. I left my collection at home, and you know how I love hats. Besides, this heat is killing me. What are your plans for today?"

"I'll pick up my Suphcar that's supposed to be fixed today; it's funny that you mentioned that you are going to buy a hat because, in my dreams, there is always a guy wearing a hat."

"Oh, that is a coincidence, Jardnn loves hats too. That reminds me that I should buy something for him as well. Good call, Gavriel. What kind of hat was the guy in your dream wearing? It might help find one for Jardnn."

"I don't know, I'm not familiar with hat styles. It was gray and had a rounded crown and brim, and the man always wore a floral shirt too."

"That's interesting because Jardnn usually wears a floral t-shirt when dealing with our garden. Maybe you guys met each other in your dream," Theena said, a little bit excited about the coincidence.

"So, tell me what's the dreams about?"

"It isn't anything special grandma, he just appeared in my dreams for some nights in a kind of sequel, and it looked like he knew that he was actually in my dreams."

"Wow, this is bizarre. What was he saying? What was the topic of your dreams?"

"Apparently, I knew his daughter, and I was supposed to tell how much he loves her. For my sake, I don't know him or his daughter," Gavriel said sighing.

"Oh, weird, wait a minute Gavriel. I want to show you something, this is a picture of Jardnn," Theena projected a little image on the palm of her left hand. Gavriel paled and couldn't hide his discomfort.

"Can I see it better, grandma?" he asked, touching her left palm with his index finger and sliding the projected zoomed image down toward the surface of the table. "It's him!" Gavriel said in a mix of confidence and perplexity.

Gavriel was shocked because he couldn't find any reasonable explanation for the coincidences. He zoned out and was shaken from his thoughts by his grandma's conversation on the live line.

"What do you mean he is not among us anymore? Where is he?" Theena asked while walking away from the kitchen. Two minutes later she came back to the kitchen, her face pale, and announced that Jardnn was dead.

"Apparently, he terminated his life in one of the available clinics on Zyon five days ago, just after spending the day with his daughter. They delivered his ashes about two hours ago, and the poor girl is devastated," Theena said, looking down in a mix of shock and disbelief.

"What you mean five days ago? Why has nobody contacted you since then?" Cillia asked, raising her eyebrows.

"I don't know. We agreed that we would take our cryogenic freezing together. I can't think straight right now, and I need a private moment. Can you lend me your car, Cillia? I'm not planning to come back for dinner."

"Of course," Cillia agreed, as her mother made her way out of the kitchen.

"Well, now I will need your car, Gavriel. I need to talk to Hallan face-to-face," said Cillia.

"Sure, I'll call the office and ask them to send the car in auto-mode."

"Thanks, I'll pay the delivery fee," said Cillia

"ok. I need fresh air, so I'll walk on the trails," he said, looking down and heading to the elevator.

CHAPTER 5 – *The Micro Planet Acqua*

"I HAVE SOMETHING FOR YOU," Cillia said, handing an envelope to Gavriel. He opened it and read a note in unidentified writing, so he needed to use the automatic translator to understand it.

I need your help with something you might be familiar with. Can we talk privately? Peace to your heart, Hallan.

"He wants to talk to me. Do you know what this is about?" Gavriel asked.

"I don't know. Are you coming to the Day Seven meeting? You can ask him then," Cillia said.

"Yeah, why not?" answered Gavriel.

The death of Jardnn wasn't supposed to cause any impact on Gavriel's life, he didn't even know him, but having those dreams about that guy was creepy. He needed some answers, and any source was welcomed. Although he wasn't eager to talk to Hallan, it was his only option so Gavriel would try to include the dreams about Jardnn in their conversation.

Day Seven came, and as usual, Gavriel didn't pay much attention to the message. After the end of the service, some people remained outside to talk to Hallan or each other. The rain that fell over the night caused it to be a bit cooler, and people lingered in the pleasant weather. They were all gathered on a large concrete slab attached to the building.

People enjoyed sitting on the wooden benches scattered throughout the area. Each court overlooked exotic gardens built inside raw wooden boxes. The boxes contained different flowers with distinct scents, all meticulously cared for by Hallan. Gavriel was seated on one of these benches waiting for his moment to talk to Hallan, while his mom and grandma spent some time talking to some Novus Mundurians.

"Good Morning, Gavriel, how are you doing?" Hallan approached, his hand extended. He spoke in a smooth and confident tone that immediately put Gavriel at ease. He stood up and extended his hand, knowing that this was an ancient way to greet people before a conversation.

"Good morning, my mom said you would like to talk to me. What's up?

"I'm going for breakfast, are you available for the next two hours?" Hallan asked.

"I'm free," Gavriel replied.

"Ok, let's go. Do you guys want to join us for a coffee?" Hallan asked Cilia and Theena as they passed by them.

"We will pass. Thanks anyway," Cillia replied.

Watching Gavriel and Hallan walking away, one might have assumed they were somehow related. They were the same height, had the same body shape, and even shared a similar gait. Even their vocal mannerisms were the same. If Hallan weren't bald, and with darker skin, one would swear they were related to each other.

"Come on my son. Let me show you my private garden," Hallan said, heading for the elevator to reach the ground level. "I used to go down by the stairs, but you know, we get lazy as we grow older. Even the most rooted, healthy habits succumb to laziness."

They reached the ground and started to walk across an open field. It took ten minutes to reach a little entrance at the beginning of the woods, with a narrow trail running into it.

Hallan stepped up front and said, "Follow behind me, the path is too restrictive in places, and we won't be able to walk side-by-side all the time. I've heard that your grandma is spending some time with you guys and I also heard about the loss of her husband. I'm very sorry to hear that," he said moving ahead.

"Yes," replied Gavriel, while following him, "and I don't know what is going to happen now. She has to work for some time here in Novus Mundus, but she will eventually have to return to Zyon, and I can't foresee a future for her over there. She doesn't have any other relatives in Zyon."

"You probably don't know about this Gavriel, but your grandma and I used to spend a lot of time together, chatting and sharing our dreams. I'll be honest with you. It delighted me to spend time with her, and I'm looking forward to meeting with her again."

Gavriel was surprised. Grandma had never mentioned that she used to have real conversations with Hallan. They kept walking and chatting about everyday matters. Gavriel noticed that there were many forks along the trail.

"How long until we reach our destination?" Gavriel asked.

"Well, it can take up to two hours to reach my site. All I need for my breakfast is in a cabin somewhere in the woods, so every morning I need to walk a certain distance if I want to have my breakfast. I use this trail not just for exercise, but also to feed my soul with spiritual food. Does it make sense for you?" Hallan asked.

"Yes," Gavriel answered, some disdain finding its way into his voice.

"Good, I'm glad you get it. It means that you've learned something wise," Hallan said.

"I'm sorry, what did you say, I just got the wise thing? My mind was wandering," Gavriel said, clearly showing a lack of interest.

"Wisdom is something like reason and spirituality walking together for the purposes of creation, separate they are useless. If you learn something wise and use it to make a difference in your life or that of others, you are living a life of purpose. If you learn but do not apply, you are wasting the life you were given, or you are not even living, "Hallan said, stopping at a dead end.

"And why all these forks?" Gavriel asked.

"I did not build or trace these paths, a friend of mine who shares the same lifestyle, did it for me and I do the same on his property. The bifurcations are options of ways to get to my cabin," Hallan said and passed Gavriel, taking the lead again.

"When you reach a dead end like that one, the solution is to go back and start over. Bifurcations look like decisions we make in our lives. If we make the wrong decisions, there is always a point of reference where we started, so we can go back and try a different route to continue the journey. And of course, you learn from your mistakes, so you better watch and learn if you want to avoid the same mistakes. "

"Interesting, but how do you make a decision when you find a new fork," Gavriel asked.

"Then you have to learn to listen to the voice of your heart and for this you need wisdom," said Hallan, when they reached their destination.

"It looks interesting, in theory," Gavriel said, noticing that they had arrived at the breakfast site. Hey! Look at this, I thought it was going to be just an opening in the woods, but you have premium service over here," Gavriel said, looking at a half egg-shaped construction made of wood and surrounded by dome-shaped glass doors.

They entered the breakfast space, and Hallan took the coffee from the coffee maker, a loaf of bread from the wooden china cabinet, and placed them on a rustic table. He also put some fruit that he had picked from the trees along the way on the table.

"I like the Spartan and rustic decor. I'm a bit surprised."

"Good, I like to surprise people."

"Did my grandma come to this place? How did you manage to talk about your religion with her? She definitely doesn't like the subject," Gavriel asked, biting a slice of bread while Hallan poured coffee.

"Your grandma came here a couple of times. We didn't talk about religion." Hallan said, sipping his coffee.

"How come, it's your ministry, isn't?" Gavriel asked, curious.

"I don't like to use the word religion. In our society, the word religion brings back memories of abuse, extremism, war, deception, death, and many other things that distract people from the real purpose of life."

"Well, but what you preach in the spiritual services is religion."

"That's not correct. What I do in my services is to guide people to find the truth, to have a meaningful life."

"Changing the subject, you wrote in a note that you are looking for some help. How can I help you?"

"Yes, I do need your help. I had a dream about you a few days ago, and in this dream, you were dark skinned, and you were anxious. Do you have any idea what it means? I'm studying dreams, so I wonder if you could help me in this case. Tell me, has anything unusual happened in your life lately that might be connected with this event?"

Gavriel's displeasure was evident. *I was getting along with this man so well, and suddenly he comes out with this nonsense about having a dream about me as if I was stupid enough to believe that he wasn't warned by my mom about them. I won't allow other people to interfere in my life,* he thought.

"Listen, Mr. Hallan, I believe we should talk like adults. I respect you as a person. Hence, you should be more direct about alluding to my dreams. You preach about helping people to find the truth, so you should practice it. Pretending you had a dream about me, preying on my emotions to drag me into your religion, that's not helpful, it's not even valuing truth," Gavriel said, agitatedly, his back straight against the chair and his palm pressed down firmly against the table.

"Bringing your dreams up? I'm baffled," Hallan said but was interrupted by Gavriel.

"We can talk another day again, but I'd be better going now," Gavriel said, as he stood up.

"Ok," Hallan agreed, standing up, "but I'm staying for a while. To get back, just follow the trail, it'll lead you to the entrance, there's no way to make a mistake."

"Ok," Gavriel said confidently, making his way," have a nice day."

"You too," Hallan said, as he watched Gavriel walking away. "He'll be back," Hallan said to himself. "As sure as the sun will rise tomorrow, he'll be back."

As Gavriel found his way down the trail, he was submerged in his own thoughts. *I can't believe how Hallan and my mom tricked me into this meeting. This is ridiculous. They are treating me like a child."* Immersed in his thoughts, he barely noticed that he had reached the end of the trail.

As if on autopilot, he found his way into his vehicle and made his way home. The minute he arrived back, he unleashed his frustration on his mother, which was standing by the kitchen sink.

"How dare you treat me like a child?" He pointed his finger at her, barely noticing his grandma sitting in a chair near him.

"What did I do?" his mother asked, surprised.

"You know very well what you did. Who gave you permission to tell Hallan about my dreams? Do you need to share my personal life with a stranger? This is a breach of my privacy!" Gavriel said, turning his back to her. He tried to leave the room but was stopped by his grandma who stood in his way.

"Now you just calm down and lower your voice right now," his grandma commanded in a determined voice, and put her hand on his chest, firmly directing him into a chair.

"Listen, and listen carefully," grandma demanded, with authority in her voice, "This is not my house, and I have no business here. But that's my daughter, and I have every right to protect her and to preserve her, the same way your mom has been protecting you. So, you will never again point your finger at your mother. Or you will have to answer to me."

"Yeah but," he tried.

"There's no but. You have the right to question and make your points in a civilized and adult manner, but I will not tolerate disrespect to your mother or me. I hope you realize that we can make your life tough until you learn how to treat people with respect. Am I clear?" Theena said calmly, but with a stony glare in her eyes.

"Yes, it's clear. I'm sorry but I, uh," Gavriel mumbled to his grandma.

"Now can you please clarify what's going on, in a civilized way."

"Yes…" he paused, "I was just upset that she shared my dreams with Hallan without my knowledge and," but Cillia interrupted.

"What are you talking about? Who told Hallan about your dreams? I didn't!"

"You didn't? What are you talking about? You went to talk to him on Day Five, and when you came back, you said I should ask for some help in regards to my dreams. Remember? You gave me his invitation. Look," Gavriel said, waving a piece of paper in front of his mom. His voice faltered, which did not go unnoticed by Theena.

"Civilized manners, remember?" Theena said in a reproving tone.

Cillia took the piece of paper. "He wanted to check with me to see if I was willing to volunteer for a new program he is starting," she said while reading the translated note. "This note just says that he wants to talk to you. I had no clue what the subject was. Besides, I never mentioned your thoughts to him."

"So, you never talked to him about those creepy dreams?" Gavriel asked, confused.

"No, I never talked to him about that."

"Rats, I feel so stupid," Gavriel covered his face with both hands. "Now I understand why he was surprised when I mentioned my dreams, I feel like an idiot."

"Ok, we are all subject to make mistakes, yet there's always an opportunity to go back and take the right path if you are willing to," Cillia said, looking sweetly into Gavriel's eyes.

"So, what do you think you should do to correct your mistakes?" Theena asked.

"Yes, you are right. Sorry Mom, sorry grandma. I was making assumptions," Gavriel said, deeply ashamed. "I'll ask forgiveness from Hallan as well," Making a move to make a call.

"Wait, sweetheart, this is not a subject you deal with by live line. I suggest you wait for a proper time to talk to him in person. Knowing a little bit about Hallan, I know he would not be offended, no matter what you have said to him. Also, I suggest you ask him for some help with your dreams, they weren't random. It's time to find some answers," his grandma finished.

"Yes, thanks, I'll do that," Gavriel said, kissing his grandma and mom before heading to his room.

Once they were alone, Cillia turned to her mother. "Thanks, Mom. I think I could have handled it, but you being here and saying what you did help out in a big way."

"Oh honey, you're welcome. After six husbands, I am getting pretty good at handling a variety of personalities. Although some, apparently, couldn't handle the pressure and decided to leave without notice," Theena said, turning her head toward the window and looking out at the horizon.

Theena was a strong woman, and the loss of her husband didn't affect her daily life. Still, it was evident that something had changed. She was more contemplative, and her usually talkative personality had quieted somewhat. After all that had happened, she had decided to settle on Novus Mundus. She had her own private dwelling, although she still found her way to her daughter's house at least two days a week. Gavriel's upcoming move to the artificial micro planet for the military camp was also an excellent reason to spend more time with her daughter.

#

Gavriel spent the week at the UCD site learning take-off and landing procedures on the spaceship that would travel to the micro planet. He also prepared his military backpack and received his gun, which was engineered to be connected to his brain. Holding the weapon for the first time gave him an excitement he never felt before. It only lasted a few moments, though, as his instructor began to talk.

"So, you like her?" the instructor asked, taking the gun from Gavriel's hands and holding the device in the shooting position.

"Yeah, it's kind of weird holding it for the first time."

"I know, I like this weapon," said the instructor. "It brings back good memories just holding it again."

"You mean you had a gun like this one?" Gavriel said, receiving the weapon back.

"No, I mean this one specifically was mine. I received a new one, and this was relegated to being used for training purposes. Take care of this baby, it served me in many missions and never screwed up."

"Wow," Gavriel said, looking admiringly at the gun.

"Yeah, you should be proud! It put down many people, and it never failed."

"What? What do you mean it put down many people? I don't recall our planet being in a war lately."

"Oh, although we are receiving training for war times, we can also be assigned to small missions, it happens all the time. This gun has followed me on many missions to Zyon to deactivate rebel cells, and it did the job the way it was supposed to do. I'm telling ya, this is a killer machine, take care of her," the instructor said, as he moved away.

Gavriel stood paralyzed. He had never held a weapon that had been used to kill people and experienced a sense of repulsion. Suddenly the gun seemed more cumbersome than before. To make things worse, he was trying to process the information about Zyon rebels. He couldn't recall hearing any news about it. The instructor calling out his name aroused him from his thoughts. He needed to stay alert as a lousy mark during training could reflect poorly on the rest of his professional career.

On Day Seven, Gavriel decided to attend the spiritual service to clear things up between him and Hallan before heading out to a military camp. After the ceremony, he waited patiently for everyone to finishing chatting with Hallan.

"Hi Hallan, how are you doing?" Gavriel asked, offering his hand for a handshake.

"I'm great!" Hallan said, shaking his hand.

"Listen, I'd like to apologize for my attitude last week. It was childish, and I'm sorry."

"Apology accepted, you are a good man, Gavriel."

"Thanks, I also wanted you to know about some dreams I had two weeks ago. They may or may not be related to the dream you had about me," Gavriel began. They started to walk around the suspended area by the building as Gavriel shared his dreams about Jardnn.

"Hum," Hallan muttered after Gavriel finished his story. "So, you said that this week you are heading to the micro planet for your military camp, right?"

"Yup."

"This is a complicated subject, I suggest we talk when you come back from your military service. Meanwhile, just to try to find the meaning of your dreams by yourself."

"How can I do that?" Gavriel asked, opening the palm of his hands, "Is there any procedure or training, because I have no clue?"

"You will need to find the truth, find the truth and the truth will set you free," said Hallan in a gentle voice.

"The truth will set me free from what?" he insisted.

"Will set you free from the answers. After finding the truth, you will notice that your soul has all the answers you need. To help you, I'll ask you to bring something with you to the micro planet to read. Hold on a second," Hallan said, going inside the building and coming back with a worn, leather cover book.

"This is an ancient manuscript, and you won't find anything like this around, so please be careful because it's my only copy," Hallan said, handing it to Gavriel.

"We are responsible for our decisions, and any decision we make has to pass through our rational minds. Otherwise, anybody can fool you with false concepts. If you are seeking answers from a spiritual perspective, you have to look or answers from the spiritual source that lives in you," said Hallan raising his eyebrows.

"Ok, I'll keep that in mind, and thanks for the book. I'll take a look at it," Gavriel said, and headed to his car.

CHAPTER 6 – Back to Planet Earth

IT WAS MORE THAN TEN MONTHS since Clara landed in Miami, and as many landed immigrants do, she decided to change her name. This was to help her feel that she belonged to the new culture and also to set the point of a new beginning. Clara wanted a fresh start, so she registered herself as Claire.

As soon as she was settled, she enrolled in English classes to bring her language skills to an academic level. When she lived in Chile, English classes were expensive, so she used to take online courses and had to use creativity to improve her skills.

She got a part-time job as a stock girl in a big chain store. Although she knew it was temporary, she felt the heaviness, as she woke up early in the morning to spend hours alone in the stark, windowless storeroom. Her aunt had lost most of her Latin culture and barely stopped for a conversation with Claire before work.

The camaraderie and family-like atmosphere that dominated meal breaks in Chile were replaced by fast food meals that Claire ate alone. The solitude that was imposed on her was dictated by a culture that valued business, and the acquisition of wealth. Her relatives in Florida were barely at home for meals, and spent their leisure time in shopping centers, spending the money they had worked so hard to gain. The little time that she had with her family for conversation was often spent reminiscing about all of the fun they used to have.

"How's your adaptation to the Promised Land going?" her aunt asked while both were unloading the dishwasher. Although her aunt was her mom's sister, they didn't look alike at all. Aunt Mirna had gained weight after moving to Florida, and her coloured-red, curly hair starkly contrasted her black eyebrows, giving her the appearance of wearing a wig.

"It's fine, although I don't really feel like I'm living in the Promised Land. I can see a lot of good things here, but also miss good things from Chile."

"Yeah, it'd be nice if we could just choose the good things and send the bad ones to hell," her aunt chuckled.

"Well, I'm not expecting to live in a perfect world, but trying to achieve good social, political, and moral standards should already be well defined in developed countries. Yet even here I see so many wrong things, humanity is weird," Claire said.

"Is there something I can do to make you switch your preference from Chile to the Promised Land?"

"Oh no, don't worry, I have to get there eventually. In my personal life, however, I'm having dreams about earthquakes. Actually, they are more like nightmares, and they are draining my strength, making it difficult to wake up in the mornings for work. I thought they would go away after a while, but they haven't," she said, closing the dishwasher door.

"Let's deal with that. I'll set up an appointment with a psychologist. I'm pretty sure this is a medical case, so let me find a doctor, and I'll make it work," her aunt said, opening the freezer door and taking some food, "are you staying for supper?"

"Yes, I am. I have no commitments for tonight."

"Good," her aunt said, taking one more portion from the freezer.

They kept talking while Claire did some cleaning around the kitchen. Her aunt had a different standard of cleanliness than she did, but she was grateful for her aunt's help and tried her best to minimize the clutter she found herself in the midst of.

Three days later Claire was by herself talking to a doctor, and there was no surprise in the medical analysis. She was diagnosed with post-traumatic stress due to her experiences in Chile. To help with her sleep, she was prescribed pills that she knew she would never take. To avoid confrontation with her aunt, she decided to pretend she was taking the pills and stopped telling her aunt when the dreams came.

Her social life wasn't too different from the one she used to have in Chile, but she began to feel an intense desire to have meaningful conversations with someone. A few months ago, she decided to attend a church, and on her second visit, a guy from the youth group invited her out for a coffee. She refused, as her experience with Rodrigo was still fresh in her mind.

Monica, her English teacher, would suggest every so often that they should have a coffee together, so Claire accepted the offer to go to a local parade with Monica next time she was invited.

"So, did you like the parade?" Monica asked after the event while they were looking for a place to have a coffee.

"It wasn't what I had in mind. I was taking for granted that it would be a huge event, but it was more like some bands and a bunch of mascots entertaining children. Don't get me wrong, the kids seemed to love it. It was just my expectations were different."

"Yeah, I understand, here," Monica said, pointing to a small coffee shop in front of them, "let's get in."

As they were seated, Monica continued, "I was touched by what you wrote in your assignments. I can't imagine how tough it must have been to survive the earthquake and then find yourself in a new country. I don't mean to bring up painful memories, but I just want to let you know that if you need someone to talk to, you can always come to me. It might be helpful to share what you've gone through."

"Thanks. It seems like I've gotten used to dealing with challenges. As I told you before, the only thing remaining are these dreams that come very often. Actually, I'm having other dreams lately, not connected with Chile, but with people here in the United States. I wonder why am I having so many of these dreams here?"

"Hmm, my mom dreams a lot as well. She's had a lot of dreams since she was little, so I've done some research on it. It seems like everybody dreams every night, but some people have this ability to remember them the next morning."

"So that means your mom and I are actually like computers with a good memory," Claire joked, and they both laughed.

"You should talk to my mom, she might know a way to help you, or at least you guys can have fun together. Friday is our girls' night out, and you are coming with us, no excuses!" Monica said quite persuasively.

"Well, it seems like my options are limited, so I'll say yes," Claire agreed, receiving a hug from Monica.

Friday came, and they met in a restaurant. Meg, Monica's mother, ordered some food and a bottle of wine. Meg looked a little bit older than her forty years; she had a tired expression on her face that aged her. Monica didn't resemble her mom whatsoever, she coloured her hair dark brown, to contrast with her blue eyes, whereas her mom kept her natural blond colour. The meal was served, and conversation ran from Claire's adaptation to the American culture to the Chilean earthquake. Monica emphasized how much of an ordeal Claire had undergone before coming to the US. Finally, they went to the subject of Claire's dreams.

"So, Claire," said Monica, "tell my mom about the dreams you've been having, as I said, Mom might help you, she's a dreamer too."

"No, I'm not a 'dreamer,'" interjected Meg, "I just have dreams once in a while."

"Oh, C'mon mom, you have all these connections with spirits as you say, and you have dreams as well," said Monica.

"Hey, this is way different. My connections with spirits are part of my life. When I need advice from the supernatural, I do my work, but dreams come without my invitation," Meg said.

"Do you think you can help Claire in this matter? She's been having these earthquake nightmares. Is there a way to help her to stop them?" Monica asked eagerly, "hey, why don't you work with your connections to help Claire?"

"Well, it isn't a bad idea, we can try that, or maybe we can check the meaning of her dreams. I have a book at home that has meanings for some symbols. We can go through the dreams, search in the text for the elements of each one, and try to make sense of them."

"Great idea, if we do both, the connections with spirits and the book, we might be able to get everything sorted out," Monica said.

Claire was zoned out for the conversation; the subject was heading to an uncomfortable zone. Spiritual connections like crystal balls or black magic weren't an option for her, and she missed an extended part of the conversation.

"Claire, are you ok with that?" Monica asked, bringing Claire back to reality.

"What, ok with what?" Claire asked, confused.

"For my mom to consult her spiritual connections about your nightmares, and try to find an answer for them. We can go to our place and do it tonight. In fact, you can also sleep over and," Monica was excitedly talking nonstop when she was interrupted by Claire.

"Thank you, but I'll pass. I really need to get a good rest, and besides, tomorrow is Saturday so I can sleep longer. I'm pretty sure we won't get to bed early if we go to your place," Claire said, sparking some laughs from Monica. "Yeah, the night was fantastic guys! Oops! I meant girls, we are girls," Claire said, getting more laughs from Monica, "but I'd like to go if you don't mind."

"Yeah, not a problem," Monica's mom agreed, asking for the bill.

They dropped off Claire at home and said goodbye. Before going to bed, Claire received a message from Monica. *It was a fantastic night! Sweet dreams! See you tomorrow!* Claire didn't respond to the text. Monica was probably trying to be a good friend, but she felt that the maturity level difference between her and Monica was significant, making the friendship a bit of a challenge.

Claire had a good rest that night, despite having a dream about an earthquake again. This time, the scenario was different than the previous ones. After waking up, she decided to find a solution that would address both her body and soul.

Saturday morning, Claire had brunch and decided to go shopping, before heading to a performance in her local community. "This is a beautiful town to live in," Claire said to herself as she arrived early for the meeting. She decided to wait on one of the benches at the picnic area. A well-dressed woman, probably in her fifties, was walking around. *She must be praying,* Claire thought and was reminded of how her spiritual life had withered. After a quarter of an hour, the woman showed up at her table.

"How are you doing, young lady? My name is Johanna Smith, and I'm a volunteer for tonight's event."

"Hi, I'm Claire!" She said, shaking Johanna's hand.

"Your face looks familiar, have we met before?" Johanna asked.

"I don't think so, maybe from the Sunday services? I'm Mirna's niece."

"Oh yeah, I remember now. Your aunt once came to talk to me about some dreams bothering you, is that correct?"

"Well yeah, but why did my aunt tell you my dreams?" Claire asked, frowning.

"Oh, maybe because I'm a psychologist. Don't get me wrong, your aunt never told me the content of any of your dreams, she just said that some dreams were bothering you lately, and she was asking for some professional advice. Maybe you want to share them with me," Johanna said in a gentle voice.

"I don't know," Claire said with mixed feelings. She was glad to know that the lady was a doctor, yet she wasn't feeling comfortable. "I had some issues sleeping through the night, and I went to a doctor already… I don't know, don't get me wrong but I just don't think I need a second opinion," Claire said, hoping she wasn't too rude.

"Oh, don't worry, you don't need to apologize for being honest," Johanna said, sitting by her side. "I feel fortunate and respected by a young lady like you. I came to the gathering earlier and started to walk around. When I saw you looking at your phone, I said to myself, 'Tsk, tsk, what a waste of time, I'm going to talk to this young lady to save her from this evil technology," Johanna said, laughing.

"So here I am, I need to rescue you from the evils of microchips."

This caused Claire to smile, and she relaxed.

"Well thanks, that's really encouraging. What exactly is your position in this gathering?"

"I'm a volunteer, I offered to share my expertise as a medical professional over any raised issued. After the event, they always open it up for questions and comments. Usually, people bring up personal issues, some attribute everything to faith or a lack of faith. However, many people have misguided faith, and it detracts from its real meaning. Some believe that religion will help them to lose weight, yet religion by itself doesn't melt fat, effort and perseverance are also needed," Johanna said.

"You're right. How did you develop such extensive experience? You look young," Claire said, more as a way to indulge Johanna for her volunteer work.

"Oh, you really made my day. I'm fifty-six. Now I know why I should come here earlier, it was for you to make my day. Thank you so much," Johanna said, "now tell me, what's bothering you in your dreams? It's ok if you don't want to share anything, just talking to you has been a treat for me."

"Oh no, it isn't a secret. According to a doctor, I've developed post-traumatic stress disorder after the earthquake," and Claire summarized her experience for Johanna. "She prescribed some sleeping pills, but I'm not eager to take them."

"Well, I'm pretty sure your doctor gave you the correct prescription according to the information she had at the time of your appointment. Having said that, I'm pretty sure she would have asked you to go back for a follow-up appointment, have you gone back for a follow-up?"

"No, it isn't due yet, but I'm not taking my pills, so why bother?"

"Well, what about a second opinion then?"

"Hum, yeah, it's fine. I just can't afford long-term treatment. Besides, I don't want to take pills for something I understand can be treated with an alternative option, I'm talking about dreams, not nightmares."

"Now we really have something to start with. Listen, if you feel comfortable coming to my office, I think I can help you. I don't work for free, so your payment is to keep saying those nice little lies about my age, that'll keep me happy. Do we have a deal?" Johanna said, extending her hand for a handshake.

"Yes, we have a deal," Claire said and shook Johanna's hand.

"Now we should get into the gathering room, there is a handsome young fellow in this performance, and you don't wanna miss it. Here is my card with my address, I'll wait for you on Tuesday at twelve o'clock, does that work for you?" Johanna asked, handing Claire a business card.

"Yes, I'm free on Tuesday at noon."

"Now let's get in," Johanna said. Claire stood up and noticed that Johanna was about five inches taller than her. She gently took Claire's arm, and both walked toward the building, Johanna talking nonstop.

On her way home, Claire told her aunt, who was at the gathering as well, about her encounter with Johanna and her offer to help her.

"Really?" Mirna said, "Johanna Smith is a famous psychologist. I didn't even try to get an appointment with her because her agenda is jam-packed. Besides, she is really expensive, so that's why we opted for a doctor from my health insurance."

"Oh, that's fine. I know you've been trying your best to help me out, thank you so much. So yes, I have an appointment for Tuesday at noon."

"So, you'll miss part of your English class, by the way, your teacher Monica called three times looking for you today. Apparently, she couldn't reach you on your cell, and maybe you should call her back."

"Yeah, thanks, I'll do that, not today, tomorrow maybe," Claire said and made her way to her bedroom, right after they got home.

The next morning, Claire's aunt knocked on her door with a telephone pointing at Claire. "It's for you," her aunt said, handing it to Claire, and leaving the room.

"Hello? Oh, hi Monica! What is going on? It's eight thirty in the morning," Claire said looking at the clock.

"Hi, yeah I tried to reach you yesterday, but no success, so I decided to call your home, am I bothering you?"

"No… it's ok, anything else?" Claire asked, trying to finish the conversation.

"I'm planning to go to the Pop Art Gallery today, and I'm wondering if you want to come with me?"

"Well, I'm planning to spend the day with my family here. It's been a busy week, and I need to catch up on my home duties as well, so I'll pass, thank you."

"Ok, you're welcome, see you tomorrow."

"Bye," Claire said, hung up, and went to join her aunt.

"Wow, what a lovely day!" Claire said, lying on a lounge chair, sunbathing in their backyard.

"I agree," said her aunt, laid in a chair beside her.

"I'm glad Maria found some friends to hang out with, she's timid," said Claire.

"Yes, this job at the local store is helping her to make friends. You seem to have a good social life as well."

"Yeah. What about you?"

"I chat a lot at work, that's my leisure time. Besides that, I have no expectations. I decided to stay alone after Jorge left me for that younger woman, that son of… sorry, excuse my language," Mirna said, looking to the other side, avoiding Claire's eyes.

"It's ok. I'm sorry to bring up such a painful subject."

"It's ok honey, let's enjoy the day, what's passed is passed," and they started to talk about life in Florida.

#

Monday's class was weird because Claire noticed that Monica was picking on her, and she had the impression that the entire class saw. At the end of the lesson, she quickly left the room without a word.

On Tuesday she decided not to attend the English class, going straight to Johanna's office, and *What a place!* She thought to herself. The building entrance was so large and well decorated that she was afraid it was the wrong address.

"Is it your first time here?" a young man, at the reception asked, after entering Claire's personal information in a database.

"Yes!"

"Lovely! Please keep this card with you. When you notice it buzzing and blinking, take any of the elevators over there and insert the card into a slot at the bottom of the elevator's control panel. The slots are illuminated, so you can't miss it. The elevator will take you straight to your doctor's office. Over there is our waiting area," he said, pointing to a glass door behind the reception. "Drinks and snacks are complimentary. Welcome to the United Services," the young man finished with a smile.

"Thanks," Claire said and made her way toward the lounge. The place was more like a five-star hotel lobby than a doctor's office. Waiters offered natural juices, fruits, and many other snacks. In the center, there was a fifteen-foot waterfall cascading into a beautiful tank filled with Japanese carp, and above the cascade, there was a widescreen picturing the underwater life. Claire chose a classic leather sofa and sat down.

"Would you like a coffee?" asked a uniformed lady who was passing by, pulling a small cart.

"No thanks."

"I can bring you a hot chocolate. It's delicious," the old lady said, whispering and winking.

"Sure, I'll have one," Claire smiled, and the woman brought a steaming cup a few minutes later.

She noticed some people watching a concert on a big screen inside a room with tinted glass walls, and the place must have been soundproofed because she couldn't hear a thing. Around her, many people were chatting as if they were familiar with each other, but there were others who sat alone texting on their cell phones. After fifteen minutes, the card buzzed, and she made her way to the elevator. Johanna welcomed her when the elevator stopped at the right floor.

"What a pleasure to see you again!" Johanna said, shaking Claire's hand.

"Wow, congratulations! This is a beautiful place," Claire said, "and the elevator stops at your door. Is this floor all yours?"

"Oh thanks, but this floor isn't just mine, I share it with seven other tenants," Johanna said, leading Claire to a couch and seating herself in a leather chair on the opposite side.

"Well, let's talk about you," Johanna said, putting on a pair of glasses and opening her notebook. You told me that you are looking for some help over your dreams and had mentioned that they make you feel tired. You also said that they were not bad, can you explain that to me?"

"Yes, I clearly remember my dreams," Claire said, still looking around and taking in the classy French décor. "In the dream, about earthquakes, I try to protect myself, yet I don't feel life-threatening. It seems like it isn't me. I don't know if it makes sense for you?"

"They don't need to make sense for me, they are yours, and probably only you can make sense of them. I can clinically digest what you are saying, but in the end, it's all about you. Do you have the same dream, in the same place? Can you detail one of them to me?" Johanna asked.

"Yes, I'm in this building about four or five stories high. The building is shaking, and I look outside. I see the seacoast and the street cracking open right before my eyes. The crack deepens and eventually swallows up some trucks. Some co-workers from a company jump on the cars that have been swallowed up to rescue their fellows. Suddenly I find myself no longer in the building, but on the street and I see that the building is shaking and cracking from top to bottom. The building actually moves up about three feet above the ground as if there is something underneath pushing it up. I continue to run along the street and see small waves coming from the sea toward the streets. They aren't big, but I wonder how they got there," Claire paused.

"Are you making notes about these dreams?" Johanna asked.

"Nope."

"Well, for our sessions I'll ask you to write them down, ok? Don't forget to include the details. Nothing is too insignificant."

"Ok," Claire said, "then I reach these townhouses," but she was cut by Joanna.

"You mean the dream goes on?" Johanna asked.

"Oh yeah," Claire said, "it will probably fill ten pages of your notebook. Well, as I was saying, I reach this townhouse building; I have a house at the end of the row," and Claire continued for twenty more minutes.

"Wow, I understand now why you get tired during the day. Your dreams are quite in-depth. You are subjected to a fair amount of stress during your sleep. As you were speaking, you recounted many details. In the beginning, for instance, you said that some co-workers from a company jumped into the crack to help their friends. How do you know it is a business?"

"Oh, because the trucks are all the same and they are parked side-by-side in a parking lot. They look like UPS trucks, except they are red, and the company's employees are wearing uniforms. Besides, in dreams, you just know these things, even if you can't see, you just know," Claire explained.

"Can you locate where these dreams occur?" Johanna asked.

"Yes, I noticed that lately, all of my dreams with earthquakes happened in the United States. However, there is one old dream that shows a massive earthquake happening from North to South America. I'm watching a small TV, and the anchor illustrates the damage from the US to Chile."

"Well, we will explore these events in a future session," Johanna said, looking at her watch, "I'll set up your sessions on Tuesdays and Thursdays at noon. Then we will reduce the frequency as we move along. Is that ok with you?"

"Yes, it's fine."

"Great, I'll walk you to the elevator, and again, make notes about your dreams," Johanna said, standing up.

"Yes, thanks, see you," Claire said, getting into the elevator. She quietly hummed a song to herself as the elevator descended, and felt that a weight was taken from her shoulders.

CHAPTER 7 – *Gavriel in Acqua*

GAVRIEL WAS READY for his military camp at the micro planet Acqua. He remained in his room until the shuttle from the UCD arrived to pick him up, he knew his mom was emotional, and he didn't want to prolong her tears for a long time. When mom came to his room to announce that the shuttle had arrived, he had just enough time give her a hug and say goodbye. From her red face and puffy eyes, he guessed that she had been crying.

"Bye Mom, take care of yourself, I'll be back soon. It's just three hundred days, and I'll call you whenever I can," he said while walking away.

"Ok, you take care of you too," Cillia said, as he walked away. He turned back to wave, as he boarded the shuttle. He could see she was trying to be brave, although he could fell, she was emotional.

"Just three hundred days," he said to himself and braced for the journey ahead.

After a six-hour trip, the spaceship descended onto the planet and docked at the central station. There was no way to view the building from inside the vessel, and the official information said it was for security reasons, but it seemed more likely that it was to build anticipation for visitors as they entered the station.

The place was huge. The main building was about three miles long and a quarter of a mile high, with an enormous glass dome supported by buildings on each side. The internal part of the buildings had slanted balconies facing an ample open space in the middle. There were also lateral openings about every two hundred feet along the main street, leading to the side streets. From an aerial view, the structure looked like a giant glass centipede. The view was impressive to any visitor, especially since the Novus Mundus legislation didn't allow buildings of this size on its surface.

Due to the variation in natural light on the micro planet, the station had artificial day and night periods synchronized with Novus

Mundus, to help the operational teams to keep their usual patterns of sleep and work.

Gavriel was granted a special room on the top of the building, which allowed him to see both external and internal environments. He clearly saw that his grandma had pulled some strings, as it was definitely not his educational efforts that afforded him this luxury, and he didn't believe in luck. He was excited to explore the site; however, the enforced sleeping curfew postponed his plans until the next day.

Gavriel had one of the best sleep of his life that night, although it was one of the busiest ones regarding dreams. It seemed like he was dreaming all night long and they were so vivid and real that he could describe everything down to the minutest detail. The one he liked most was the one in which he was flying over mountains, valleys, and rivers on a bright sunny day. The landscape was filled with different types of trees, brilliant colours, even a purple lake. The sights were breathtaking, and the best thing about his dream was that he could control it. He was able to fly up and down and, could even feel the wind against his face.

He was amazed when he awoke. Just before heading for the group breakfast, he remembered Hallan's suggestion to write down his dreams, and wrote it on his screen palm, while a mouth device was brushing his teeth. He dressed for his first outdoor mission, ran toward the gravity-controlled tubes made of glass, and joined his group.

"Hi Noah," Gavriel said, looking at the organic screen tag on a guy beside him, "that's an unusual name." Noah was about one inch taller than Gavriel, was bald and had bright golden eyes that contrasted with his smooth, dark skin.

"Yeah, everyone says that. It seems like people are not familiar with strange names over here, I'm from Zyon," Noah said.

"From Zyon? What a surprise, I don't recall hearing about students from Zyon coming to this program, that's awesome!" Gavriel said followed by an excited smile.

"Yes, this is just the second time our planet was invited, it's a dream come true for me."

"This is Miller, we just met," said Noah, pointing to a guy next to him.

"Hi, Miller, nice to meet you. I can see from your eyes that you are from Novus Mundus, am I correct," said Gavriel to the fellow beside Noah.

"Yes, you are right, nice to meet you too," Miller answered, raising his hand.

"Good to hear that! How did you guys sleep last night?"

"Oh, although we had prepared for this time zone, last night wasn't easy," said Noah.

"Mine wasn't easy either, what about yours?" asked Miller.

"Fantastic, I feel like I'm in heaven. What should I request for breakfast? Hmm… they have such different options here," Gavriel said, looking at the many holographic meals projected on the table.

"I don't know about your usual breakfast, but they included something from my planet, look over there?" Noah pointed to an image, two feet from them."

"What exactly is this meal like? I don't want to waste my time watching their video explanation about the food."

"That one is made with regular bread and eggs that come from a domesticated bird. The unique flavour comes from when the eggs are fried on a sea rock."

"Sounds yummy, I'll order it," Gavriel said, touching the option.

After the right amount of time had been allowed for breakfast, their organic screen tags started to buzz, indicating that it was time to gather at the scheduled meeting point for the outdoor program.

"This isn't a vacation," barked the Chief in command. "This is the time of your life when you are cut from the umbilical cord of your childhood. Today is the first day of the rest of your life, and I can assure you everyone will agree after completing the program.

There are no failures or successes in this journey, this isn't a contest. You are here to grow in knowledge and character. You'll train night and day, there will be no time for distractions.

Take the time to get to know your team because from now on you are not only recruits, you are one body," he paused.

"How long," Miller started to ask but was cut off by the Chief.

"This is not the time for questions, I will tell you when you can speak.

We are about to leave, so be careful out there. This environment is controlled, yet hostile. We will be travelling by foot from here and will return at night. Keep in mind that this planet is artificial, so weather variations and changes in the air composition are common.

Stay together and squeeze your organic tag if you find yourself in a life-threatening situation. I will then evaluate the situation before triggering the central emergency team service. Also, don't even think about stepping off the trail.

There is a zero-gravity barrier between our trail and the forest to keep wild animals at bay. If you step away from it, there are no words to describe the dangers you will face," the Chief said, which elicited some nervous laughs from the crowd. "That's it, you have all the information you need. From now on, keep your mouth shut and your senses sharp," he finished his speech as he opened the outside door.

They took a hard trail that led them inside the dense forest, coming across many forks along the path, which reminded Gavriel of his journey with Hallan. They encountered animals along the way, some were startled by their appearance and scampered away; others stopped whatever they were doing to observe the troop marching through the forest. The smell of burnt wood and wet soil permeated the air.

Using the organic communicator, the Chief relayed to them that the alien species had adapted very quickly to life on Acqua. He also told about the factory of spaceships located on the other side of the globe, which was four times as big as the station they were registered at.

"Stop! Don't move," the Chief commanded through the organic line of communication. As soon as he had spoken, what appeared to be black arrow-shaped birds whizzed above their heads and disappeared over the horizon. "Those birds are black-razors, and they attack their victims by making a cut on the victim's upper body. The cut, made by their razor-sharp claws, deposits a toxin in the victim's body that usually leads to death."

"They look too little to target us for food," someone from the group said.

"That's the problem, these birds aren't carnivores. They don't target their victims for food, they kill them for sport. Most of the animals and plants on this planet are alien, and we don't have a full understanding of their previous environments. Of course, we have treatments for the wounds caused by these creatures, but nobody here wants to spend your time in a hospital bed, do you?"

"No!" everybody replied in unison.

That night, Gavriel crashed out on the bed, but he didn't have a good rest. He remembered waking up twice to drink some water, and he was sweating, so he decided to change his shirt, and went back to his bed, he saw the rare manuscript given to him by Hallan, on the nightstand. He opened and noticed that it was a handwritten text and decided to read.

It began, *'In the beginning, the Creator generated the heavens and the muller.'* It was an ancient vocabulary, and he was able to read about four pages, before realizing that the content wasn't from any nearby planet. The characters had foreign names, the stories were simple and lacked a recognizable structure. The landscape described seemed different, and the relationship between people was really primitive.

He kept reading until he fell asleep. He dreamt about black-razors flying over him and trying to cut his scalp. He ran frantically with worry, and went into the woods, losing grip on his feet due to lower gravity. He was desperate and tried to cry for help, but he could only manage to whisper, "Please, someone help me, please!"

"Help!" he finally cried out, waking, and finding himself soaked in sweat. He got out of his bed, showered and then looked at his watch, to see it was almost breakfast time.

He got dressed, but before heading for the common area, he decided to check the video recorder about his sleep, as the government had their lives recorded for research purposes. He started from the beginning of his night, and saw himself tossing and turning in his sleep, until he reached the morning, crying out "Help me!".

He was puzzled because he clearly recalled waking up twice during the night, but nothing like that was recorded. What really bothered him was the fact that it didn't show him reading the manuscript, which he clearly remembered doing the previous evening.

Gavriel was set for another day in the woods. The team received tasks to be completed by groups of three people. Miller and

Noah were his partners, and they spent all day working on their assignments and building a relationship. Gavriel even shared parts of his dreams with them, but they seemed disinterested, so he kept quiet until the end of the day.

Another night came, and Gavriel fell asleep, finding himself dreaming about the same place he had dreamt the evening before. He was flying again, but this time, he also noticed that the landscape in his dream resembled Acqua. Gavriel flew over what seemed to be a long distance and saw animals precisely like the ones he saw during his exploration time over the past few days.

He also spotted what looked to be another person, way down by a lakeshore. Getting close, he noticed that it was a woman, and approached her. Instinctively he stretched his hand to her, and she gently held it. They both slowly took off and flew over the lake, increasing their speed, going up and down as if they were flying over invisible mountains and laughing like children playing.

When he awoke, he again noted down his dream and the one from the night before. He was getting excited about having these dreams, mainly because he was able to control them, and he found great pleasure in this woman, who had now become part of his dream world.

CHAPTER 8 – *Clara in Miami*

CLAIRE ANXIOUSLY WAITED for her Thursday appointment with Johanna; she was excited to talk about her last few days.

"So, how's been your life Claire?" Johanna asked her during the appointment.

"I'm happy! Even this rainy day isn't bothering me. I have had two beautiful days since we last talked."

"That's great news. What an accomplishment in just two days! You are soaked, though! Let me bring you something to dry your hair," she said while heading to the bathroom and coming back with a small towel in her hands.

"Oh, thanks. Wow, this smells Eucalyptus," Claire said, deeply inhaling the scent from the towel.

"Yes, I like this smell too," Johanna answered with a smile, "so, what has made you so happy?" Johanna asked, putting on her glasses and grabbing her notebook.

"It's not just about the good days I had, it seems like something else happened. I feel like I have the joy back. I've had some good nights, but there's this joy that I can't quite explain," Claire said serenely as she dried her hair.

"Wonderful, let's find the source of this good feeling so we can make sure we have something to pursue. Did you meet someone you liked? Have you received good news?" Johanna asked while making notes.

"No, nothing like that, well, let me see… I had a short dream two nights ago. In it, I am walking by a shore of a beautiful lake on a bright sunny day," Claire answered.

"Nice, was the water dirty or clean?" Johanna asked.

"I didn't pay attention to that. Actually, it was beautifully purple, nevertheless rough."

"Was there something different happening to you in this dream?"

"Hmm… nothing that I can recall."

"Ok, what about last night?"

"Last night was fantastic! I was in the same lakeshore, and I knew it wasn't Earth because there were some weird animals, and the scenery something vivid… I don't know how to explain it. Anyway, the sunshine has beautiful hues of red, orange, and yellow. I am walking, and a guy is floating in the sky, a little bit away from where I am. He comes down, looks at me, reaches out for my hand, and then we take off, flying up and down over the lake and through the forest, laughing, filled with pure joy. The sensation was incredible! I awoke to feel alive and good!" Claire gushed, filled with enthusiasm.

"Wow, sounds great to me, I'm glad to hear that. Now, it seems we are getting to something here because even your expression changed when you told me about this specific dream. What about the guy? Do you like him? Does he resemble someone you know?"

"I don't remember meeting someone resembling him. I didn't have any feelings for him, although I recall the feeling of pure joy during the dream. The only thing is that we didn't need to talk, we were communicating with no words."

"Excellent, I'm going to ask you for some details about your dreams because I'm trying to find some association with your life. That's why I have to be picky sometimes."

She paused to sip some water, excusing herself, and continued, "In the past, dreams were objects of psychology. Many scholars used dreams to give them a deeper understanding of a person's life.

Studies were done, and most led to the conclusion that dreams were subjective experiences related to the dreamer's life. Some dreams are connected with everyday events, and some are linked with traumas a person has experienced. Let's try to find out what dreams play in your life. I can't promise any conclusions, yet I must say that we have made progress already because you are happy!" Johanna said, and both smiled.

"Yes, I understand. I remember having dreams in the past, and I never bothered to pay attention to them. The ones I'm having now are different, they are vivid, and I can feel the environment. It's not just like something playing on a screen, I feel like I'm actually living them."

"Yes, and that's why we need more information. First, we want to give you deep rest and peace in your sleep. Second, we want to see if there is some message in your dreams."

"Sure, whatever you say, works for me!"

"Now, don't think you are getting off easy. I'm going to guide you through this process. You are still going to have to think through some of these things for yourself."

"I know, I understand," Claire said. Suddenly, her tone shifted. Looking down she continued, "There's something else, I'm planning to quit my English classes."

"Why?" Johanna said, peering at her from above her glasses.

"I no longer enjoy my teacher, and I can't learn anymore."

"And how do you think you should deal with this situation?"

"As I said, I'm planning to quit," Claire said, showing the palms of her hand

"So, stopping the classes will solve your problem with your teacher? Is that what you think?"

"Yes, I think so. Why are you suggesting it's not an acceptable thing to do?" Claire asked, raising her eyebrows.

"I'm not saying that it isn't acceptable. You reached that conclusion on your own. Listen, Claire," Johanna took off her glasses and continued in a smooth voice, "my job is to make you think through these situations so that you can come up with your own conclusions. You need to be responsible for your own decisions, this will help you grow and bring peace to your life. I have seen evidence that you are mature enough to deal with situations like this. So, I'm asking you, do you think quitting is the right thing to do in this case?" Johanna asked, stretching her arm toward Claire.

"I don't know, maybe I should look for another challenge?" Claire said with some hesitation in her voice.

"All right, and what would this new challenge be?"

"I believe that I should pursue post-graduate studies, maybe," Claire said.

"Okay, you have a new challenge already, let's follow up this decision in our next meetings," Johanna said and took some notes.

After routine questions, they finished the session and confirmed their next appointment. The very next day Claire went to her English classes and said to Monica that she was quitting. Monica tried to persuade her to continue the course, although she knew it was better for Claire to move forward. They said goodbye to each other, promising to keep in touch, but Claire knew they were two worlds apart. The very same day, Claire started to research options for an MBA.

CHAPTER 9 - *Dying Where Nobody Should Die*

GAVRIEL'S MILITARY TRAINING was almost done. He had built a good relationship with Noah and Miller, sharing academic and personal life. In the last mission, named Surviving in an Alien Wilderness, Noah's team of six members was supposed to reach a previously determined position on Acqua. Afterward, they had to spend the night and come back without leaving any trace of their presence on the field. The team read the coordinates and headed to their target. After a journey of eight hours through a dense forest, they achieved their goal without incidents.

Gavriel looked surprised at the landscape, and said to Noah, "Hey buddy, this is the place that was in my dreams about three months ago. As soon as I arrived here, I recognized it. It looks so familiar to me. This is the place where I met that woman, remember?" he said while pointing his arm toward the lake.

"I… I remember you mentioned something, but honestly, I don't recall what it was exactly."

Gavriel then looked at Miller who also shook his head.

"This is the place! Isn't it amazing?" Gavriel continued to look around in awe, "it seems surreal to me because I had never been here before."

"It looks like an ordinary place to me," Noah said, looking up and around, while Miller just nodded, like trying to be polite.

"Ok, time to prepare for the night. Maybe you can find a way that we can all dream and fly back to the base, this mission was tough," said Noah.

"Attention everyone, here is the site to spend the night, let's set up the camp according to our instructions and let's get some sleep. We need to get up early tomorrow to finish our mission on time, " he said out loud, looking to the rest of the team that was a bit behind.

The night fell upon the team gathered by the lake, they were chatting and laughing around the fire pit when they heard a whizzing sound above their heads. Suddenly, one of their peers started to scream, blood was gushing from the top of his head, and quickly covered his entire face.

"Black-razors! Grab your guns and turn on the flashlights, circle formation, and facing out. We need to protect Miller!" Noah yelled, "Gavriel, you take care of Miller's wounds."

They could hear more black-razors approaching, but it was hard to see them in the darkness. They began to shoot randomly, but that seemed to only attract more birds, as the noise of flapping wings increased.

"Noah, Miller's bleeding isn't responding to the first aid. We need to request an emergency rescue!" Gavriel yelled.

"Ok, proceed with the emergency request," Noah replied, and Gavriel hurried to contact the base.

"To shoot isn't working, I'll protect Miller and Gavriel, the rest of you grab your laser sabres and wave them above your heads," Noah commanded and went down on his right knee beside Gavriel and Miller. The others did what they had been told, and soon the sound of the black-razors faded into the night.

The emergency and rescue vehicle came in minutes and lifted the wounded trainee to the hospital, while the others remained at the site. They managed to get inside the shelter and tried to get some sleep. About an hour later they woke up by the noise of a vessel landing just outside, and their Chief came toward them.

"We need everybody to get on board. We are returning to the base, no questions! Quickly pack your things and Let's move!" he yelled, and everyone got on board. After arriving at the station, they went straight to the board room for an emergency meeting.

"We want to hear from you what has happened on the site. Our cameras don't show anything other than the black-razors attack, but Miller has passed away," the Chief in Command said.

"What? What do you mean, you stated that we have an antidote for that poison? What's happened?" Noah questioned, clearly distraught.

"What?" The others joined in disbelief.

"Miller didn't die because of black-razors attack. His body had an unknown reaction and his internal organs melted. Something else happened, and we need to know. Tell me everything that happened since your troop left. What have you eaten? What did you drink?" he said, looking straight into Gavriel's eyes.

As the leader, Noah relayed everything they had done, and the others agreed with his report.

"If there was any wrongdoing, it was entirely my fault. I'll take all the blame and consequences," Noah said, his head hanging down.

"This is the initial inquiry. Nobody who has followed orders will be punished. I believe you did everything possible to protect Miller. We just need to go through the protocol. You are dismissed and will be contacted individually for further questions. Stay in your rooms and try to rest, dismissed," the Chief ordered, and everyone left.

The death of Miller was devastating for Gavriel, mainly because it wasn't explained and results were kept confidential. The feeling of losing someone close to him made the second part of training even more challenging.

The training was entirely based on simulating battlefields, where androids mimic a human enemy. To Kill wasn't in his plans, and he was shocked to see targeted androids bleeding like a human because it was impossible to distinguish them from real people.

One night, close to the end of the military camp, he looked in the mirror and didn't recognize himself. Gone was the innocent, new recruit. Instead, a pair of deep, cold eyes peered back at him.

He had grown a strong personal relationship with alien people, thanks to Noah's friendship. Close to the end of the training, while celebrating in one of the local pubs, Gavriel invited Noah to pay him a visit on Novus Mundus so they could play some zero gravity games.

"You are so selfish because you know that we barely have zero gravity courts on our planet, and you want to challenge me to a game that you are good at? You want to win, don't you? That's not fair! All right, I do accept, but only if you take my challenge. You pay me a visit on my planet, and we'll visit a pub. I'll choose the girl you're supposed to get, and you'll choose the one for me. The first one to get a kiss win," Noah said.

"Deal, although I'm not an expert in Zyon girls, I'm definitely the better-looking one among us, challenge accepted!" Gavriel said, and both laughed.

Gavriel recalled having many dreams while in Acqua, most of which were recorded in his personal files. The last two were really something out of this world. He recollected flying again over the same landscape he had dreamt before, just to find that woman in the same spot. When meeting her, he recalled their conversation, and although they weren't speaking, they could understand each other's thoughts.

"I remember meeting you here before!" Gavriel said.

"Yes, we have met here before," she answered.

"Do you live here?"

"No, do you?"

"No, I'm here for a military camp. Why are you here?"

"I don't know, I'm just here."

"What's your name?" Gavriel asked. He heard something, but the dream was fading, and he awoke.

On another night, he found himself on an entirely different planet and flying over some sand hills, when he made his way, at high speed, into the ground through a hole on its surface.

Inside, he found himself in a kind of illuminated freeway tunnel and landed on the road. He barely managed to avoid being hit by a floating car coming toward him at high speed. Another car coming from the same direction stopped by his side. The window on the driver's side opened, and one of the two women inside the vehicle offered him something to eat. The minute he bit into the food, he regretted it, it was horribly bitter. "This is all we have to eat over here. It feels awful, but it is the only way to survive," the woman said.

The last day on the micro planet was a special one. Every student was granted permission to take one animal to bring home as a pet. Although choosing a pet wasn't mandatory, the officials strongly recommended it to develop respect for the animal kingdom and a sense of responsibility. In the pet room, there were different types of animals, and all of them had been tested and certified to be sent to Novus Mundus. Gavriel didn't feel any connection with most of the alien animals except for one with a tiny, fluffy, white, rounded face, and four legs. It came close to him by the little fence, and the pet's eyes seemed to look at him, begging him to be chosen. It was impossible to resist, so he got that one.

CHAPTER 10 - In Miami Again

ALMOST TWO YEARS PASSED since Claire immigrated to America, and the excitement that accompanied her first year was replaced by a routine of work and slow improvements.

Sometimes she felt down because of the distance from her dad, but she knew he was doing well at the copper mine and used that feeling to comfort herself.

She was disciplined and having a well-organized agenda left no room for procrastination. She poured herself into her family affairs and duties, making sure she was there for the family in good and bad times. Claire even took responsibility for the income tax return for her aunt, helping her find options to increase her tax deductions. This made her aunt happy.

The decision to apply for an MBA program was another substantial step that helped her to build confidence. However, after months of waiting, she had yet to hear from any of the colleges she had applied to. She knew her application was delayed because of the certification of her Chilean diploma. She felt like her life was filled with waiting.

"So, what's the good news now?" Johanna asked during a therapy session.

"It came to my mind that I've been in these sessions for a year now. Even having just one session a month, it seems like a long time."

"I totally forgot that, let me see," Johanna said, searching in her notebook, "You are right. It's been one year, time is flying," Johanna said and looked to Claire, waiting for the answer.

"In my daily life, everything is fine. I don't know what to say, it seems normal."

"Normal is good news to me, I love to have patients like you. However, I might go bankrupt if everyone got better with just one session a month," Johanna said, chuckling.

"I wish I could say the same thing for when I'm sleeping. I had another dream about the ground shaking, but in this one, I'm not in the city. I'm driving on the road, and there is a four years old girl about in the back seat right behind the passenger's seat. The road starts to move like a wave, and it feels like I'm driving on an ocean. I'm not scared, and the girl seems to be fine with the situation, but I know there is something wrong."

"Do you know the girl?"

"Yes, in my dream the girl is someone close to me," Claire answered.

"No, I mean, in real life. Do you know the girl?"

"No, I don't!"

"Are you familiar with the landscape in the dream?"

"No," Claire said.

"What is the feeling in this dream?"

"It's happening."

"What is happening?" Johanna asked.

"The feeling, the feeling is *it's happening*, as if something that was expected, is finally going on."

"Ok, any other dreams?"

"Oh yeah, I'm watching TV, and there is breaking news about an American military base located in a Central American city being attacked by terrorists. Afterward, business people from the town are actually pleased because the US government addressed extra resources to that town, which was having some economic issues.

"There is another dream about the Vatican being destroyed by terrorists, using a weapon in a large black cylinder that they stole from Russia. There is another one about an American missile launched at a North Korean city, in this one the US government said it was an unintentional launch. They had taken a military drill from North Korea as a real threat and launched a missile as a counter-attack," Claire said, reading notes from her notebook.

"Wow, busy month for your dreams! When was the dream about the Vatican?" Johanna asked, looking above her glasses to Claire.

"It was actually last night. Why?"

"Haven't you heard the news? The Vatican was attacked last night, it was a massive explosion, and they have no clue what happened. It's all over the news, but there are no details about the motives, the area is cordoned off right now."

"Wow, this was really close. My dreams usually take a while to come to pass. There is more actually, remember a dream I had a long time ago about a guy flying and coming down to a lake where I was, and we both took off and flew over the landscape?"

"Yes," Johanna answered, searching her notes for where she had recorded that particular event.

"Well, I had the dream again, but not quite the same idea. In this one, the guy lands on my side and talks to me. We get into this conversation, and we both remembered that we had met before and so on. He asks my name, and I tell him, but then all of a sudden I awoke."

"Interesting," Johanna said while looking at her notes. "I've heard about people dreaming about the same subject over and over again. I've heard about people going back to the same dream on the same night, although I don't recall hearing someone who went back to an old dream and continued the conversation with another character."

"Not the same dream, but in the same place and we talked as if we both were aware of the situation."

"Yes, I got it. Well, I think I need to do some research on the subject. In the meantime, just keep taking notes about them and let me know," Johanna said, looking at her watch. "We will need to shorten our appointment today because I'm going to have lunch with my lovely daughter.

Unfortunately, we can't wait another month," she said, checking her agenda, "so I wonder if we can set an appointment in two weeks?"

"Ok, works for me, see you in a couple of weeks," Claire stood up, said goodbye mage her way to the elevator.

At the end of the day, Johanna took some time to review her notes. Looking at Claire's file, she decided to do some research about concatenated dreams. She hadn't recalled studying them before, so she decided to check if there was any material about this subject over the internet.

The search came across many video links. Without enthusiasm, Johanna clicked on a random link, which opened a short recording of a young, brown-skinned woman.

"Hi, everyone. Yeah, I had another dream about an earthquake. This time, my four-year-old daughter, Jessica, and I were driving down a road in the countryside. The road started to move up and down like waves in an ocean. My daughter thought it was cool, but I knew it was serious. I pulled over to wait for the shaking to stop." The video ended a few minutes later.

"Intriguing, maybe Claire has been watching too much YouTube videos," Johanna said, bookmarking the address.

CHAPTER 11 – Back to Novus Mundus

Cillia was thrilled to have Gavriel back, she didn't realize how much she would miss him until he was away for more than three hundred days.

"So, how was your camp? Did you miss me?" She asked, noticing that he had definitely changed. He looked more like a man than the son she had said goodbye to."

"Yes mom, of course," Gavriel answered, somewhat unenthusiastically, while hugging his grandma.

"Oh, boys never change. They want to show strength, but deep in their hearts there is a cry for mom's lap," Theena said.

"Oh Mom, you know that I love you," he said hugging his mom again.

"Yeah, I know that. So, tell us about your experience."

"To be honest," Gavriel said, "it was good and sad at the same time. Everybody says it is a pleasant experience, but for me it was painful. We lost one of our team members in the middle of the training. It was hard to keep going with that burden on our minds."

"Yikes, I'm sorry to hear that. I am sure it is rare to have a death during training camp," Theena said, looking down while shaking her head. She knew a fatality could affect the new plans of Acqua as a military camp option for many planets.

"The real cause of death was not officially released. It seems like he had a bad reaction to something.

On the other hand, I was in awe of the site. The main station is massive, and the on-the-ground missions were exhausting but completely worth it. And…" he paused, lifted a cage from the ground and took out the pet he got from Acqua, "I have a present for you," he said, opening the box, and handing the pet to Cillia.

"Oh my word, what a cute!" Cillia said, taking the fluffy white animal into her arms. "Is it a he or a she?"

"He is a boy, and he doesn't have a name yet. The doctors said his genes came from an alien planet, and he is not supposed to be aggressive. His genes were modified to eat the same food we eat, so he isn't a carnivore."

"Great! So, how are we calling him?" Theena asked.

"I'm not sure, give me a couple of days to think about it," Cillia said.

"How is work, grandma?" Gavriel asked.

"It's fine, although we haven't made much progress on my new mission to the Sick Planet. We have a plasma screener that reached that planet many years ago, but we haven't received the results of the screening yet. It takes many years for the signal to get back to us. We also have a permanent nuclear scanner that was sent to the same planet a few years ago, which is supposed to reach its target in a couple of weeks and remain there indefinitely. But it is going to take another thirty-five years to receive that signal. In other words, I'm stuck," Theena finished.

"Sorry to hear about that. How are you doing apart from your work?" Gavriel asked his grandmother.

"I'm doing well," Theena said, understanding that Gavriel was interested in her emotional well-being after Jardnn's death. "But you are on the spot now, and I have some news. There is an opening to work at the Alien Research department. It's located right beside my office, interested?"

"Wow, of course, I'm interested! But, am I qualified to work there?"

"Well, you have to have completed your military camp on Acqua, which you just did. And you have to have a recommendation from a high-ranking member of the body, me. So, it's yours if you want it," Theena said, not hiding her pride in her position.

"Great, so when do I start?"

"On Day One you will come with me, and I'll take care of the rest. Now, I have to go, see you tonight," Theena said, heading to her car.

"I got a job!" Gavriel celebrated by pumping his fist in the air.

"Yeah, but you'll have company," Cillia said, still holding her pet. "Lennah is working over there too, not in the same department, but still close enough to you."

"What? What do you mean? She was planning to go to Zyon. Why is she working here now?"

"Lennah and your grandma seemed to get along very well, especially after Jardnn's death. Your grandma decided to stay on Novus Mundus indefinitely and ended up finding a position for Lennah to work at the government too. So welcome to your new-old life," Cillia said, rubbing her pet's head.

"Great, like if I don't have enough challenges in my life. Why not another one? What the heck?" Gavriel said sarcastically, heading to his room.

"It seems like our baby is not happy with his new job already," Cillia said, talking face-to-face with her new friend.

Gavriel's sleep was tormented by another weird dream. His grandma and many other people from Novus Mundus were being sucked up by golden-coloured tubes coming from above. One of the tubes came toward him, and his mom, making the noise of a violent tornado, but passed beside without harming them.

He awoke from his sleep to realize that it was the spiritual service day, and he felt motivated to talk to Hallan, to share the news with him. He got dressed and went to the kitchen for breakfast.

"Good morning handsome! We missed you for supper yesterday," grandma said.

"Yeah, I was exhausted, and I crashed out. Hey, Mom, are you going to the spiritual services?" Gavriel asked while grabbing a fruit.

"We are going," grandma answered.

"What? You're coming as well, grandma?" Gavriel asked, really surprised. "What else happened since I left? It was probably the most exciting time this house has ever seen."

"Nothing major, I just decided to make company to your mom, and make sure I saved your spot at the church while you were gone."

"Well, great, thanks for thinking of me, but I didn't know you liked religion," Gavriel teased.

"I said that religion is not my area. Yet, as far as I am aware, Hallan doesn't preach religion at all," Theena said.

"Well, it is a complicated subject, and it seems like I'm a newbie in the area. I'm getting used to it though," Gavriel said, enjoying his first sip of coffee.

"Yeah, and I do like Hallan's preaching, the problem is that he never stops talking about his spiritual life, which didn't help to keep us together," Theena said, looking slightly to Cillia.

"What the heck, were you and Hallan married?" Gavriel burst.

"Not exactly, we weren't married according to the protocol. We were young rebels at that time, so we just decided to live together," Theena said, bracing herself for another round of questions.

"Ok, I'm done. I'm really feeling disconnected from this family," Gavriel said jokingly, while Cillia and Theena shared some laughs.

The message from Hallan about fulfilling our mission in this life was really profound, and Gavriel wondered why he had never paid attention to his words before. After the service, he went to talk to Hallan, who welcomed him with a hug.

"Welcome back young man! You have no idea how good it is to see you again. Hey, why don't you come and have breakfast with me? I haven't eaten yet, so I have a long walk up to my source food."

"I don't know. I came with Mom and grandma and,"

Hallan interrupted him, "even better, invite your mom and grandma to go with us."

"Ok, I'll ask them," Gavriel said, releasing Hallan to talk to the others.

He came back and waited for his turn again. "They said yes, so I will be having a second breakfast today," Gavriel said.

"Good for you. You can never have too much coffee, just give me a few moments, I have to make myself available to others, and then we can go," Hallan said, excusing himself and going toward another group.

On their way to the breakfast site, Hallan and Gavriel were walking together and chatting while Theena and Cillia followed about thirty feet behind, lost in their own conversation.

"So, I heard that you and my grandma used to live together."

"Oh yeah, I left it at her discretion to tell you about it because she's your grandmother. And while I don't see a problem in this kind of relationship, others do, do you?"

"Oh no, absolutely not, it just makes me feel closer to you. It could be worse," Gavriel joked, and both laugh.

"When I was on Acqua, I had many dreams, and some weird things happened."

"I see, well, tell me about the weird things and the dreams, I'm interested in both."

"One night I couldn't sleep, so I started to read the manuscript you lent me. The weird thing is that, when I decided to check my video recordings in the morning, it didn't show my incursion to the bathroom or even my reading time. I also had two dreams that seemed to be related to one another," and Gavriel told Hallan his dreams by the lake.

"Well, dreams are mostly symbolic and personal, so most of the time they have a meaning for you, and they come in symbols that make sense to you. We have the technology to scan your brain and tell if you are having dreams, what type of dreams, but we can't decode the information, you are the code and the decoder, and there's no short cut," Hallan said, smiling.

"About your ordeal with black-razors, I can infer that you are facing challenges related to your personality, and you'll find a way to deal with them, as you manage to deal with your fears.

About the developments during your sleep, I've heard of many events in which a person thinks they are awake, but they are actually sleeping. However, I never heard about someone who was reading a text while sleeping. Are you sure you were awake?"

"Yes, I am. I can even tell you the content!" Gavriel said seriously.

"Ok, so, it might be a fail in the recording system. About meeting someone in a dream as if it was a continuation of a previous event, that's a bit mysterious for me too, and I'm curious to know about the meaning. Hey girls, breakfast time, we have arrived!" he said, extending his arms toward the cabin, and Gavriel realized that he would remain without answers.

CHAPTER 12 – Our Life is a Roller Coaster

"I WAS ACCEPTED!" Claire relayed to her aunt enthusiastically, after opening the letter from a college she had applied for an MBA. She read on, until finding the tuition amount, and realized that it was impossible to fit in her budget. Aunt Mirna did everything to convince Claire that there were many options she could try.

That night Claire went to bed frustrated, and inconsolable fell asleep. The guy came down flying again, although this time he didn't land. He gently grabbed Claire by her hand and flew up to the sky. She could see the landscape of the planet, where she was, fading in the distance, as she found herself heading to a giant world right in front of them.

For a brief moment, she had a flutter of fear, but it soon disappeared when she began to soar over the planet's landscape. It seemed like the guy was showing her the place, and it was daytime so she could see a long and bright train crossing the skies, Whizzing way above the ground. She could identify what seemed to be floating buildings scattered around, and vehicles moving between them.

Night descended, and she identified spots of light way below, what she supposed to be vehicles running in many directions. He suddenly went down, and she found herself in front of what looked like a giant mushroom surrounded by glass walls.

"I live here," he said.

Claire just nodded, to convey that she understood what he said.

"My name is Gavriel. What's your name again?"

"Claire. Where am I?"

"You are in my house on planet Novus Mundus. Are you from Acqua?"

"Acqua? No, I don't even know what Acqua is. I'm from Earth."

"Acqua is the planet where we came from. Where is Earth located?"

"I don't know where we have the moon and the sun," she said in a tentative to locate Earth, but she couldn't.

They were interrupted by his mom's pet brought from Acqua, which came toward them in the room.

"What a beautiful dog you have," Claire said, extending her hand by the dog's nose.

"A dog you said? Do you have dogs on your planet?"

"Yes, we do, and this is a beautiful fluffy Yorkshire," and she tried to grab the dog, but she awoke.

My Lord that was a fantastic dream, she thought right after waking up, and grabbed her notebook, and recorded every detail about the dream.

Claire spent her day trying to find some alternatives for her MBA tuition but found nothing. It was a disappointing situation, but she was known for her perseverance, so her mind and soul were committed to finding a solution. *You can do it, you can do it*, were the words hammering her mind. She decided to make an appointment with the principal to ask for financial support. *Things will get better*, she thought to herself and jumped out of bed, for another day of work.

It was an ordinary work day, and she was alone as usual. The dream from the previous night kept replaying in her mind. She even brought her notebook to go over the details of the dream. During her break, she went to the computer and tried to search for images she recalled from her dreams. She found some exciting drawings resembling the buildings, but couldn't find anything really close to the many things she saw on the planet. It was just noon, but she was anxiously waiting for the night, and for the dreams to come. That afternoon, time felt like an eternity.

#

In Novus Mundus, Gavriel met her mom at breakfast and recalled his last dream.

"Mom, you won't believe it," Gavriel said during their quick breakfast. "I had a dream night, and I meet this woman that I have met in a dream before. The woman said that this animal is a dog," Gavriel said, pointing to the puppy. "She also said that he is common in her world, and he is a kind of fluffy York... something. I don't really recall the full word."

"Really?" answered his mom, "maybe it's a hint about the name we're supposed to give to him. Let's call him Fluffy. Hi, Fluffy, how are you doing?" Cillia said, petting him and getting a bark from the dog.

"See, he likes it. Your grandma was in a rush, so she went to the office already, and she is waiting for you. You know she is an early bird, so finish your coffee and move on," she said while petting the dog.

Gavriel arrived at the central government building and was automatically scanned by the entrance. He followed the floating orb in front of him, knowing it would lead to his grandma's office.

"You are very early for tomorrow's shift," Theena joked as Gavriel arrived.

"Let's work," she said, getting out of her floating cocoon chair, where she managed her daily duties. She moved to another room separated by glass. The huge room was filled with 3D images and people. Gavriel wasn't surprised, he had visited this place before as part of the UCD studies. She introduced him to another young woman, who was supposed to be his supervisor for now.

"This is Zenya. Zenya, this is Gavriel. You are both familiar with the policies and protocols, so please proceed with your duties," Theena turned her back on both, and went back to her floating cocoon chair.

"Yeah, that's the grandma, straight to the point," Gavriel said, getting a little laugh from Zenya.

He spent the day familiarizing himself with his duties and was very excited to learn that he had the freedom to research alien life. Nevertheless, he knew, he was expected to follow the procedures and bring some consistent results from his work. If he didn't, he could be sent to another department, or worse, go back to the UCD lectures to recalibrate his skills.

That night, during his sleep, Gavriel found himself in Acqua, and he decided to get straight to the point. He wanted to gather information that would help him find another planet. If Claire really were someone from another world, the implications of this discovery would be profound.

He came down from the skies again, but this time, he didn't take her for a flight. Instead, he stopped for a while, and looked at her carefully. She also paid attention to him, and his face became more natural. His initial glowing appearance faded, revealing a handsome man.

"Hi, Claire. It seems like we live in different places," Gavriel said, acknowledging they were in a different dimension.

"Hi, yes, I guess, but I'm a little bit confused."

"You said that you are from planet…" he said and waited for her to complete the sentence.

"Earth," Claire answered, completing the sentence.

"Tell me more about Earth."

"More like what? I don't know what to say."

"Something like, what honeycomb system it belongs, how many planets there sustain life, and how many luminous starts are in the system," Gavriel said.

"What's a honeycomb system?"

"We divide space in honeycombs, forming a hive, to understand and locate the stars and the planets in the universe."

"Oh, we don't use a honeycomb system. The only thing I know is that we have some planets, and one star in our system which we call the sun," Claire answered in an attempt to bring the conversation toward something she had a knowledge of.

"How many planets do you have in your system? Are they all the same? I mean, size and shape?"

Now Claire understood that Gavriel was trying to pinpoint Earth in the universe.

"I think we have around nine planets, but I'm not sure. They have different sizes, but I don't recall them by size. Saturn has rings around it, like a ball with one large disc around."

"Our planet is two-thirds water," Gavriel said, just to be interrupted by a flock of black-razors coming toward them.

"Let's get out of here!" Gavriel abruptly said, grabbing Claire by the arm. He tried to fly but his feet didn't move from the ground, so he pushed Claire, and they started to run.

"What?" Claire asked confused, and panic started to build up.

"See those black dots in the sky coming toward us? They are black-razors, they are poisonous, and we need to hide from them," Gavriel said, heading toward the woods.

They both reached the woods, yet black-razors were getting closer. They took a swipe at Claire's head but missed. She tried to keep them away from flapping her arms above her head, and then she awoke.

#

"When I extended my hand to grab the dog, I woke up," Claire said, explaining her dream to Johanna in her therapy session.

"You said the guy is from a planet called Novus Mundus?" Johanna asked, checking her notes.

"Yes, and as I said, I had a glimpse of his planet while heading toward his house," motioning with her hands as she answered.

"Can you say something about the buildings on Novus Mundus or something that caught your attention?"

"I was flying at a fair distance from the ground, but I could see that all buildings had a dome-like shape, and they were floating above the ground. They resembled mushrooms and had large glass doors around them."

"Go on," Johanna said while making notes.

"On the following dream, we were at the lakeshore, and the scenery looked more realistic. I noticed details about Gavriel, like his multi-color eyes, and large rings on his middle fingers and thumbs," Claire said.

"What else?" Johanna asked, just looking over the glasses.

"In this last dream, he asked me details about our planet, like how many planets are in our system, whether we have other planets sustaining life, etc. He was clearly curious about trying to locate our planet. We couldn't go further in our conversation because we were attacked by some black birds," Claire stopped as though waiting for further questions.

"What kind of birds?"

"I don't know. Gavriel just said they are poisonous, and we started to run. Then I awoke, and that's it," Claire said, hoping Johanna would focus her attention toward the specifics of the story, rather, than just trying to find a rational connection with dreams.

"Do you see any connection between your dreams and your real life? For instance, you said that the guy looked handsome. I wonder if you met or came across a guy lately that you saw as attractive. Or the birds, any situation from the past relating to birds that might have caused some trauma?"

"No, not at all," Claire said. "I don't think I have been in a situation that would lead my mind to have such unusual dreams, especially having them in a sequence. I don't think I have that power," Claire said with a different tone in her voice. She seemed to be impatient about the direction of her sessions.

"Do you see any connection between your dreams and that signal from outer space detected from NASA a few years ago?"

"No, it didn't come to my mind that there could be a connection," she said raising her shoulders.

"You know Claire," Johanna said, noticing Claire's frustration. "As a professional, I have to go after the facts, even knowing that these dreams build up a lot of emotions on you. I can help you find some answers, but at the end of the day, you are the only one who can understand the meaning of your dreams.

The sources I have are based on studies, and these studies lead me to conclude that your dreams are projections of personal situations.

There are studies about collective consciousness dreams, but it is hard to find conclusive evidence that dreams can predict future events or communicate with life on other planets. We just don't have the data to verify that this is even possible.

Theories based on quantum physics might give us some understanding of relating to other dimensions. Astronomy is also proposing that there are plenty of planets hosting life, but there is no link to associate dreams with these scientific studies, for now.

In your case, we aren't supported by any previous surveys, because there are so many variables that are difficult to fit into the fundamental scientific methodology. So here we are. We are in this thing together, and as I said, I'll do my best to help you," Johanna said, trying to reassure her.

"Ok, I understand," said Claire in a frail voice.

"Let's do this, I'll check some notes from my previous sessions, and dig into non-academic sources of knowledge about this subject. I might find something to help us. Does it work for you?"

"Yes," Claire said, opening her hands.

"Last Saturday you told me that you were accepted into an MBA program and that you're trying to find money for the tuition. Any news on that front?"

"Yes, I'm trying to set up an appointment with the principal, but he's busy. I could only schedule an appointment to see him in about three months, so I have to wait."

"Good Lord, three months?"

"Well, they asked about the subject of my request, and I told them it was in regards to my tuition. Apparently, that is a low priority for them, so I have to wait."

"Good job, don't worry about the delay in your appointment. It's always a good procedure to talk to someone face-to-face. Speaking of appointments, I'm afraid to mess up your agenda again, but I'll be away for vacation next month, and you have given me a lot of information to digest. I wonder if we can have another session before my leave. Does the beginning of next week work for you?"

"Yes."

"Ok, let's close our session for today, see you next week," Johanna said, stood up and followed Claire, out to the elevator.

#

Gavriel couldn't stop thinking about his dreams. His last conversation with Claire was a massive breakthrough in the quest to discover a new planet. At the very least, he would be able to build a case for an unexplored world using a different approach or maybe a sophisticated method of communication.

I'm probably close to decoding the organic wave structure and might be able to communicate in real time with the entire universe. This discovery could boost my career in the Alien Research department, and I might even be promoted to a very high level in the government and, he was thinking.

"Hello Gavriel, are you there?" He lifted his head and saw Zenya standing in front of his cocoon chair, bringing him back to reality. "We have to accomplish four tasks this week, and I sent you two of them to start, please check your messages. Questions?" she asked.

"No, thanks for letting me know," Gavriel said, leaning back into his floating cocoon chair. He couldn't wait for Zenya to leave so he could continue his research on Claire's planet.

Let me see, Claire said that they have nine planets in their system, one planet with rings, one star providing light, and the results are... Rats, above three hundred thousand planets just in our lower body receiver. I need more information to get this right.

Gavriel spent the rest of the day working on his own project. At the end of his shift, he was leaving the office when he heard Zenya from her desk shouting.

"Hey Gavriel, don't forget," she was saying but was cut off by Gavriel.

"I know, the tasks, I've been working on my duties," he replied.

"No, I'm talking about the haircut. You know you are expected to show loyalty to the government, so if you don't mind, just do it," Zenya finished.

"Oh yes, the haircut," Gavriel said, rubbing his head.

He was aware the haircut was not mandatory. Still, it was a personal gesture to show loyalty to the government, and of course, he was aiming to get a higher position. He sat at one of the haircut floating cocoon chairs available on every level and leaned his head into it for a scanner.

"Welcome to our midst, Gavriel. Your loyalty is much appreciated" the robot said and began to cut his hair, designing a semi-circle pointing up, just above his neck. "Congratulations, you are now part of the family. I'm looking forward cut a higher rank shortly," the robot said.

"Yeah, me too," said Gavriel, standing up and making his way to his Suphcar while touching the cut. He could feel the outline of the seven stars that were now shaped inside the semi-circle. The configuration of the stars indicated his rank. *Soon those stars will change their position,* he thought to himself.

#

Night came, and he dreamt again. This time, he was already by the lake, right beside Claire.

"Hi Claire, let's walk by the beach?"

She promptly accepted, and they started to walk along the shore close to the woods.

"It's ok if I hold your hand?" he asked.

"Yes. Does it have a meaning in your culture?"

"Kind of, and I'm also trying to keep you in this dream if we were to be bullied by those nasty birds. So, tell me, do you know how much water you have on your planet?"

"It's two-thirds."

"Do you guys have artificial gravity?" he continued, making no room for her talk.

"I don't even know what artificial gravity is, why are you asking things about my planet all the time?" Claire asked.

"Oh, I need it for a research project, and I need to know where you are coming from," Gavriel answered without further explanation. Listening to a weird noise, he turned his head and could see black-razors coming toward them.

"Oh no, what the yapoo!" he said, released her hand and ran away, yet Claire decide to stay put, watching him disappear inside the woods. She awoke.

At Johanna's office, Claire was finishing her report about her last dream with Gavriel, "…and he ran into the woods, looking for protection."

"Is there anything else particular in this dream?"

"Yeah, this time, there was something different about his hair. He had a regular haircut except that at the very back of his skull there was a kind of half circle with six stars inside it and one in the middle."

"It was a tattoo?"

"No, just the hair was cut in a way that formed that layout."

"Why did you stay put and didn't run with him when the birds attacked?"

"I don't know, I didn't feel threatened by them at all."

"Do you have an idea why these birds frequently pop up in your dream?"

"I don't know…" Claire paused for a few seconds. "Listen, Johanna, I know you are trying your best, and you have to do this professionally, but I think I need some time to myself. I'm planning to stop my sessions for a while if you don't mind."

"I can't interfere in your decisions. If you think this is the best choice for you, we can take a break," Johanna said, putting away her notebook.

"Yes, I think I need a break. Besides, you said that I need to find the answers myself, and that's what I'll try to do. I need to find myself before looking for answers, and I think I'm stuck right now.

I understand that we have already accomplished our goal, which was to help my sleep. The earthquake dreams had gone, so that goal has been achieved," Claire said.

"Ok, let's have a break if this is the best for you. Feel free to come back whenever you want, just call me, so we can adjust our schedules."

"Ok, thanks," Claire said, standing up and heading to the elevator.

Johanna followed her up to the elevator and then went to the window to watch Claire cross the street, disappearing behind a building. *She sure has grown up,* Johanna thought, smiling.

As she headed home, Claire submerged her thoughts. *'I'm stuck and I need to get out of my routine if I want my life to make sense. I need to do something different, but what? Nobody has gotten back to my dreams and even this Gavriel seems immersed in personal ambitions. Maybe it's not even real and it's only in my subconscious, what an irony, it seems that even my subconscious conspires against me.*

I doesn't matter, I will not live under pressure from frustrations, I will go after my dreams, I will overcome this. And mentally Claire sketched out her next steps:' *Find a new job, strengthen your self-esteem, find a goal in your life. That's it, it's a good start."*

CHAPTER 13 – Locating Earth

RATS, HOW STUPID I AM! How could I forget to ask Claire about the planet's calendar? How? Gavriel thought to himself, frustrated by his forgetfulness. *The number of days in a calendar year would give me the needed information to tabulate the data and find her planet's location, damn it!* Gavriel thought, punching the inner wall of his floating cocoon chair. *Now I have to wait for another dream to meet Claire, and deal with those terrible birds. In the next dream, I have to be quicker and walk even closer to the woods.*

The sleep came without any dream, and the next few nights were dreamless as well. *What's going on?* He thougt.

"Good morning Gavriel. What happened to you? Are you sleeping ok? You're pale and look tired," Zenya said by the beginning of day 4.

"I'm fine, I'm just not having a good sleep."

"Ok, don't forget our weekly report. We need to present at ten o'clock."

Oh no, I'm screwed! He thought, passing his right hand over his hair. He had forgotten about the report deadline, and there was no time to even start it. *Well, at least it's Day Four, and it's almost the weekend,* he sighed

"Hi everyone," Theena greeted her sixteen team members. "Let's start, team one, what's the news?"

"We have good news. Yesterday we received the transmission from our plasma screener vessel that was sent thirty-five years ago to explore the planet 6H365Y24T, which we kindly nicked-named Sick planet," the team leader reported.

"We spent part of the night checking some of the data, and we found some significant information already.

The planet runs on a 365-day calendar, confirming our previous information. It had around one hundred million human-like people at the time the scanner collected the data. However, we can't predict the population today. Keep in mind that every year here in

Novus Mundus is equal to three and a half years on the Sick Planet. More than one hundred years have passed on that planet since our plasma screener collected the data.

The basic atmosphere composition is basically the same as what we have on Novus Mundus, although the biodiversity scores point to levels never before seen here on Novus Mundus, and this goes for both their botanic and zoological life. That's it for now." The leader finished, receiving some applause from the crowd.

"Good job. Now team two, what do you guys have?" Theena asked.

"We have the confirmation that the nuclear scanner will reach the planet in about ten Novus Mundus days, but it will take another thirty-five years to receive the information back. Hopefully, we will have news from our Organic Waves Studies Department in less than thirty-five years," she finished, and everyone present laughed.

"Team three, my attention is all yours," Theena said.

"Yes, we know for sure there is no way to reach this planet in time to avoid a catastrophe.

Our latest simulations about the outcomes for that world forecast some, or perhaps all of the following consequences: first, the continued deterioration of the biomass, detected by organic waves, will probably change the layers of the atmosphere on the planet, decreasing or even destroying some layers. Our historical data suggests that in this case, the other layers will adjust their thickness to protect the remaining biomass.

This event would drastically affect population growth as well as human health conditions due to a decrease in natural light, and stellar radiation exposure.

Second, an increase of the surface temperature on the planet will trigger its self-protection program, forcing its core to expel ashes into the atmosphere.

There will be interference on the organic waves. Light speed space travel will be almost impossible, and our real-time detection systems will be muted," the leader finished.

"Very good, or perhaps I should say, terrible," Theena said, getting some grim faces from the audience. "Team four?"

"Well, we have finished two tasks delegated to our team for the week; however, we are still behind on two others so we won't be able to present the results today," Zenya said.

"Ok, thanks, everyone, by the end of the day, I'll assign your new tasks for next week. Team four, please remain in my office while the others are dismissed."

"So Zenya, what's happened to your team?"

"Well, I think Gavriel might need extra training, or extra time for his tasks because it seems like he's struggling to meet the deadlines."

"Ok, Gavriel, you stay. The others are dismissed, thanks," Theena said in a calm voice, holding the palms of her hands together.

"What happened Gavriel? What might be affecting your work?" she expressed in a controlled voice.

"Well, I just didn't have time," Gavriel said.

"That's it, you didn't have time?" Theena asked, exasperated.

"I was expecting something more convincing. Listen, Gavriel, you are starting your professional life, your career, and you are very, very lucky that you are under my supervision.

In real life, your boss would check your weekly records and you'd be screwed. I know you enough, to save my time double-checking it because I can see you sitting in that chair all day long doing something, but your work." Theena said, now with some anger in her voice.

"I know that there is something else going on, but it's time to understand that there are parts of your life that don't belong to you. Your professional life at the government doesn't belong to you, *Capeesh*?" Theena firmly said.

"What?" Gavriel said, confused about the word.

"Oh. *Capeesh* is just an alien word for, 'do you understand?'"

"Yes, madam, I'm sorry, I screwed up, it's entirely my fault. I was probably selfish and even naive about a fast-track career. I'll make things right by working through the weekend, to have the results by Day One. I'm sorry to disappoint you," Gavriel said, his face downcast.

"Ok, I can see that you have grown up. People make mistakes, yet just a few recognize it. Welcome to deadlines, welcome to real life. You are dismissed, although you should clear things up with your teammates," she said while heading to Zenya's floating cocoon chair.

"Good job," Theena said, taping Zenya's cocoon chair when passing by, then making her way out of the office.

CHAPTER 14 – The Universe is Full of Life

SINCE SHE HAD BOUGHT A BIKE, Claire was able to fit more commitments into her day. On her way back home, she stopped by the library. She met Rachel, the library assistant who helped her.

Claire also searched the internet, and tried to be selective in what she learned, "garbage in, garbage out," she perused an article about technology, so "no garbage in" she said to herself.

Rachel announced that the library was closing, so Claire got her bike and took off. When she arrived home, her aunt was already sleeping, and she felt terrible to realize that the price for her pursuit of a better life, was taking precious time from her relationship with her loved ones. This thought filled her with some regret while going to bed.

Claire was watching a parade from a building, and she knew she was in a dream. She saw military vehicles and personnel passing by a crowd of people watching the show. Flags waved high in the air, as a massive fire truck passed by. Its siren was wailing as it moved down the street with the procession, and it was draped with a huge white and red flag with a red leaf.

She looked beyond the buildings and saw a rogue, black wave coming toward the shore. She yelled and waved to the crowd on the streets to alert them, but nobody acknowledges her. She frantically ran down the stairs, which seemed to never end, when she awoke.

It was a vivid dream she had, after just a week away from her psychology sessions. She knew the dream was warning her about something that was going to happen in the future but didn't have Johanna to share with, so she decided just to take notes.

During the day, she went to the library to return the books she had borrowed. Stopping by the counter, waited for Rachel who was talking on a cell phone.

"I need to hang up now, bye," turning to Claire, Rachel apologized, "Sorry about that, it was my boyfriend."

"It's ok, I don't have these problems," Claire said, realizing that she said something that might be misunderstood by Rachel. "Oh, sorry Rachel, I didn't mean your boyfriend, I mean a cell phone, I don't use cell phones."

"Oh, it's ok. Boyfriends can be a pain in the neck sometimes, so you are forgiven," Rachel said, laughing.

"I feel stupid for saying that crap."

"Don't worry, did you like the books?"

"Yeah, kind of. You can always learn something when you read a book, but this one is too theoretical. I'm looking for something more practical, so I guess I'll have to come up with my own solutions."

"What are you looking for?"

"I'm looking for something efficient on how to develop new ideas. I feel like my life has been stuck in a routine.

I read in this one that, in theory, technology can help us on our everyday tasks, on the other hand, it doesn't benefit our brain to develop in areas that we are supposed to keep active. So, I made up my own plan, I gave up my cell phone, and I'll see if it's possible to live without it."

"Are you nuts? How can you live without a cell phone? You're gonna die, I can't survive without mine," Rachel said, shaking her head.

"That's the idea. I'll try to get some useful results from this experience, and maybe I can publish my results and become famous," Claire said jokingly. "I still keep the device with me, but I no longer have service, so I just use where there's free WI-FI, or to call 911 in an emergency."

"Hum, why don't you start to publish your thoughts in a blog? You might help other people who are looking for ideas on the subject."

"I don't know, it seems too complicated, especially if I'm trying to get away from technology. Besides, I don't even have a camera."

"Well, that's the point. If you can prove that it's possible to live a balanced life using the resources available, you will be successful in your mission. Listen, the library has a booth you can use to record your videos and computers to edit them. Why don't you come back in a half hour? I'll have a helper in a few minutes so I can dedicate some time to give you basic instructions," Rachel suggested.

"Sure, why not? I'll stick around, and we can talk later," said Claire.

While she was waiting, Claire took out her cell phone and made a note in her calendar about the topics she would use for her first video. After half an hour, Rachel came to her table and invited her to go to the soundproof booth.

"See, it's hushed, and as long you don't feel bothered by people watching you through the glass wall, you are ok.

Now, this is the equipment you can use. To start recording your message, click here. After finishing your recordings, the app will automatically load the video editor so you can make adjustments. The app has video tutorials you can access if you need help. Do your first recording, then call me. I'll show you how to publish it," Rachel finished.

"Ok, thanks."

About two hours later, Claire called Rachel, who went through the recording. "Great job! Now let's publish it on your own channel. People can subscribe if they want to follow you… there, done!" Rachel said, watching the video on Claire's own channel.

"I'll subscribe to your channel. I want to be the first one," Rachel celebrated.

"Ok, let's upload this other video too," Claire said, clicking on another file.

Rachel watched the uploaded video and asked, "Is this part of your practical advice? It sounds like you are narrating a story."

"It's a dream, I'm having lots of dreams, and I'd like to publish them as well," Claire said.

"It's interesting and well done. Why did you put that maple leaf at the end of your dream?" Rachel asked.

"It's an image I saw on the top of a fire truck during my dream. I didn't know it was a maple leaf, so I just searched images with a red leaf, on the internet, and I found this one," Claire answered.

"Well, I'm from Canada, and this is the leaf that belongs to the Canadian flag. Tell me more about this dream," Rachel asked Claire, and she did so.

Days later, when working on her blog, Claire read some feedbacks and regretted. She felt punched in the stomach over some awful comments. *They are probably coming from the dark side of the soul, where envy and jealousy reside,"* she thought.

The bitter comments weren't easy to swallow, and she got frustrated. She was tempted to put an end to this blog thing, but then she remembered a lesson learned many years ago. She decided to use the experience as her answer for some of the mean comments and wrote:

'I will never forget what I learned in high school. The teacher called it the "love one another for dummies lesson."

One day, our teacher came to the classroom with a paper split into two columns. Both were numbered from row one to twenty-four, the exact number of students in our classroom. He also projected the class list on the screen, with students' names and their respective number in the class list.

"Before starting our regular class, I'll give you an opportunity to say whatever you want to say about your classmates," the teacher said.

"On the left column of this sheet, you will write down everything you like about each student. So, for number one, which is Diane, write positive words about her. You could write, friendly, beautiful, etc. On the right column, you can write down whatever you dislike in that person. Whatever you want to say, as bad things, horrible things, nasty things, it's entirely up to you.

This will be completely anonymous, you don't need to sign it or put your name anywhere on it. Bring this sheet back to me without any identification, and place it on my desk facing down so nobody can identify you, and nobody will know who wrote it."

'That last part of the instructions brought frenzy to the classroom. So many of us wanted to share our opinions about others in our class, and our teacher had given us the chance to say every bad thing we thought anonymously.

At the end of class, the teacher said, "Now I'm going to read the lists of what you've written about your peers to the entire class."

A sound of surprise swept through the classroom. Some students cheered, others were a bit more reserved.

The teacher started with the good feeling's column: "Diane people see you as beautiful, intelligent, mature, honest, and hot."

"Woohoo," cheered the classroom.

"Someone is in love here," said another student. It was a lot of fun. Each student was entitled to receive his or her good feelings words.

"Now the bad things," said the teacher, raising the pile of sheets up in the air, and tearing them apart. He took the negative column and tossed it into the garbage.

"If you keep this lesson for your life, I'll feel like I've accomplished a mission. Remember, always tell people how good they are, and always keep your negative opinions to yourself. In the end, good feelings will always encourage people. However, bad feelings can kill people and whatever doesn't kill them might leave scars forever. Whatever comes from your mouth is what you carry in your heart. Keep in mind that the bad feelings are more an indication of what is inside of you, than anything having to do with that person. Think about this."

It was a lesson I will never forget. That's exactly what I want to do as my "love one another for dummies lesson. Thank you all,' Claire finished.

After a while, Claire's subscribers reached a stable rate of growth, and she felt rewarded. She managed to add many videos into her *Talent's Brainstorming* blog. Although she wasn't making money, felt honoured to be invited to talk about her experience in different online chats and some local radio stations.

#

It hadn't been a good month for Gavriel. He felt swamped by work, and joy seemed to avoid him.

To make things worse, he felt betrayed by Zenya and pressured by Lennah, who worked near to him and was always sitting by his side in the cafeteria, during their breaks.

After days without having any dream, his plan to find Claire's planet was postponed.

"So, what's up? What's the news about the Sick Planet?" Lennah asked.

"No news, we are stuck," Gavriel answered grumpily.

"Well, maybe I can help you?" Lennah said, looking up, and trying to gauge Gavriel's interest in the subject.

"What you mean you can help me?" he said, uninterested while looking to his sandwich.

"It's not that I know something in particular, but I have an idea that might help you guys to get more information about the situation. It might help you come up with a more accurate analysis."

"So, what's your idea?" he said scratching the back of his head.

"There are other sources of information for the planets we have screened before, and you probably don't have access."

"What sources?" Gavriel asked, still not showing much interest.

"In the database," Lennah said, raising her hands as if it was a no-brainer question.

"So, what's the secret?" Gavriel asked in a mocking tone.

"Well, all the plasma screeners receive directives to reach a particular target, and to do so they travel in a random motion. Also, after finishing their primary task, they fly off into space at a ninety-degree angle from their origin and keep sending collected information along with their route indefinitely. We call this process extended missions.

The catch is, we cross-reference our data and the information collected in extended missions, so we can get accurate details about most planets during their evolution. We might have up to date information about the Sick planet, not just the thirty-five-year-old you have."

"Sounds interesting, how can we have this information?" Gavriel said, raising his eyebrows.

"Data from extended missions aren't open to the public, or even to our level of access. Only someone with a high rank can have access so you will need to ask permission from someone like your grandma," Lennah said, crossing her hands again like she was waiting for his input.

"Lennah, it was a pleasure to have lunch with you. I'll talk to my grandma right away," Gavriel said, excited. He stood up, and was about to leave, but not before saying, "See you tomorrow at lunch."

Gavriel was informed that Theena had left for the day so he would have to wait until Day One. Grandma made it clear that she didn't want to talk about their work at home. Due to her position in the government, they were aware that they would be monitored all the time.

That night, Gavriel went late to the bed, and his sleep was filled with nightmares. He dreamt being followed by black-razors all night long until he woke up.

That's enough! He thought to himself. He needed to return Hallan's book so he would take the time to talk to him about the latest developments of his dreams. He tried to contact him many times, but he was unreachable.

After his work, he went to Hallan's place in a try to find him. Getting there, he grabbed the book and headed toward the cabin.

By the woods, he noticed that the old entrance was blocked by trunks, and there was another one, not far from where he was.

He called Hallan again but had no answer, so he decided to use the new entrance to reach the cabin.

Ten minutes into the woods, he came across with a fork and took the left way. After another fifteen minutes, he found another one and, following it for a while, ended up in a dead end. He made his way back and took another direction, just to find himself at another dead end. *Rats, now I have to go all the way back to the first fork*, he thought, and kept walking, taking different directions, but always coming to dead ends.

He thought to hear weird noises, like black-razors flying, and although he couldn't see anything up in the skies, getting anxious, he sped up. After a while, he found the cabin, but Hallan wasn't there and panicked. *Am I in the right place?*

Afraid of getting lost, he decided to get back before the dark, so he got inside the cabin and left the book on the table. He was about to go, when Hallan called him using the live line.

"Hi Gavriel, sorry, I missed your calls. What's going on?"

"Hi, I wanted to return your book and talk to you about some dreams I'm having, but it's ok, we can talk another time," Gavriel answered, and sighed.

"Hum, I can feel that something is bugging you. The challenges and triumphs you are having are a mirror of your personal strengths and weaknesses, and you won't find peace before dealing with them.

Once I told you to seek the truth, and the truth will give you the answers. I'll give you some tips about finding the truth. Find in your workplace all the government records about what we are talking right now."

"What? What you mean?"

"Just do it, and you'll notice that not everything people tell you, is actually true. Lies can make you blind. If I give you the answer, how do you expect to learn about truth?

Well, I have to hang-up, and I suggest you spend some time with oneself, bye" Hallan said, and abruptly hung-up.

Shocked, and having no choice, he left the cabin downcast. As he walked back, his concerns started to fade, and he found himself not thinking at all, just serene and walking like in an autopilot mode. He lost the reference of time, just coming back to reality, when he saw a dim light from an illuminated area by the main entrance of the woods, and realized he had been walking fearlessly in the dark.

#

Claire got home, turned on the TV, and heard that San Francisco, California, was rattled by an earthquake. The shock caused a lot of damage to buildings, and infrastructure. The quake also triggered a tsunami on the west coast, hitting many cities in both, the United States and Canada. Although it was long due, according to experts in seismology, the devastation was something nobody expected or wanted to experience.

The story covered the airwaves for many weeks until traffic was restored, and the rebuilding had begun.

Her life took a huge turn when she found her email box loaded with hundreds of emails.

Apparently, one television station discovered that, in at least three of her published dreams, there were connections with the earthquake, including the date it happened, July 1st, Canada Day.

The publications on her blog were enough to bring a deluge of media attention. She arrived at the home and found a few television station trucks waiting for her.

She couldn't escape, and for more than an hour, had to answer questions from reporters.

"How did you know about it?", "Are you a clairvoyant?", "Do you have more predictions?"

Those were some of the sensationalist questions she had to go through. Claire managed to answer most, and made her way inside the house, promising that she would report any new dreams on her blog.

She was so happy about not having a cell phone. Her limited social media helped her retain a balanced perspective, and she looked forward to having her life back to normal again. As a result of this event, she had to quit her job, to manage new commitments in her life.

Everything seemed to be going along smoothly, and she was rattled to discover that everything on her web page had been deleted. She contacted the provider and was informed that they had a technical problem, her subscription didn't include a backup feature, and everything had gone.

In a fraction of a second, she felt struck by a train, because she hadn't backed up her files either.

The only strategy that came to her mind was to inform subscribers and recreate her videos and posts. She remembered having shared some comments through emails, so she decided to begin by searching through the email box. She opened up her account and found to her dismay that all of her messages had been deleted as well. A feeling of dread filled her, as she realized that this had been done intentionally.

She called a friend who worked with computers, hoping he could help recover something. All she got, though, was the realization that her accounts, all of them, had been hacked. Whoever had done it, made sure to erase all her data from history. For the first time, she hated technology.

#

Coming back from Hallan's cabin, Gavriel went straight to the bed and fell asleep. As if it was only a few seconds later falling asleep, he awoke to feel different than the day before. He was feeling great, he wasn't tired, and it seemed like the entire planet was quieter.

He went to work and saluted everyone who crossed his way. Zenya came to talk to him, and he didn't have that weird feeling about her. He just felt fine.

"Hi, Gavriel! Good morning! Apparently, we have news about the Sick Planet."

"What news?"

"We just detected a spike in its organic waves, a signal about an intense event. We analyzed all the variables and concluded that it was a massive earthquake.

According to historical data, the size of this event indicates that the planet has tremendous internal pressure due to the surface temperature. This event could trigger a systemic reaction."

"What do you mean reaction?"

"The signal indicates that this event was localized, which means that a worldwide reaction might be underway."

"Yikes," Gavriel said. "Good job. It seems like right now there's nothing we can do but wait, right?"

"Yes, you are right. However, let's not forget about our next steps, if there are no signs of temperature decrease."

"Yes, I understand. Thanks for keeping me up to date, I feel honoured to work with you," and Zenya turned back, raising her eyebrows while leaving. *What the heck? Is this guy high?* She thought to herself

The afternoon meeting brought news about the Sick Planet event, as well as the next steps for the team.

After everyone had left, Gavriel talked privately with Theena. He was careful with his words, as he was aware everything he said would be monitored.

"Hi, Theena! It came to my mind that we should try to find additional sources of information about the Sick Planet," Gavriel said, looking deep into her eyes.

"I agree. What do you have in mind?" she asked, noticing Gavriel's unusual look.

"I wonder if you could authorize Lennah to have privileged access to the database. She works in a department that might have additional information that pertains to our research. If we get it, we will need to spend some time creating algorithms to search for sensitive information about the Sick Planet."

"That's a good idea, I'll do it right now," Theena said, making changes to the system, anything else?"

"No, thanks," he said, and went back to his post.

Gavriel finished his work and left the building. Once at home, he skipped supper, talked to some friends from his military camp for a couple of hours, and then went to sleep. That night, he found himself on Acqua, right beside Claire, who was walking by the lake.

"Hi Claire, where have you been?" he asked excited.

"Taking care of my life," she said roughly, without stopping or looking at him.

"Have you been here since we talked last time? I'm asking you because I don't recall coming here lately," Gavriel said, noticing the resentfulness.

"No, I've been busy with my life and my country. We had an earthquake, and I was caught in some weird events," Claire said stepping up her pace. It was noticeable that she was trying to find her way out.

"Are you serious? Do you mean a tremor?" he asked, and stopped, catching her attention. She stopped too and looked back at him.

"Yes, exactly, a violent tremor that destroys buildings, roads, and lives," she said, now facing the lake.

"Wait a minute? How many days are there in your planet's calendar?"

"Oh no, here we go again with your planet's quiz. Listen, I don't know how we are having these dreams, and I just can't control them, but if I could, I'd make sure they wouldn't happen again," Claire was saying, clearly stressed, when she was cut off by Gavriel.

"No, please don't get me wrong. I really apologize if I was mean to you during our last encounter. I like to share my life with you, and I want to keep meeting you during my dreams.

Right now, I just want to confirm some information about your planet, because it's a proof that we are both real and we aren't just dreaming," he said as humbly as he could.

She was surprised by his apology, yet it seemed like his answer was sincere, and she had no reason to doubt it. It looks like emotions were easily perceived by the other person, and you couldn't hide them even if you wanted to.

"It's ok, apology accepted. We have 365 days in our year."

Gavriel was so excited that he felt himself being carried away for a moment. For some reason, he knew he needed to keep it together, or he would leave the dream.

"Listen, Claire, we have detected an event on a planet that I'm pretty sure is Earth," Gavriel said, calm and focused on Claire's presence.

"Our records show that Earth's surface temperature has been increasing at a rapid rate in the last few decades. This earthquake could possibly be a reaction to correct this anomaly."

"How do you know this? How did you detect it? Can you see us?" she asked, confused.

"We can not see you, yet can listen to your planet through organic waves," Gavriel said, knowing she needed more information.

"I have no clue what you are talking about."

"Let me try to explain. Organic waves are a kind of real-time communication between planets with systemic organic life. Like in our body, the organic waves, are the nerves of the universe, and defy the laws of space and time.

"Our civilization has decoded some information from the waves, and that's why I'm saying that we can listen to your planet.

We know that something happened recently because we have detected something from a distant planet that matches with the information you told me about Earth. Do you understand?" Gavriel asked patiently.

"Yes, I get it. Ok, but how can I know, that what you are telling me is real, and not just the product of my imagination?"

"I am not sure how can I prove it right now, but I'll think in something. For now, you can ask something that might convince you."

"Let me see, do you believe in God?"

Gavriel stopped and raised his eyebrows.

"I wasn't expected that. You are probably talking about the Creator. Yes, I believe, although I know very little about Him."

"How old are you?"

"I'm eight Novus Mundus years, which means twenty-eight years in your planet. We live about one hundred years, which translates to about three hundred and fifty years on Earth."

"Wow! That's quite an age! Does everybody live that long?"

"Most, we don't have diseases. When our lives degrade, we are putting to sleep."

"Sleep?"

"Yes, until they discover a way to extend our lives."

"Are you married?"

"No, didn't find my better half yet."

"Can you come to my planet with a spaceship?"

"Yes, we have the technology to physically reach you guys in about forty years. We have some devices that travel at the speed of light and can reach you in thirty-five years, but we can't carry anything solid on these devices. They only contain instructions in a plasma state. They collect meaningful information, and send it back to us."

"I remember that about two years ago, we detected a signal coming from outer space. Are you guys sending messages to us or other planets?"

"Not that I'm aware of. We have no reasons to broadcast signals indiscriminately. The universe is full of life, and there are good and bad people out there. We don't want to attract the bad ones."

"How can I find you in the universe? That will probably convince me that this isn't just my imagination," Claire said.

"You have the information you need. We have two suns and one micro planet in our orbit. Our calendar runs on a 1290-day cycle, and we have the same climate and atmosphere as Earth. This should be enough to locate us in the universe if you have the proper technology. That's enough for you?"

"One more question, how, and why do we meet in dreams?" Claire asked, and suddenly they both woke up.

#

Claire couldn't believe what she had just dreamed, so she took notes about everything she could remember. There was a lot more this time, and she didn't want to miss anything.

She felt burdened by what she knew, because she had a lot of followers on her blog, and presenting this dream exactly as it unfolded would be hard for them to believe. She decided to create a different topic on her blog and called it "Talent's Cove." There, she would insert her own ideas taken from the dreams. Just before heading to the library she received a phone call from Johanna.

"Hi, Claire! How are you doing?"

"I'm fine, how are you?"

"I'm fine too. I was reading my notes from your sessions, and I noticed that most of your dreams about earthquakes were pointing to the one we had last month.

I did some research and noticed that other people had dreams of similar details. I've applied for an academic grant to research this further and was wondering if you would be willing to be part of the study. It would take only a half day a week, and you'll have a chance to make your point."

"Yes, I can do that. However, I want to have access to the findings before they are published, to avoid misunderstandings."

"I think that is a fair request. Let's work on an agreement that is fair and equitable for both of us," Johanna said.

"Ok, Thursday at noon as we used to do?" Claire asked.

"Sure, see you on Thursday."

Her life seemed to take off, but she got sad knowing that Rachel was going away for a full month. She was heading to England to spend some time with her boyfriend's family.

"Hey! I don't buy this new section on your blog, what's going on?" Rachel said, referring to the new topic Claire had posted, so Claire decided to tell her about her dreams on Novus Mundus.

"I believe in you, but it's a little bit over my grounds. I'll be leaving tomorrow, and I'll follow you daily. If I smell something weird happening with you, I'll contact you right away, deal?"

"We have an agreement," Claire said and hugged her.

"Oh, by the way, I have some good news for you. Since you've been here almost every day, the library has been getting a lot of good press.

The City hall has decided to offer you a dedicated space over here. It won't be yours, but it will be booked for you full time. It's like the booth you have right now, except bigger. What do you think?" Rachel asked.

"Wow, sounds great! Yes, of course, I accept. It means that we will be working together from now on, that's great!" Claire said, again hugging Claire.

"There are some rules though, you can't talk to the media over here. Also, you can't create personal cards with the library address. Basically, you can use the space, but you can't run a private business here."

"Not a problem, I don't want to do any of that. I don't need another thing to be added to my load right now."

"Good, I'll bring some coffee for you, later. Now I have to catalog some books into our database."

#

"Sorry for this short notice Theena, but I need to talk to you," Gavriel said, standing nine feet from Theena's floating cocoon chair.

"Yes, Gavriel. What can I do for you? By the way, before you start, I have to say that you're doing a good job, and I'm proud of you."

"Thanks. Earth, the name of the sick planet is Earth," Gavriel said, smiling.

"I'm guessing that you want to rename the Sick Planet."

"Yes, and I'd like to stop calling it Sick Planet, Earth is its real name," Gavriel said, as he explained further about his dream.

"Ok, Gavriel. Changing the planet's name is easy, and we can do this without major problems. However, to use your dreams as the basis for this decision, well it's not going to happen. We can deal with the idea that there are many mysteries in our universe, but I can't make decisions based on your supernatural trips."

"Theena, it's not just a dream. It's a real thing, I can assure you. We are probably close to witnessing the breakthrough of a new technology, or at least, a confirmation this is something real. It might even be the key to help decode the organic waves, who knows?" Gavriel said with confidence in his voice.

"Hey, not so fast. Even if we can get something from your dreams, there is a long road ahead. The protocols in the system are stringent, and it takes time and resources to have something certified as scientific. What if we get nothing? How can we keep ourselves even working here?

For now, let's just collect evidence for further studies," Theena said.

"You have to believe in it, if you don't, then there is nothing we can do," Gavriel stressed.

"I trust in you, Gavriel," Theena reassured him, "but that doesn't change the systems in place. We have a lot of work to do. Keep up the excellent job you are doing.

If you get something consistent, we can point some of our efforts in a new direction.

I'll take the step to change the planet's name, and that's it for now."

"Yes, Mme," he said, putting his hand by his forehead, mimicking a military salute and leaving office.

By the end of the day, already in his bed, Gavriel was stargazing while thinking about how to convince everyone that his dreams weren't an illusion.

I actually have nothing but vapour. How am I sure that Earth is the Sick Planet? If it is, how can I know that Claire even exists on Earth? Is this just an illusion? Is this just craziness? He asked to himself.

He fell asleep and met Claire at the lake. He paid attention to her appearance and looked deep into her eyes. She had an inexplicable beauty that seemed to come from inside of her. Her eyes appeared to smile, and Gavriel felt attracted to her.

"Hi, good to see you again," Gavriel said.

"Likewise."

"How is life on your planet?" He asked.

"Busy, a lot of things to do, and little time. How's life on your planet?"

"The same, but I learned that I can't use the lack of time to avoid my commitments. Later one I can give you details. Right now, there is something about your planet that I need to tell you. It isn't something selfish such as a personal project, it's something that might affect your life."

"Don't worry about explaining the reasons to me, it seems like I can read your mind and everything around. Let's use our time wisely, and be direct with one another."

Gavriel stopped for a few seconds, his mind digesting what Claire had just said, because he also felt connected with the entire environment, including Claire.

"Well, we have detected that Earth is heading toward a catastrophic event due to its level of deterioration."

"Nothing new to me," she said with some frustration in her voice, "people from Earth know about this, but it seems like we don't care. Even facing the undeniable evidence that a catastrophe is about to unfold, we remain resolute in our fidelity to making things worse."

"Well, I can understand why people make poor decisions, but it makes no sense to foresee a life-threatening disaster coming your way, and persist on a path that would ensure the destruction of your civilization.

This isn't about just making things worse, it is about the annihilation of your planet. Doing nothing is purely irrational," he said aggressively, hurting her feelings.

"I understand what you mean, but I don't know how to change it. Though we live in a wonderful world, we are immersed in corruption. A few greedy people perpetuate the poverty of millions and propagate the diseases of the soul. We daily witness wars, sexual abuse of children, abandonment of the elderly, and annihilation of mother nature. I'm over it, I feel helpless, and you expect me to save humanity," Claire was angry and did not contain the tears. Both woke up.

Gavriel went to work feeling depleted. He was quiet, and everybody noticed that he was downcast. Theena called him into her office.

"What's wrong? You look terrible! Was it one of your dreams again?"

"Yeah, it seems like we argued in a dream. Can you believe it?"

"Well you better find a way to stop them, or this is going to hurt you."

"I'm down, but it isn't just about the argument. It's also from what I've heard about Earth. It seems like corruption is the source of its destruction."

"Wow, what a different set of words you are using. Since when you are familiar with corruption?"

"I remember it from a manuscript Hallan lent me."

"What has happened in this dream?" Theena asked, so Gavriel told her.

"Well, I have reasonable grounds to think that we should avoid any contact with them. If what you say is correct, we have to rethink our strategy in regards to that planet," said Theena.

"I have to disagree with you. There are good people over there as well, it's not simply filled with corruption. Remember that we are also concerned with the planet, and the effect of its collapse in our system."

"Yes, I know, let's not take any drastic measures. If you really have this controlled connection, ask Claire about the primary source of energy they use for transportation and power generation. Ask about the planet's population and its average life expectancy. Also, inquire as to whether or not they are planning to have a scheduled major event in their environment, like an artificial flooding or a contained large fire, for instance. Capeesh?"

"Yes, I will, but why should I ask about a major environmental event?"

"Well, that Gavriel is our ticket to success. If we can predict something happening on that planet and confirm it through organic waves, people will trust us. It will give us credibility, and we will be able to further develop this project," Theena finished "That's all. You are dismissed," and he went to his cocoon chair

#

Claire woke up crying. It had been one of her worst dreams ever, and she felt the heaviness of being in an argument with Gavriel. She didn't know what had happened. They just got together, and in a fraction of seconds, they were arguing and going ballistic.

She had no motivation to work; instead, decided to walk to a nearby park. She couldn't track how long she was walking and meditating. She was trying to get some answers from God but didn't hear or remember a word of consolation or motivation. Heaven seemed to be silent.

It was almost noon, so she decided to go to the library to blog. She was scanning the comment section quickly when some words caught her attention.

He was from planet Novus Mundus.

"What?" she exclaimed, going to the beginning of the text.

I had this dream. My sister and I were in my floating car in one of the underground roads we have on our planet. We have to live underground because of the high levels of star radiation on the surface of our world. We feel depressed because I know it wasn't this way before, and I know there is a better life on other planets around us. I saw this guy not far from where we were going. He was almost struck by a car in front of us, and we also managed to stop before hitting him. I knew he was from the planet Novus Mundus. I handed him a piece of what is supposed to be food on my planet, and I said, "This is all we have to eat over here. It tastes horribly bitter, but it is the only way to survive." I don't know if he was aware of our ordeal; however, I want to show him that we are suffering because of all the bad things Novus Mundus's people did to us. I want him to know because I have a feeling that he is not aware of. He seems to be a good man, and I don't feel threatened by him.

The text went on to another dream. Claire was really confused. *If Novus Mundus exists and they are the cause of the misery on this planet, does Gavriel have good intentions to help Earth?* This question hammered her mind until she went to bed that night.

#

"Hi again," Gavriel said with a smile.

"Before we go any further, I need to a know something from you," Claire said, taking control of the situation. "You've said something about peer planets in your system. What can you tell me about them?"

"Well, I don't know what you want to know. You need to be more specific. I can inform you that Zyon looks like our planet, but it is less developed technologically.

Sion is different because people live under the ground at most time. Although they are technologically more advanced than Zyon, they have many limitations due to their planet's issues. Is that enough for you?" Gavriel asked, confused.

"Yes, I mean no. One more question. What's Novus Mundus's relationship with Sion? I mean, what kind of relationship have you guys had with them in the past?"

"What?" Gavriel said, with an expression of confusion. "Well, in the past we helped them overcome their environmental issues. It happened a long time ago. I just learned about it through history classes, why?"

"Nothing, it's ok for now," Claire said, knowing that he was telling the truth.

"Ok then, can I ask you some questions about your planet?" asked Gavriel.

"Yes, but first tell me how you guys are planning to help us. Are you travelling to Earth?"

"We don't know how we can help you yet. We can't reach you in a short time. I might not ever be able to see you face-to-face," Gavriel said with an expression of sorrow.

"Yeah, the universe seems to have its own dynamic," Claire said with a slight expression of frustration. "So, what questions do you have for me?"

"What's Earth population, and what is the life expectancy on the planet? What kind of fuel do you use in your vehicles? And finally, is there a significant artificial environmental event planned to happen soon on your planet?"

"Uh, let me see… we are around seven billion people, the life expectancy should be around seventy-seven years. About the fuel, we mostly use oil, that black thing, mostly extracted from underground.

A significant environmental event happening or planned, hum… let me see, the only thing that comes to my mind is the construction of a big dam in one of our countries. They are planning to deviate a river and create this huge artificial lake, but I don't know when it's supposed to happen."

"I think I memorized everything," Gavriel said.

"Now it's my turn. Can we revisit your planet? I'm curious to know how you guys live."

"Ok, he said and grabbed her hand. They quickly floated up until they reached outer space. Claire stopped in front of Novus Mundus, as she noticed hundreds of shiny golden dots spread around the planet. She pulled Gavriel closer to one of them, staying a few feet away from a device as tall as a ten-story building.

"What is this? It looks like a huge leaf," she said, watching the object.

"This is a quantum receiver. We have many around the planet and some bigger ones on the poles. They are stationary, which means that they don't move while the globe runs in its orbit. We use them to collect information sent from our plasma devices around the universe.

"Why do they have all those irregular holes on their surfaces?"

"The units are custom made by artificial intelligence and the holes are placed exactly where the direct signal from outer space reach the antenna's surface area. This way, the noise from the nearby stars doesn't interfere with the information coming from beyond their position. Because of this, we are able to detect signals from very distant places."

"Interesting," Claire said, and they started to move again toward the planet, and this time, they reached a city.

While hovering over the buildings and floating vehicles, Claire looked around in many directions as if looking for something specific.

"It's strange, isn't it? There is nothing here beyond buildings and floating vehicles. What about people, where are they?"

"To get together, we come to the arenas," Gavriel took her hand and flew into a building resembling two half spheres, joined back-to-back. One of the openings pointed up, the other pointed down toward the ground, and they were hovering above the building.

"Sports is one of the pillars of our society, and we have many games happening year-round. Arenas are one of the few large buildings allowed for gatherings because government policies won't allow large places for meetings for security reasons."

"Security reasons? What kind of security reasons? People like to get together to express their voice."

"The government says that large gatherings were the source of social unrest and violence in our history, so now they are forbidden."

From her vantage point high above the arena, Claire was fascinated by the zero-gravity game that was taking place.

"Te players look like monkeys jumping on trees," Claire said, laughing while looking them jumping from one tree-like structure to another, quickly passing a football to each other.

She floated close to someone on the watchers who was watching the palm of his hand while talking. She noticed that there was an image projected onto the palm of his hand, and got curious. "What's this?" she said, pointing to the man's hand.

"It's the way we communicate. No screens, just projections on any surface. The rings on our thumb and middle finger control everything. And when I say they control everything, I do mean everything. They store personal artificial wealth and regularly scan your body to detect health issues. When you need to order clothes, you don't need to provide measurements because the device does that automatically."

They continued onto the micro planet, and Claire noticed that she was sensing holding Gavriel's hand. As they neared the lake, they flew through a torrential rainfall. Claire could feel the raindrops falling on her face, and could smell the aroma from the mud below. It didn't seem like a dream, and she felt alive as she never felt before, when she awoke.

#

"That's the information I got. What do we do now?" Gavriel asked Theena after he reported his conversation with Claire from the night before.

"Well, we have something to work with. Tomorrow I'll bring something to our weekly meeting, and we'll see what we get from our co-workers," Theena said. "I got a call from Hallan, and he wants you to pay him a visit today."

"Why did he call you instead of me?"

"Oh, because he wants to talk to you as soon as possible. It seems that he has a community restaurant appointment tonight, and he asked me if I could release you to go during the day. So, you are dismissed," Theena said, stood up and went to another room.

Gavriel arrived at Hallan's home a short while later.

"Come on my friend, let's go to the cabin. I'm starving," Hallan said, waving his hand to get Gavriel into the elevator so they could go to the ground floor.

On their way to the entrance, Gavriel noticed a machine cutting down trees.

"That's the new trail to the new site," Hallan said.

"It looks like your friend has another challenge for you," Gavriel said.

"He does indeed, and he is supervising from Sion."

"Do you have friends on Sion? You never told me."

"So, what's the problem? Don't you have friends from another planet as well?"

"Yeah, but, forget it," Gavriel said. "So why did you ask me to come?"

"How's been your life? Any news?" Hallan asked while increasing the pace.

"I'm fine. I'been having some unusual dreams with this woman, and she is beautiful," and he kept telling Hallan about his latest dream until they arrived at the cabin.

Once they arrived, Hallan interrupted him and asked, "Did you do your homework?"

"What homework?" Gavriel asked, surprised.

"Don't you remember our conversation about the government records?"

"Yes, I remember now. But why should I go after these things? Do you think that it's related to my current dreams?" Gavriel asked.

"Gavriel, you have a unique talent, and this isn't by accident. There is something significant to all of this. If you have received it and you are just using it for your pleasure, like meeting up with a hot woman, or using it for your own personal purposes, then you aren't using it wisely. That's why I told you that you should seek the truth," Hallan urged, with some stress in his voice.

"Ok, but what is the connection here? Why am I supposed to go after the records about our conversation?" Gavriel asked curiously.

"Because if you had looked for it, you would start to find part of the truth. Let's start from the beginning. Let's speak of the recordings of your sleep when you were on your military training."

"Ok, go ahead," Gavriel said.

"I know that the government is scanning people during their sleep. They wanted to read quantum signals over people's dreams but had no success so far, because the signal disappears when scrutinized." Hallan said and paused for a few seconds.

"I'm pretty sure your recordings on the micro planet were edited, maybe to cover up the scanning of your brain. They are probably using that record to collect information to decode organic waves."

"Interesting, but why are you interested in this subject? What's the connection between your spiritual services and what the government is doing?" Gavriel asked.

"Well, we are pretty sure they are hiding something sensitive from us," and he paused for a more extended period, looking to the ceiling as if he was not confident about going on.

"Wait! You said 'we'?" Gavriel said after digesting what Hallan just said.

"For now, let me tell you that it is me, your grandma, and my friend on Sion."

"My grandma? What do you mean my grandma? She works for the government. She has a high-level position there and can get any information she wants. Further, why does it involve someone from Sion?"

"Your grandma joined our cause through Jardnn who was also from Sion. You are right, she has a high position in the government, and that's why we are keeping her away from anything that can connect her to our investigations. We don't want to raise any suspicion, so she can use her power to get information at critical moments," Hallan said.

"What's your cause? What are you talking about? If this is so secret, we shouldn't be talking freely about this, you know that the government can track us at all times. What makes you sure that they aren't listening to this conversation right now?" Gavriel asked.

"That's why I told you to check if the government had any records about our conversation. I can give you answers, but ..." Hallan stopped again.

"But what?" Gavriel insisted.

"I can answer all the questions, but keep in mind that after hearing the answers you might be in danger. I need you to understand this before I go on. Do you understand that having access to this information could cause harm to come to you, even death?" Hallan asked in a calm voice.

"Hey, that's bullshit," Gavriel said, in a frail voice.

"No, it isn't BS, it's just serious. This is part of life, and you have to make decisions in your life. Do you understand?"

"But you said that we can always go back on our decisions," Gavriel replied sarcastically.

"Yes, as long as you are alive," Hallan said. "Do you understand or not?"

"Yes, I do," Gavriel said, his curiosity getting the best of him.

"The government cannot listen to us, on this site. That's why we've been meeting here."

"What do you mean?" he said, frowning.

"This is considered a blind spot, which means, it can not be hacked by the government. The pattern of these trails isn't just for fun, they work as encryption for us to communicate freely between Novus Mundus and Sion. The trails are built with an active material connected to this cabin that sends out signals that cannot be detected."

"Sounds smart, yet what's the reason to communicate with Sion in such secrecy?"

"Something is going on in the system, and the political class of Novus Mundus is covering it up.

This behaviour is typical when there is an imminent threat. Sion and Zyon are convinced that this is a threat to the two planets. But we have no active voice, and any sign of rebellion against the system is discouraged ... or eliminated.

You will not find in the history books that Zyon was looted by Novus Mundus after our planet was covered by ashes due to the solar storm. With the excuse of helping us, Novus Mundus also took over all the scientific discoveries, as well as abducting our scientists, then abandoning us without any help or hope."

"Wait, are you telling me that you are from Sion?" Gavriel interrupted.

"My father was. Sion used to be a beautiful planet, and now it's dead," Hallan said.

"Yikes! It's hard to believe."

"The conditions on our planet aren't capable of sustaining life, so one of my missions on Novus Mundus is to forge an agreement of migration. We have tried everything already: politics, commercial agreements, but nothing seems to work. The last resort will be a military intervention, we have nothing to lose."

"What about Zyon? Why don't you guys move to that planet?"

"We are doing it already, but on a smaller scale. The Zyon government is helping us in every way, and we have open border agreements with them. But don't forget that their planet also has food shortages due to climate and soil issues. Moving over there would just increase the misery for both peoples."

"All these things don't make any sense. What you've said is just ... well ... it's hard to swallow."

"Yes, I understand," Hallan said, his face down, "and I'm not asking you to believe me just because I'm saying this. I'm just asking you to search for the truth. If you find it, you might feel inclined to help Sion and Earth instead of just enjoying your dreams," Hallan said.

"What does Earth have to do with Sion or Novus Mundus's issues?"

"From what we know, Earth is on the same path as Sion. The signs the planet is sending now are the same signs we had on Sion. We are sure that Earth will collapse, and life might disappear from it very soon," Hallan said, his face downcast.

"Ok, but what do you want from me and why are you trying to help Earth? The government have a lot of departments working on this subject," Gavriel said.

"I need you to find who is above the formal structure of our government because some decisions aren't coming from the appointed members.

As for the government being concerned, do you think Novus Mundus's government is actually trying to save Earth's population? If so, why didn't they help Sion when they could? Why did they refuse to rescue us from our dying planet and bring us here when we were struck by a solar flare? Why, until today, do they not allow us to immigrate here when Novus Mundus has an abundance of land and resources? Why? If you explain all that to me, I'll be the first one to apologize for any self-righteousness," Hallan said, his voice rising with anger.

"Well, I don't know what to say," Gavriel said, a bit lost.

"Well, do your homework. You can get information from Lennah without triggering any alarms. She will have to memorize it though because she won't be able to carry anything out of the building. It's like your dreams, you can't take any proof from them.

You can invite her to come here so you can talk without raising any flags, but you will have to hurry because I don't think we have much time on Earth or Sion issues," Hallan said.

"Ok, I'll try to help. I'm going home, I have a lot to digest," Gavriel said and left.

The next day, Gavriel joined the follow-up meeting Theena had scheduled the week before.

"Hi, everyone! Let's get straight to the point because we have a big problem and little time.

I received classified information that the Sick Planet we are now studying is called Earth. So, from now on, we will call it Earth.

I was informed that they use oil from the ground as fuel, and this only exasperates the problem.

Under these circumstances, I need to know what are the options, and how much time we have. This meeting is open to ideas from anyone. Any questions?" Theena said, looking to her team.

"The planet is heading for a cooling process, and it might be expelling ashes on its surface," one team member said.

"How much time do we have? I know we can't predict it exactly, but give me a window."

"Between now and ten Earth calendar years. It won't be longer than that," the leader of team three answered.

"What if we try to transfer some technology to them?" someone from team one asked.

"Earth is thirty-five light years from us, so this option is pointless. Don't forget that we also need approval to transfer technology. Right now, we don't have that permission," Zenya said.

"It seems a remote option, but I'll take care of any approval if we need it. Anything else?" Theena said, looking at her team.

The room was silent.

"Ok, you're dismissed. You have twenty-four hours to bring me something, or we will be in trouble. Let's get back to work."

"We need some spiritual advice. Let's go to Hallan's place," Theena said to Gavriel with a wink.

"Ok, but I need to talk to Lennah before leaving."

"Bring her along. She can receive some advice as well," Theena said.

#

Six people joined at Johanna's office when Claire arrived. She was surprised to see that the number of scholars seated in chairs, forming a circle in the corner of the room.

"Wow, I'm feeling spoiled here. I didn't know you would have so many doctors involved in a simple study," Claire said as she made herself comfortable.

"Well, since you had your blog published, other government programs contacted me and asked to participate in this meeting. You don't mind, do you?" Johanna asked.

"No… it's ok. Let's do it," she said with some hesitation in her voice. She was feeling uncomfortable talking to so many people without knowing the nature of the questions precisely. Johanna handed Claire a non-disclosure agreement that she signed and gave back to Johanna.

"Won't you read it?" Johanna asked.

"I trust you," she said and was soon introduced to everyone.

"Nick Martins from NASA? Why is NASA interested in my dreams?" she asked a young guy who claimed to represent the space organization.

"The signal that Earth got from outer space two years ago opened a new dimension in our research and all the options to decode that signal are welcomed. We are collecting any credible information from people with information related to alien matters," answered Nick.

"Ok, but how do you know about the alien subject of my dreams?"

"You have made some allusion to it on your blog, and you have proven to be a reliable source of precognitive dreams."

The doctors reviewed the dreams she had, her connection with the earthquake and other past events.

They were surprised when she informed them of her recent dreams about Novus Mundus, and were amazed by the amount of information and detail she included.

Some doctors questioned her harshly as if they didn't believe in her, but when they repeatedly asked about specific information, they found no apparent contradictions.

The meeting was so intense that they ended up going late into the night. They finished the session agreeing to meet again soon.

The next meeting did not happen as planned. One of the interviewers was actually an undercover reporter from a local television station, and two days later Claire's face was all over the media. Headlines around the country made sensationalized claims of aliens preparing to invade Earth. Claire was devastated.

Her aunt called from home saying that, again, there were some media trucks parked outside her house.

"I'm so sorry Auntie, I didn't mean to cause all this trouble for you."

"Don't worry honey. These dogs won't dare to come into my house. I'll make them run back as quick as a flash," her aunt said, laughing. "You take care of yourself, and you're welcome to come home anytime. However, it might be best if you lay low for a while, at least until this dies down a bit."

"Yeah, you're right. For now, I need to be away from home if I want to escape from the media circus. I'll think of something and call you back." Claire hung up the phone and looked outside. She saw a police car protecting the library premises. She knew the media was not allowed to come in, so she was safe for now.

The telephone rang, and she was afraid to pick up the incoming call. She checked the display and found that it wasn't an American number, so she picked it up.

"Hello?"

"Claire it's me, Rachel."

"Hi, Rachel! It's good to hear from you. How are things there?"

"Everything is wonderful, I got engaged!" she cheered.

"What do you mean? My God, really?"

"Yes, indeed, but listen, I didn't call to talk about me, this is about you. I've seen these junk articles someone published about you, and I thought you might be feeling under pressure over there."

"Yeah, it's not my favourite way to spend my days. Right now, the media might be waiting for me outside the library, and they're at my aunt's home as well."

"Here's an idea. I just sent my office a message requesting a leave of absence. Some opportunities have developed for me over here, and my fiancé and I want to pursue some of them.

Listen, I know that you can't go to your home for a while, so go to my apartment, the only thing you have to do is pay the utilities while I'm out. The keys are inside my car under the passenger's mat. What do you think?"

"Is the car unlocked?"

"Just the passenger door. Thieves won't bother to steal that piece of junk. By the way, you can use the car as well, the key is inside the ashtray."

"Are you nuts, in the ashtray?"

"Yes, in the ashtray, I don't smoke, remember?" Rachel said, laughing, "so do you wanna go for that?"

"I don't know what to say."

"Oh, come on, don't worry about it. You need some privacy now."

"Ok, thanks, I'll do that."

"There you go, and listen, I'm travelling now, but as soon as I get to the hotel, I'll email you, so I can send you some more information about living at my place. Let's keep in touch, okay?"

"Ok, bye for now."

Wow, the universe seems to cooperate to help me when I need it most. How are these coincidences possible? Claire thought and immediately called her aunt to tell her what had just happened.

"Hi, Aunt. A solution has just presented itself. I'll be staying at my friend's apartment. She works at the library, and she's away travelling right now. She just called and offered me her place. Isn't that amazing?"

"Yes, it seems like little miracles are a regular part of your life, and I'm happy for you. Send me the address, and phone number, as soon as you can. I won't be able to sleep not knowing where to find you."

"Ok, I'll send you by email. Please pass it on to my dad as well. I'll talk to you soon, bye for now."

Claire asked the library assistant if she could accompany her off the premises. She would hide in the passenger's seat and crouch down for a few blocks until they had cleared the reporters.

They managed to reach Rachel's building without any incident and, as expected, the keys were inside the car.

After checking the apartment, she opened the fridge and realized that she had to go grocery shopping. She turned on the TV, only to turn it off right away. Claire couldn't bear the garbage that was coming from the media, and to avoid being part of sensationalism, she decided not to go to the library for the next couple of days.

She turned on the computer, sitting on a desk, in the corner of the small dining room. On her blog, she found some people congratulating her, some calling her sick, and others saying that she's a demon, and there was even a death threat.

She went to bed late, feeling awful. Gavriel was there, waiting for her at the lake.

"Hi, I missed you a lot!" Gavriel said.

"Yeah, I missed you too. How've you been?"

"Life has this ups and downs, but I think I'll overcome it. Listen, Claire, we put together the information you gave to us, and we cross-referenced it with the information we received from organic waves, and we have some bad news. If we put the data together, it points to a strong reaction from the planet to cool down the surface temperature.

The use of oil from the ground makes things worse because it deteriorates the biomass and, at the same time, reduces the planet's thermal regulation provided by the oil."

"So, what's the bad news exactly?" Claire asked as they walked by the lake.

"Your planet will probably expel ashes in the air. The ashes are supposed to reach the first layer of the atmosphere and block the sun in some parts of the planet. This will cause the temperature to decrease abruptly, but it will also kill the organic life in areas covered by the ashes. Many people will die due to this toxic atmosphere, and the survivors will die due to contamination of water and starvation. Very few will survive; unfortunately, life isn't going to be easy for survivors.

The planet's biomass will eventually come back, but a lot of animal life will disappear. It will take a hundred years to rebuild a sustainable life. This is what has happened with Sion, the only difference is that they were struck by another event after the first one. However, the outcomes would be almost the same for Earth."

"But you guys can help us, can't you?" Claire asked, frowning. *Of course, I'm dreaming, this is going too far,* she thought.

"What do you mean, this is going too far?" asked Gavriel.

"Oh nothing, I'm just wondering," she answered, and remembered that their thoughts communicated in that environment.

"We are trying to help, but we couldn't find anything yet." As they walked along the beach, Claire played with the flowers of some trees that stood outside of the woods and extended their branches close to the sand.

Claire felt something like a bite in her arm and saw an animal like a snake moving away between the branches. She stopped and noticed some bubbles popping where she had been bitten, and blisters started to burn like fire.

"Poison, the snake is poisonous," Gavriel said, looking at her arm, and pulled her into the water to wash it and try to minimize the pain.

Claire awoke, and her arm was burning. She immediately looked at it but realized that the pain was because she had slept on her arm. As the blood started to circulate again, she felt the pain go away.

#

"Lennah, thanks for coming," Gavriel said while they made their way to the breakfast site. "I really appreciate your willingness to help us."

"Ok, don't worry. How can I help you?"

"You work for the database department, and you have access to a lot of information. I was wondering if I can ask you to look something up for me."

"I can help you as long as it is not something illegal. You know that my options are limited. I do have full access to the database, and I am unable to copy or remove anything."

"Yes, I know about your limitations. I just have some questions. You can bring me the answers tomorrow. We'll have to meet here because this is the only place we can talk, without being monitored by the government."

"No, it's not the only one," Lennah said.

"What do you mean?"

"There are many areas on the planet that we call blind spots where it isn't possible to hack or monitor," Lennah said nonchalantly as if the information was not that important.

"Come on, really?" Gavriel said, surprised.

"Yes! What else?"

"Well, I need to know about how Novus Mundus discovered Low-Density Artificial Gravity. If you can get this information," and Gavriel was interrupted by Lennah.

"We didn't discover it. We stole it from Sion," she said naturally as if the information was trivial.

"What?" he said, jaw-dropping.

"Why are you always surprised about certain things, Gavriel? People inside the government have access to sensitive information. Novus Mundus was an intermediary in an agreement between Sion and Zyon to supply Zxylon for battery factories. From Sion, our intermediation service would be paid by the transfer of artificial gravity.

Then Sion was struck by the ashes in its atmosphere. We had received the documentation about the technology already, so we offered asylum to all Sion scientists, just to make sure the technology would work. They didn't have a choice, so the scientists migrated to Novus Mundus. That's it, we basically stole the technology without giving anything back. We didn't even offer humanitarian aid."

"Why didn't you tell me this before?"

"You never asked. I do recall offering you the option to explore the database, but you didn't get back to me."

"Well, now I feel ridiculous," Gavriel said. "What else do you know?"

"I know a lot of things. You'll have to be more specific."

"Ok, what else do you know about Earth?"

"Earth? Are you talking about the Sick Planet?"

"Yes, but let's call it Earth from now on, ok?"

"Yeah, we have its name registered as Earth as well."

"What? Stop! How do you have information about the name?"

"We keep the names given to the planets by their locals, and we do that by listening to the plasma devices from our extended missions."

"So, you are telling me that we have complete information about Earth?" Gavriel asked, frowning.

"Yeap. We also share some information with other developed civilizations for scientific reasons. What else do you want to know?" Lennah said, holding her chin between her thumb and index finger.

"What about the issues Earth is having right now? Is any other planet inclined to rescue, or help them?" Gavriel asked.

"As far as I know, there is no way to help them. However, they are not the first, and they won't be the last planet to have this problem. I found information suggesting that this is probably the sixth or seventh known planets have faced similar issues. They all had severe damage in their development, and their people were, or have been, partially annihilated."

"Unbelievable. Why has nobody ever tried to help them, and why is this such a big secret?"

"Good question, but I don't know the answer. We didn't help Sion, which is very close to us, so why would we save planets far away from us?"

"So why do we have all these departments working on new discoveries, if we have all the information we need?" Gavriel asked, bug-eyed, and raising his voice while opening his arms.

"I believe that this is just to keep the status quo. And it's really all about power. If leaders have run things this way for thousands of years, they will keep running in this way forever."

"Who are they?"

"It's not me, that's for sure!" Lennah said. Theena and Hallan arrived, interrupting them.

"Listen, guys, I had a chat with Lennah, and we are definitely the ones who know the least," Gavriel said, summarizing what he had just learned from Lennah.

"Well, that doesn't surprise me. I have access to this kind of information, but try not to poke around too much, so that I don't raise any flags on the system," Theena said.

"I have an idea," Gavriel said while looking at Theena and Hallan. "Why don't we transfer some technology to Earth during my dreams with Claire?"

"Wait, now I'm surprised. Who is Claire and why will you transfer technology to her?" Lennah asked, and Gavriel told her about his dreams.

"Wow, I'm impressed. The more I live, the more I realize that I know nothing," Lennah said, after listening to Gavriel's explanation of his dreams. "So, you are probably using organic waves to communicate with each other in your dreams."

"That is our best guess, although we don't know how to decode it yet. We don't have full control over the dreams, but it is pretty clear that they aren't happening by coincidence," said Gavriel.

"We need to think of a way to transfer technology, but it won't happen by memorizing an entire formula," Theena said. "The low gravity process, for instance, is huge and will take forever to complete the task using dreams."

"Theena is right, we need to find a feasible solution, and we don't have much time," Hallan said.

"I have an idea, however, to be successful, authorities on Earth have to believe in Claire. "Theena said and continued. Nobody will pay attention to what she says even if she lets them know about the dreams she's having.

The only way to get their attention is to anticipate an event, I mean, if she predicts an event. There is a plasma permanent nuclear scanner that is supposed to reach Earth in about a week. If we can give her instructions to trap the device, they will keep trust in her afterward."

"Good idea!" Gavriel said.

Theena continued, "Meanwhile we can start transferring the synthetic fuel formula based on water to her so they can begin to use this instead of their current source of energy. This option is supposed to cause a minimum impact on its current economic structure.

It's going to take a while because we need to transfer the formula based on their chemical structure. We will have to translate it, and it won't be easy. Nevertheless, I can't see another way to solve this problem."

"I'm in, but we need to try other options to speed up the transfer and increase the amount of information Claire can memorize. How about talking to her and see if you both can synchronize your sleep twice a day, at night and at noon. If you can have two daily contacts, this will help us," Hallan said.

"Just one more detail," Theena said to Gavriel. "because of the circumstances, I'll tell the government that you have requested a leave of absence, to deal with some personal issues. This should give you the time you need to complete data transfer."

CHAPTER 15 – Are we in Paradise?

CLAIRE AND GAVRIEL MET AGAIN by the lake. She still had her arm swollen from the poisonous snake bite.

"That's so weird. We are in this thing that is supposed to be a dream, but we are also feeling the effects of the environment," Gavriel said.

"Yeah, it's really surreal," Claire said. "Anyway, I'll keep washing it and check if it gets better." They went close to the water, and she splashed on the rash while talking.

"Wait a minute," Gavriel said, while Claire was washing her arm. If this is environment get more real than our reality and we become trapped here?" he said, looking at Claire.

"I don't think so… anyway, back to our reality, or dream, do you have news about Earth?" Claire asked.

"Yes, and I would say it's good news," Gavriel told her about their plan. "So, are you willing to try it?" Gavriel asked while they got out of the water.

"For sure I want, but I'm stuck in an apartment, and the articles from the media are making me into a person that I can't even recognize. I believe I'm doing the right thing, nevertheless, some people are seeing me a liar, and I don't know what else to do. I was hoping to have some peace in my life, but here I am, fighting poisonous snakes in my dreams, and in my real life," she said while tucking her hair behind her ear. Her expression was downcast, and her eyes were sad and dark circles were beginning to form under them.

"What do your parents have to say about this?" Gavriel asked.

"My mom passed away seven years ago, and my father is living far away from where I live. I moved to this new country a while ago, and I decided to take some drastic steps to start thriving, but I'm almost regretting it. I wish I could go back to the place where I was born and just live a simple life."

"Maybe it's better just to forget everything and go back to your normal life. Don't worry, I won't judge you," Gavriel said, he was touched by her ordeal. Living away from her family, and her native land couldn't be easy.

Gavriel came over and tenderly embraced her. Suddenly their hearts seemed to merge, it was something inexplicable as if in reality they pulsed synchronously. Their minds blended like a whirlwind of energy. The feeling was that time did not exist and that this was an eternal condition.

Claire felt her heart slowly sucked into a universe of peace with an indescribable sense of love, and tears of immeasurable joy flooded her eyes without, however, affecting her vision. It was when a lump of consciousness reminded her of her mission on earth and slowly returned to the dimension in which she was dreaming. Clutching Gavriel's shoulders, she slowly disengaged himself from the embrace.

"Wow, what is it?" She whispered, looking directly into Gavriel's eyes, which still seemed to be immersed in another reality.

"Wow!" He exclaimed, now showing himself in the dimension of his dreams and both realized that their eyes had a smile.

"I do not know what that was, but I remembered that I have a mission on Earth and I'm going to finish," she said, still looking into his eyes, and concluded, "There has to be a way to save that planet."

Gavriel could not express himself and, in an involuntary gesture, calmly took her hand and went to the sand, took a piece of bamboo that was on the floor and gave it to Claire.

"Write in the sand the formula of water," he said with a serenity that could be perceived in their consciousness, she wrote H2O.

"This is the way you will transfer information to me, by writing it down. Does Earth have twenty-four hours per day?"

"Yes," answered Claire.

"Our planets are probably synchronized regarding time because we meet each other during the same sleeping time. You'll try to get to sleep at twelve o'clock in the afternoon, and I'll do the same. Let's try to synchronize our schedules and meet each other here twice a day."

"Sounds like a plan to me," Claire said, ready to awaken. Nothing happened.

"Wow, it seems we have more time to talk," she said, and without any planning, they began to walk hand in hand along the lake, not exchanging a word because they had a feeling that all her thoughts were shared.

Claire awoke and made a phone call to Johanna right away.

"Good morning Johanna."

"Hi Claire, I'm so sorry," she started to say but was interrupted by Claire.

"Listen, Johanna, we don't have much time. I know you didn't do that on purpose, and I forgive you anyway. Right now, I need a favour," Claire said, getting straight to the point.

"Yes dear, what can I do for you?"

"I need the phone number of that guy from NASA. The one present at our meeting." She wrote down his name and phone number on a piece of paper, and after she had hung up with Johanna, she called him.

"Hi Nick, this is Claire Luan. We met briefly at Johanna's office. I would really like it if we could meet up and talk."

"Sure, when?"

"Is tonight ok for you?

"Well, I work at the KSC – Kennedy Space Center, and I'll need three hours to reach Miami, so I can be there by eight. Where would you like to meet?"

"Meet me at my current address. I'm pretty sure you'll be able to find me, see you at eight o'clock." She hung up the phone. She knew she sounded rude, but she guessed Nick would find a way to get to her, or he would call her back. She needed to know what kind of people she was dealing with.

She then called a TV station, a competitor of the one who broadcast her dreams about Novus Mundus.

"Hi, this is Claire Luan. Can I speak with the producer in charge for the evening news?"

"Sorry, what's your name again? Do you have an appointment?"

"My name is Claire Luan, and no, actually I don't have an appointment. Can you please mention that I'm the person on the news that is involved with the alien dreams?" She waited for the phone call to be transferred.

"Hi, this is Diane speaking."

"Hi, Diane my name is Claire Luan. I need to talk to someone about some developments regarding the news about aliens, and I wonder if you are interested?"

"How do I know you are the Claire from the story?"

"I can send you a scanned piece of ID, as well as a picture of me holding them," Claire said.

"Sounds good to me," Diane said.

"Ok, just reply, acknowledging my email, so I know you are interested. Can we meet at the coffee shop on Main and Fifth Street, at eight fifteen tonight?"

"Yes, it works for me," Diane said, and gave her email to Claire.

At eight o'clock sharp, the bell rang. Claire opened the door and said: "HI, let's go." With that, she closed the door and headed for the elevator.

"Well, it seems like NASA and the NSA work together because you found my address," Claire said as they entered the elevator.

"It was a little bit tricky because you don't have a cell phone. But it wasn't too difficult to identify your number from the call display. I just needed a little help to connect the number with the address," Nick said. "May I ask you if we need to drive, or are we going somewhere nearby?"

"Nearby," Claire said. "That was a bit primitive, finding me through the call display. Seriously, I was hoping for something slightly more high-tech," she said, as they started walking down the street.

"I feel sorry for what's happened to you. I mean about the unauthorized broadcast. You have to realize, though, that this is very common in the media. You have to be careful dealing with people."

"Yes, I've learned my lesson. Never again," Claire said as they entered the coffee shop.

"One house coffee, please" she ordered. Do you want something?" and Nick promptly pulled his wallet from his pocket.

"Don't worry, this one's on me," Claire said.

"Ok, the same for me," Nick said to the cashier.

"You look too young to work for NASA, how old are you?" she asked, noticing that he looked similar to Gavriel, only with short brown hair.

"I'm twenty-four, but some friends call me baby because they say I look younger. I'm new at NASA as well, so my first assignments are field research, as this one now."

They chose a table in the corner. The television station producer arrived after a few minutes. Diane looked to be in her early thirties. She made a beeline to their table as soon as she spotted them.

"I'm Diane, nice to meet you," she said, shaking Claire and Nick's hands.

"I'm Nicholas Martins, but people call me Nick. Pleased to meet you."

"Wow, I'm not feeling like a little girl in the middle of wolves like I thought I would. You two are young," Claire said.

"Yes, but it doesn't mean that we aren't vicious," Diane said, making them laugh.

"Well, everyone here knows what's happened to me, or at least has a guess," Claire said, looking at Diane.

"Knowing a little bit about the journalist who broadcast your story, I have a good idea," Diane said.

"Right, so I'll update you about some things. Let me finish what I have to say, and then you can ask me questions if you want. I'm having a lot of dreams about an alien subject.

Apparently, there is an alien planet called Novus Mundus, which is very, very developed. They have information about the imminent collapse of our world. This collapse would happen due to changes in our environment, the same thing our scientists have been saying, and the scientists on Novus Mundus have reliable data to support these claims. This is not new to us, but the thing is, they think they can help us." Claire paused for a few seconds and saw their looks of indifference.

"My contacts are offering to give us a formula, or process, whatever it is, to create synthetic fuel based on water that won't be harmful to the environment. They say that the synthetic fuel, along with other cultural changes, can stop the increasing temperatures, and we can avoid the collapse of our planet.

I know this might sound crazy to you, but you two are here, and I want to make you an offer. You can say no, and we can go home and keep doing what we've been doing. I will not be upset because I did my part." Claire placed the palms of her hands on the table.

"Diane," continued Claire, "I went after you, because what that journalist did to me is an affront to what real journalism supposed to be, and I want people to know the truth.

Nick, I approached you because it seems like we will need a lot of technical information, and help from NASA as well." Claire paused to sip her coffee.

"This is the deal," Claire continued. "Novus Mundus sent a spaceship toward Earth one hundred years ago, and it is supposed to arrive on our planet by the end of this week. It's not a spaceship as we think, and they call it plasma permanent nuclear scanner. They say this device is able to scan our planet and send information back to Novus Mundus. They also say that if we use a combination of ultraviolet and infrared lenses, we will be able to see the object scanning our planet. Once we detect the device, they can give us instructions on how to trap it so we can keep it and study it for a while.

Once the scanner is captured, you at NASA," she said pointing to Nick, "convince your team to provide the resources and support to develop the synthetic fuel.

If we get everything right, I will give you, Diane," she said turning to Diane, "all the information about Novus Mundus and you can broadcast it along with the synthetic fuel formula so every nation can use it for the sake to save our planet. Questions?"

They were both remained silent, as if they were trying to digest all that they had just heard.

"Ok," Nick said, rubbing his chin, his forehead scrunched up and lips pursed together. "Is this something related to that signal from outer space we detected two years ago?"

"Not that I'm aware of. I haven't heard anything about a message sent to Earth or other planets. It might be something entirely different," Claire said.

"I still don't get it. You are offering all of this, whatever, to us and we don't even need to believe you because there will be a spaceship coming from another planet and we will be able to see it. And we can even catch this ship as proof that what you're saying is legit? And on top of that, we will save the planet? Do I have that right?" Nick asked.

"No," Claire said, "I'm sorry, maybe I wasn't clear. This is a permanent nuclear scanner. It's not actually a physical spaceship. What I said is that they are offering to help save our planet, not me."

"I don't know what to say," Diane said. "We have that signal coming from somewhere, now we have this dream with aliens, yet so far there is nothing concrete. It's hard to believe in all of this. Don't get me wrong, I'm a logical person."

"You don't need to believe me, that's why I'm offering the proof before asking you to commit. The device will circumnavigate our earth twenty-four times a day for about three days, and after that, it will be unreachable. That's the amount of time you have to make your decision. Don't forget your lenses, you can see it during the night, or during the day pretty clearly. I'm sorry, but I need to go," Claire said, standing up and grabbing her coffee. "Are there any further questions?"

"How can we contact you, privately?" Diane asked.

"For now, let's use email and the telephone."

She put her chair back and was ready to make her way out, but stopped for a moment when Nick said, "Just for the record, I'll be in Miami for a while, so if you need to talk to me face-to-face just call me."

"Thanks, I appreciate that. Bye guys," Claire said and left.

CHAPTER 16 – Everybody is Lost

THE NOVUS MUNDUS TEAM met at Hallan's cabin every evening to update their plan. They ran their regular duties during the day, and when unnoticed, used the government resources to further their scheme. Before long, Gavriel got the first set of instructions of what to ask Claire.

"You need to ask her the numbers and the alphabet. We also need to know the value of the freezing and boiling point of water, the primary colours and the colour of the sun in the sky at noon. Also, we need the distance from the Earth to their micro planet; it seems they call it the moon, capeesh?" Theena said.

"Yeah, I think so. What do I say to Claire if she asks me about the questions?"

"Well some are pretty straight forward; we need to translate our formula using their symbols and also understand their measuring system."

"Ok, I have to go. See you later," Gavriel said, going home to sleep.

"Hi, Claire! Here are the questions I have for you," Gavriel said when dreaming, and anxious about how their meeting would go.

"Those are easy questions," Claire said. "1,2, 3 … A, B, C. The freezing point is 0° C, the boiling point is 100° C. What you call basic colours should be the primary ones. They are blue, yellow, and red. The sun at noon is yellow, and the distance from the moon to the earth is 384,400 km," Claire wrote in the sand.

"Wow, a lot of different words and symbols that I am unused to. Hopefully, I'll remember everything," Gavriel said. They spent some time talking. Claire has explained her strategy to get people's attention about their project, but Gavriel was trying to concentrate on the information written on the sand.

He suddenly disappeared before her eyes, and she found herself alone. She guessed that he woke up, but she was confused as to why she was still there. She kept walking along the lake and realized that the night was coming, and the thought of being there alone at night made her quite anxious.

She couldn't be sure what kind of mysteries this place held, and she was beginning to feel cold.

For some reason, the darkness was coming faster, and she noticed some shadows moving in the forest. Sounds of animals walking and pigs snorting filled the air.

She began to rush and realized that the sounds were following her. She panicked and started to run, then she woke up.

She looked at the clock and saw that it was almost noon. *What happened?* She thought, feeling her mouth dry.

She drank some water and took a look around, but everything seemed the same. She sat on her bed, and as she looked down, something caught her eye. She picked it up and realized that it was a piece of latex, no larger than half an inch, and it looked like a part of a glove. She grabbed it and placed on the nightstand.

#

1,2,3 … A, B, C … 0°C … 100°C … red, y … 304,400 km … Gavriel audio recorded, as soon as he awoke. *Oh, how hard it is*, he thought to himself and regretted his lack of memory. He went to work without eating his breakfast.

"I can't, I can't memorize this, it is too hard," Gavriel said, sitting in front of his grandma's cocoon chair.

"What did you get?" she asked.

He made a sliding motion with his right index finger over the palm of his left hand, toward his grandma.

"Ok, give me a couple of hours," she said, standing, and walking away.

At the end of the day, they got together at Hallan's cabin.

"We will have supper, and the main dish will be a root from Sion. It is grown locally, but its seeds were stolen, oops, imported from Sion. They eat a lot of roots on Sion because, you know, they don't have a lot of open fields for crops. Most of their food comes from underground. Most roots are bitter, but this one is delicious, and you'll like it," Hallan said while preparing the food.

"Ok, let's work while we wait," Theena said, walking around the table. "Gavriel brought some information from his dream last night. I have to agree, it's tough to memorize because they use different symbols to express their language.

"I submitted the information to our decoding department, and they gave me these results," Theena said, projecting the values on the wall, so everyone could see.

"We put the information you gave us against our database, and the results are 95% accurate. We got the values we need, and we already know their scales of measurements for distance, weight, temperature, energy, colour, etc. We have almost everything we need to start to transfer synthetic fuel technology.

We also know that Earth has the technology to stop the permanent nuclear scanner, so let's give Claire the instructions. Gavriel, you have to memorize it, but you can do it in two steps, we have time. To transfer information to Claire, we will write the numbers and instructions down on paper using Earth symbols. We will leave it available on this table so, while dreaming, you guys can come to this place and memorize it. The rest is up to her, capeesh?" Theena said, looking to everyone.

"Yes," everybody answered.

"Gavriel, we need to learn from Claire the symbols for the metals with the following melting point temperatures," and Theena showed him a list. "You have two days to bring me the results. You have a lot of work to do while sleeping," Theena said, to scattered chuckles from the team.

The night went on, with Theena and Hallan preparing the meal, while Gavriel and Lennah spent some time chatting, seated on a bench outside.

"Tell me how Claire looks like," Lennah asked, looking down while swinging her right leg.

"She is shorter than you, probably one hand shorter. She has straight brown hair that goes down a little bit below her shoulders. She has light green eyes. She is thin, but very energetic and her eyes smile."

"Do you like her?"

"I don't know exactly how to describe my feelings for her, everything feels different in that place and is not like just dreaming. It seems like she's been having hard times in her life, yet she is concerned about people's fate.

I'm feeling pumped by the idea that I, oops, that we, can actually make a difference in someone's life. This experience is definitely giving new meaning to my life," Gavriel explained. "How do you feel about all of this?"

"I feel good the idea of helping someone without seeking any reward, especially because we know that people from Earth are like us.

I believe we aren't just meat and bones, and I feel something inside me begging for answers. It seems like I'm dry inside, and thirsty for something that would refresh my soul. Hopefully, this mission can bring some answers," she said, gazing up at the stars.

"Well, let me know if you find the answers. Are there other things about the government that I should be aware of? You always surprise me on this subject," Gavriel said.

"Let me see. Did you know that the government has a secret department to edit peoples' lives, and even your life was edited? Did you know that the government has secrets agreements going on, that break our own laws?" Lennah asked.

"Well, I had a suspicion, tell about these secret agreements. Who is behind them?"

"I wasn't able to identify anybody, but apparently, there is a secret organization acting above the formal government hierarchy. They divided the mapped universe into honeycombs, and they control the destiny of civilizations inside the honeycombs. If they believe civilization is a threat to their power, they halt the course of its evolution or even promote its destruction."

"How do they do this?"

"They corrupt the planet's leaders to keep that world in an eternal cycle of poverty and dependence," she said.

"I'm shocked!" Gavriel said and dropped his jaw.

"Our planet is not immune to this either. In our honeycomb, corruption is promoted in other planets like Zyon and Sion. Their leaders are manipulated, so we are able to steal resources from those planets, and people of Novus Mundus are completely oblivious to this."

"How can we know if they do this secretly?" Gavriel asked.

"We can deceive ourselves, believing that we don't know, but the truth is, we are immersed in our comfort zone, and we don't care. With a little research and some critical thinking, we would realize that numbers don't add up. How can we explain the huge gap between Novus Mundus and the peer planets' quality of life for thousands of years?"

"Interesting, now certain things make more sense to me," Gavriel said, looking down.

"Certain things don't make sense to me. I'm a little bit nervous because I can't find any of the former workers from my department. I'd like to talk to them, but they were all transferred to secret missions or died due to harmful chemical exposure, and to die scares me? Now you know everything I know," Lennah said, opening the palms of her hands.

"I just don't know what to say, but one thing I do know, we are in this thing together, and there must be a solution for this mess," Gavriel said.

"Yes, there is a solution," Hallan said by the door, "and for now, the answer has come from Sion, and it's in the shape of food. Suppertime! Come, let's eat!"

#

Claire looked at the clock, and it was almost three in the afternoon. "Yikes, I forgot the noon sleep, it's too late now."

She decided to take a look at her blog and face the truth. She had to deal with feedbacks if she wanted to thrive. *I'll try not to judge them,* she thought to herself.

To her surprise, she had a lot of likes on her posts. Most expressed their opinion in a coherent and structured way. She noticed the criticisms were usually short sentences with a couple of poorly chosen words that didn't surprise her at all. She made her own comment apologizing for the article published in the media. She explained that while her name was used, the article didn't accurately relate the truth or her opinion about the subject.

She checked her inbox and found a message relating to her that there had been a cancellation, and the dean of the MBA program had time to meet with her. They apologized for the short notice and said that if she would be able to make it that afternoon *at 3:30,* the principal would be glad to meet her. If she couldn't make it, then the previous appointment would be kept.

She checked the clock. *Oh my, God, it's 3:20 already!* Without a second thought, she grabbed her backpack and ran to the garage to get her bike. She knew that this would be the fastest way to get to the college because traffic in this part of the city was quite intense. She biked like crazy, taking shortcuts and almost running over a couple of people. The bike began to sway from side to side, and she realized that the rear tire was flat.

She locked up the bike at a bus stop sign and started to run. There was no other option at this point. She didn't pay attention to the time until she reached the college building.

"I have … uh," she panted while trying to speak.

"Take your time, breathe, breathe," the receptionist said.

"Thanks… I have a meeting with the dean, my name is Claire Luan."

"Ok, wait for a second," the receptionist told her while buzzing the dean's office.

"Unfortunately, he left already. He waited for you until 3:45, and he does apologize, but he thought you weren't coming," relayed the receptionist.

Claire mumbled her thanks and turned her back to the receptionist. She went outside the building and sat on a bench beside a flower bed. She wasn't sad or mad but felt kind of numb. The adrenaline that had been fueling her earlier had all but disappeared. She stood up and calmly made her way to where she left her bike.

She managed to get home by early evening. Claire pushed her bike with the flat into the garage and decided to grab a bottle of water from the fridge and sat on the balcony. While sipping, she looked at the thick clouds approaching, indicating an impending storm.

"Look at the bright side, Claire; you got home before the storm," she tried to console herself. It started to rain, but she didn't move. Soon it was pouring, and she felt the water soaking her hair and clothes. She closed her eyes and burst into tears. She didn't know why she was crying, but her heart needed a release. The rain intermingled with the tears that coursed down her face. It comforted her to know that Heaven was crying with her.

#

"Hi, I'm sorry I missed the noon meeting," Claire said that night as she met Gavriel in the dream.

"Oh, don't worry, I couldn't fall asleep either. I will wake up earlier tomorrow so I can fall asleep at noon. We need to be fast today; otherwise, we won't be able to accomplish our mission," Gavriel said.

"Yes, I agree. I'll wake up earlier too."

"Come, I have something for you." They held hands and flew to Hallan's house. "Listen, Claire, I don't know how our dreams work, but it seems like I can reach places that I'm familiar with. In case we don't see each other by the lake, you should come to this location. I will leave information for you on this table," Gavriel explained to Claire, showing her a paper with numbers.

"I need to know from you the symbols for each element that has a melting point at these listed temperatures," he said, showing her the list.

"Hmm… my alarm clock setup time, my coffee maker setup time, 1000, my birth time, my dad's birthdate. Done!"

"You got it already?"

"Yep," she said, looking at him, and feeling that something was about to explode inside her.

"Good for you! Hey Claire, how do you see me? Do you think something has changed since we met in these dreams?" Gavriel asked.

Despite being it being an unexpected question, Claire didn't feel embarrassed and naturally answered the question.

"The more I know you, the more I feel your presence. For instance, when you gave me a hug the other day, it was something amazing. How do you show affection on your planet?" Claire asked.

"We hug!" Gavriel answered.

"Interesting. Don't you kiss?"

"No," he said when Claire approached him and kissed him, again waking the same volcano of energy they had previously felt. This time they felt their spirits merging, finding themselves navigating dozens of different dimensions and emotions, aware that they were always part of that universe and their consciousness was flooded with a knowledge that surpassed any understanding.

"Where are we? Who are we? "Gavriel whispered, still connected to Claire's lips.

"We are..." whispered Claire, but she could not express herself in thought and felt that her consciences were connected, staying that way until they woke up.

#

Gavriel awoke in torpor as if the dream's unspeakable emotions were trying to blend in with his reality. It looked like it was in Acqua, still on the lakeside, and it was surreal. He felt a supernatural peace and trying to carry this feeling for his day, got up and went to breakfast.

"Hey! Good morning handsome! Since you started to work, we haven't seen each other much. I'd like to spend at least the weekends together," Cillia said.

"Hi, Mom. Yes, it's been peculiar and busy. It seems like you guys are getting along quite well," he said, pointing to the dog on her lap.

"Oh yeah, we really like each other," she said, kissing Fluffy. "How are you and Claire doing? What happened with you, your eyes seem to smile. Are you in love?"

"I don't know. I wondered how I ended up in this situation. I traced it back and remembered that you brought me to the spiritual services with you. That is where everything started," Gavriel said, jokingly.

"I'm happy for you. You are a man now, and I'm proud of you. I'll leave you for a while. There is a spiritual encounter at a resort in the north, and I'm going. It's going to last twenty-one days. I'm pretty sure you will survive on your own. After that, we should synchronize our agendas and make sure we have family time," Cillia said.

"Good for you. Are you bringing Fluffy along?"

"Yes, I will. I don't dare to leave without him," Cillia said, kissing the dog again.

"That's not fair; I'll really be by myself?" Gavriel complained.

"Yes, you will, I'm leaving at noon. Grandma will be around, so you won't completely starve."

"Wow, at noon? What's the reason for the rush?"

"At first, I was not interested, but I was convinced by a friend of mine who went to the last event, and I made a last-minute decision."

"Well, look on the bright side, you won't have to cook for me," Gavriel said, somewhat sad, but happy for his mom too.

"Ok, I have to go to Hallan's place to check if everything is ready for a project we are working on. I'll video chat you tonight! See you," he said, kissing her mom's face and making his way out.

Hi Theena, I'm at Hallan's place, and it seems like everything is ready for our meeting tonight. As I can see, you've set up the notes on the table so it will be available for a lunchtime dream. Bye, and have a beautiful day. He left the message for his grandma, who was probably still sleeping.

He was about to leave when he saw Hallan arriving for his breakfast.

"You are a dedicated man! Every day you are right on time, but I guess it is just because of the food," Gavriel said to Hallan, jokingly.

"You have a point, but I also get my spiritual food, and that's the one that really satisfies."

"I wish, I could believe the same way you believe. I had some moments of peace, but it seems that my beliefs are too connected to this world."

"Listen, Gavriel, people believe what they want to believe. Some people just believe in what they can physically see, and they are quite content with these facts. However, some people think that there is something beyond what we can physically see, and they seek it. It's a choice."

"Yes, I got it, but I don't see the same way you see, and I don't even know where to start," Gavriel said.

"Well, there is no formula. You don't need any ritual, scheme, rule, procedure, or even religion to find what you are looking for. It's about choices, and you made your choice already, so be patient," Hallan said.

"I understand. Well, I have to go, have a good day," Gavriel said and left.

#

Claire was awake, yet didn't want to get up. She could still feel Gavriel's kiss, and reluctant, got up. She went to the balcony, took a deep breath and enjoyed the air from the sea hitting her face. Life felt magic, and it was a beautiful day. She had been in love once, and she knew this was different, as serenity and joy fulfilled her soul.

Claire's joy arose from the fact that she now had someone to share life with, however, coming back to reality diminished that happiness, and she realized that she had a mission to accomplish.

Midday came, and she went for a nap. She found herself by the lake, but Gavriel wasn't there. The only way to get instructions was to go to Hallan's house by herself. She looked at Novus Mundus, and in a split second, she was flying around the planet, looking for a reference point to find Hallan's house. She was searching for the government compound, which she easily spotted. Then she just had to look around, and soon enough she found the terrain with trails. *Wow, I'm getting good at this thing*, she thought. She went into the cabin and found Gavriel there.

"Hi, I did this to check and see if you were able to find this place without my help. Congrats! Here you are," he said.

"Good to see you again," she said, kissing him.

They felt so connected, they didn't even need to talk.

"You'll have a visit today. the nuclear scanner will arrive tonight, so you'll be able to see that I'm real too," Gavriel said, smiling.

"These are the instructions to stop the scanner. After stopping, it will remain still for four hours and will start to run again if it doesn't receive further instructions," Gavriel said and described the steps to stop the permanent nuclear scanner.

Claire listened to him and made some mental notes to memorize it.

"This is the beginning of the formula for the synthetic fuel," he said, pointing to scientific notes on the table.

"What? This is huge, and I don't even know these symbols. This is an impossible task," she said, panicking.

"You can do this, I believe in you. We have some time so you can do it little by little," Gavriel said, knowing it was a humongous task.

"Ok, I'll try to memorize some symbols here, but I'll need some help on Earth," she sought to associate the symbols with something that was familiar to her; however these were really different from anything she recognized.

She awoke. She knew she wouldn't be able to start this task without help, so she called Nick.

"Hi Nick, I have the first part of the synthetic fuel given to me, and it's rocket science to me, so I'll need your help," she said.

"But you said we should wait for the signal; the spaceship, and then we're supposed to call you. Has anything changed?"

Yikes, I forgot about the permanent nuclear scanner, she thought. "Yes, you're right. Anyway, it's supposed to show up tonight," she said, yet the words didn't come easy.

"You can come to my place, or I can meet at yours. I don't mind helping you, and we can also have fun," Nick said.

"Well, I don't know. Can… can you come to my place?" Claire said, yet she wasn't sure what he meant by having fun.

"Sure, eight o'clock again?"

"Yes, eight is fine," she hung up.

What are you doing Claire? What if this thing doesn't show up? I'll feel like a fool. Think Claire, think! Yes, I'll call him to cancel. No, idiot! Then he will believe it is just a joke. Dear God, you put me in this situation, and I don't have any clue how to get out of this. Please help me. She was panicking again.

The lenses! I need to buy lenses. She grabbed her purse and made her way out, only to stop at the door and make her way back.

She turned on the computer and started to type. *Lenses, where to buy, photography, photography stores, Miami. There you go!* She made a note of the address. She went to the garage and found the car keys inside the ashtray, and drove up to the address.

"I need ultraviolet and infrared lenses," she said to the clerk.

"Ok, what specs and what camera are we talking about?" the clerk asked.

"Camera? Specs? It doesn't matter."

"Sorry, I don't know what to sell you if you don't know the specs. Do you want any lens? I have a pair of lenses for seven thousand dollars if you aren't sure of what to get," the clerk said sarcastically, pointing to a pair of lenses under the glass counter.

"What? I'm sorry. I know I should be more specific. I need something elementary. It's for an experiment, I don't even have a camera. I will be using just my eyes," she explained, making a circle around her eyes with her fingers.

"Actually, I might have exactly what you are looking for." He went to the back of the office and came back with two lenses.

"These lenses are damaged. The frame was entirely broken, but we kept the glass."

"How much?"

"Seven," the clerk said.

"Seven? Not thousand, surely," Claire said, raising her eyebrow and turning her ear toward the clerk, trying to hear the price.

"Seven times you have to say *thank you!*" the clerk said, joking.

"That's it? Thank you, thank you," she said it seven times, counting on her fingers, and said goodbye.

Not a bad way to start the day, she thought.

Back at the apartment, thoughts flooded her mind. *What if this thing doesn't show up? What if they can't see it? What if it's too small? What if he thinks it's just a star or satellite? What if,* and the telephone rang. *It's him, and he's cancelling the appointment,* she thought and picked up the phone.

"Hello? Oh hi, Rachel! Yes, I'm fine… no, nothing wrong. It's just me; I can tell you everything when you come back…

Really? So, you are coming back in two weeks? Don't worry, I'll make sure everything is going to be ok.

... yes, of course, I want to share the apartment with you. Great, we'll talk when you come back then, see you, bye." she hung up the phone.

It was definitely a good day. Now she could even share the apartment with Rachel.

It was eight o'clock, and sure enough, Nick rang the doorbell.

"Hi Nick, come on in," she said, opening the door.

"I brought a bottle of wine," he said, showing her a bag.

"Oh thanks, but I don't drink."

"Well..." He looked a bit embarrassed. "Yeah, I should have asked you. I'm sorry."

"No worries."

"Anyway, I can leave it for another time," he said handing the wine to her.

"Ok," she grabbed the wine and put over the China cabinet. "Here," she said, pointing to a draft on the table. On it was a few symbols, she remembered from her dream.

"They are chemical symbols. I can find some material about them so you can become more familiar with," Nick said.

"Great, that would be a good start. Why don't we go to the balcony? It's hot today, and we have a clear sky. By the way, I bought the infrared and ultraviolet lenses... to see something in the sky," she said, with some hesitation in her voice.

They sat on the balcony for a time until Nick broke the silence.

"So, I heard you came from Chile. What's life like there?"

"It was all right," she said, avoiding eye contact. She put the lenses to her eyes but saw nothing, and gave them to Nick.

"What brought you to the United States?"

"The earthquake, I moved to the United States after we had the shock. I came in that immigrant waiver program the government offered."

"So, you were there when it happened? I'm sorry, I don't want to bring up sad memories," he said, fiddling with the lenses.

"No, it's ok. I just miss my dad..." she said, trying to hold back tears. "I'm sorry about all of this. I feel like an idiot about this spaceship thing, and I'm sorry to waste your time Nick," she said, looking at the skies.

"Oh my God?" he said, with surprise in his voice.

"Yeah, I'm sorry," she said, turning her face to him.

"No way! What is that?" he said again, looking through the lenses and then handing them to her.

Claire pointed them to the sky and started to weep. A massive, bright object was travelling across the sky.

Nick immediately made a phone call. "Look at the sky, face north, three o'clock, what do you see? Nothing, right, now go and grab your camera. I'll explain later. Can you do it now, please?" and Nick explained how to see the object.

"No, it isn't Russian or Chinese. It isn't from our planet. I'll explain later. Call the air force and our people from the lab; they have to record this... yes, I know you know what to do, sorry. Bye," and he hung up the phone.

They were both silents for a moment.

"I thought you were hitting on me when you invited me to come to your place, I'm really sorry, I feel like an idiot, forgive me," he said.

"I forgive you," she said, looking again through the lenses and thinking to herself, *I can see you, Gavriel,* tears coming down her face.

"Ok, I have to go, there's a lot to be done. You stay around, and I'll contact you soon," Nick said, heading toward the door.

"Wait a minute, what do you mean to stay around? I have a lot of things to do," Claire said, eyebrows arched in surprise.

"Well, I need to contact you. What if I bring you a cell phone?"

"No cell phones, no 'men in black' wearing sunglasses and knocking on my door. Plus, your buddies from NASA shouldn't know where I am and, if they insist, I'll stop this game right away. Now, if you want to contact me, you can use the good old-fashion landline, believe me, it works. Although landlines are as unsafe as emails, so don't expect to exchange information through any device. It has to be in person, capeesh?"

"Yes, madam. When do you think we can talk again? I need the instructions to deal with that beauty over there."

"I'll contact you tomorrow, have a good night," she said as she opened the door for him.

Claire was excited, and couldn't fall asleep. Her mind was going through all that she had just experienced. She was thinking about the many hours needed to update her blog, the steps to transfer the synthetic fuel formula, and the people to contact, and it was almost morning when she finally fell asleep.

"The permanent nuclear scanner has arrived, you are real! We aren't alone in this universe. I'm so happy!" Claire said, hugging and kissing Gavriel.

"Great! I'm happy too," he said, laughing.

"Now we have a lot to do, let's check the synthetic fuel formula. I'm so excited!" Claire expressed in a frenzy.

"Here is the formula," he said, pointing to the table. "Try to memorize it. I'll wander around to avoid distracting you. If we don't meet each other tomorrow during the day, we will talk at night. Bye," he said.

"Bye," Claire said, watching him floating away.

Gavriel had something on his mind; if he could sneak into the government building while dreaming, he might be able to see who or what was behind the head of the state.

He knew that it was late at night, and there were just the security and the emergency response teams working. Besides, it wouldn't hurt to take a look.

The building was well-illuminated during the night so he could see it from far off in the distance. He felt confident crossing the glass entrance doors, yet he would never pass a wall without visualizing what was on the other side.

He floated along hallways, but couldn't get into the rooms because the doors were shut. He saw two security members chatting while walking toward him, and followed them up to the security center.

The place was filled with a large holograph image representing the universe, and walls covered with many projections, some he was familiar with.

He could see one projection showing a system with a red circle around a planet, which he guessed was Earth. He saw another projection, closer to where the guards were, and they were images circled with different colours. He stopped in front of a group of pictures circled in red, Lennah and Hallan were amongst them.

Suddenly there was a loud buzzing noise, all the lights went off, and the place was illuminated only by the emergency light. The two guards stood quickly and returned to their working chairs. Gavriel panicked and awoke.

"Lennah, I need to talk to you before heading to work, meet me at Hallan's house," he said over the live line.

He then called Hallan. "Hi Hallan, have you had your breakfast already?"

"No," Hallan said.

"Ok, can we meet at your site? Ok, bye."

A half an hour later he was at the site and was about to have a cup of coffee when Lennah arrived.

"Hi, Lennah, how are you doing? Let's wait for Hallan to come so I can talk to you both. For now, do you have any news from the database?"

"Yes, but I've been denied access to some sensitive information. I'm afraid the system is flagging me. However, before I was denied, I was able to read some policies from a group called Elite-7.

The documents were labelled top secret, and I have no idea how I ended up having access to them. Reading the papers, I got the impression that the Elite-7 group is recognized by our government as the ultimate authority, but their identity has never been made known to the public. The group pledges to be the supreme representatives of seven honeycombs.

The group is responsible for the application of what they call Strategic Policies. One of these policies, called 'Infusion Policies,' is the way governments should release information to the public. It outlines how to let people know some irrelevant information in a way that doesn't disrupt the system and keeps the population under control.

They also have the 'Maintenance Policies,' that is a clever title, yet it is very intrusive. The procedures are designed to protect the power of honeycomb governments at any cost. There is one statement that explains how to limit the level of technology achieved by planet members."

"Wow, there is something fishy here," Gavriel said.

"Every police officer gets to the level of directives and everything is nicely analyzed by assessing the risk and cost. The Corruption Method is the most cost-effective because the locals destroy their own society, and there is no need for additional resources or personnel.

The Direct Intervention directive should be used only under the authorization of the Elite-7 group, because it requires the deployment of troops, which is costly, hazardous, and proven to achieve mediocre results."

Hallan stepped into the cabin during Lennah's report and was able to get most of her updates.

"Well, that proves my theory that our government also might be behind Earth's corruption. Any more good news?" Hallan asked with sarcasm.

"Yes, more 'good' news," Gavriel said. "Last night, during my dreams, I decided to sneak into the government building, and I was able to reach some rooms.

The security room has pictures of you, and Lennah circled in red. To make things worse, an alarm went off while I was there, but I don't know why. I think Lennah can try to get something from the database so we can have an idea of what's going on."

"I'm afraid I can't help because our department doesn't have access to the security system and, as I said, my rights have been revoked in some areas. The alarm bell was a scheduled security drill, so no worries," Lennah said, looking at Gavriel.

"I'm afraid we've been flagged. We'll need to take some extra precautions," Hallan said.

You and Lennah can use one of the blind spots to talk to each other and use a blind spot to speak to Theena as well.

When we have to get together, we will meet here because my home is a public gathering place, and our gathering shouldn't raise flags. I know that being flagged won't stop the system from monitoring us no matter where we are, but at least they can't hear us. Eventually, this will escalate their attempts to track us, but it is the best we can do right now.

Tonight, go to the government building again and try to get more information. Try other rooms, we need to know what they know about us."

#

"Hi Gavriel, I was able to get a fair portion of the synthetic fuel formula. However, it's going to be a long haul," Claire said, meeting him in Acqua.

"Yes, I agree. Listen, I have trouble falling asleep at noon, so I'm afraid you won't find me here at that time. How's the permanent nuclear scanner doing? What are the outcomes? Are people taking the threat seriously now?"

"I don't know. I'll pass some instructions on to them today. Hopefully, I'll get some answers tomorrow; however, I won't be naive, and I'll be careful passing on the next steps. I have it all in my head, so I know how to control that device.

Now that you have asked, it came to my mind that even if my contacts take it seriously, I don't know how the public will react," Claire admitted.

"You mean you don't know if they will believe in you, even with all the facts?" Gavriel asked.

"Yes. On Earth, we've been bombarded with so many bizarre events, some produced by our own society. There's, so much misinformation in such a short time that I wonder if people will even acknowledge the seriousness of the current situation, and if they don't, our work will be in vain," Claire said, turning her eyes up to the sky.

"Well, at this point we don't have many choices. We either do something or do nothing, and the latter isn't an option for me. Besides, we can always meet each other over here to share our ups and downs and try new things," Gavriel said.

"Can we?" she said, looking into his eyes, and with that, they both awoke.

#

Claire turned on the computer. She had to close the windows and the balcony doors because it was too noisy outside. The internet was slow, and when the news opened, she gasped as she read the headline.

Displayed in big letters, it read: *They Are Here, As Predicted. The Aliens Have Arrived.* Her jaw dropped. She froze, and her eyes widened. The internet was so slow that she decided to turn on the TV. It showed massive traffic jams. People were streaming out of stores with whatever they could get their hands on, and panic was everywhere. The television showed the nuclear scanner doing laps around the planet and some experts on aliens being interviewed.

"They are doing reconnaissance before an invasion," one commentator stated.

"They are testing our reaction," another one chimed in.

"They are here to help us."

"They are poisoning the air."

These were just some of the theories raised. Claire kept the TV on. She too was afraid she would run out of food and went to the balcony to see the streets. *They will kill each other and let others die of starvation, this is stupid,* she thought a moment before the telephone rang. It was Nick.

"Have you watched the news?" he asked.

"Yes, you don't need high tech to realize humans are stupid."

"Wow, harsh words from someone who is committed to saving the planet!"

"Yeah, I'm sorry. I'm a little bit frustrated, but I'm human as well, so I also have this stupidity gene somewhere. Anyway, what should we do?"

"I told my boss that I received this information anonymously, but he is not buying it. With all the publicity that you've been receiving, your name came up along with others.

They are pressuring me to release the source to move forward, especially now that the entire country is panicking. They don't want to take steps that could cross legal civil rights, especially because NASA isn't an investigation agency. They will use their NSA connections if they don't have an answer quickly."

"Oh really?" Claire said. "Now that you are under pressure, you want to toss me to the wolves to solve your problem. No way, if you can't handle it, I'll find someone else who can. If I receive any indication that NASA is after me, or is hacking me, I'll forget everything I know, and I won't even feel a shred of guilt.

You know that I received my instructions in my dreams. If I am stressed, I won't be able to dream, and then you can say goodbye to getting the formula. You need to handle the pressure using your means, and I'll do my part, capeesh?" She wasn't naïve, she knew that NASA probably knew about her, yet she wasn't willing to openly allow them to get into her private life.

"Ok, don't throw the baby out with the bathwater. We are in this thing together. We will make it, ok?" Nick said, waiting for an answer.

"Ok, come to my place. I'll give you instructions on how to stop the spaceship, and you guys can talk to the media, and can you bring me some food and water, please? I don't think there is anything left in the stores," she asked.

"All right. However, I don't know how long it will take to reach you. I'm at the KSC right now, be patient," Nick said and hung up.

The internet had frozen, and the noise from the streets seemed to get louder. She raised the TV volume to hear that the United States government was mandating a curfew in certain cities to avoid looting and casualties on the streets.

They also showed the reaction in other countries around the world. The international channels of communication were broadcasting people going to grocery stores and gas stations in the main cities, but there was no coverage of out of control citizens barraging stores.

China had cut out any external communication access to its population, so the news was scarce. Five hours later, the bell rang, and Nick was at the door with two large bags.

"Greetings from NASA. We have food in stock as part of an emergency plan, and we can take it home."

"Thanks, but if NASA has a plan for emergencies, it's probably for you and your family."

"I'm not married, and I'm fine for now, so it's all yours."

"Thanks again," she said, placing the bags on the kitchen table. "Ok, I was thinking about this, and maybe you guys can calm down the population by releasing a note to the public. Life seems normal in other countries, according to the TV news.

You can suggest that everything is under control. We stop the unit, NASA captures it and brings it down to study. That way everyone wins, what do you think?"

"I don't know. I can't make any decisions regarding the media. For now, the only thing we can do is to stop the device and talk, the sooner, the better.

What you've seen on TV isn't exactly what's going on abroad. The lack of internet gave complete power to foreign governments to control the local media. They show what they want to show, and that might be way different from reality.

Keep in mind that no matter how much you say that there is no connection with this device and the signals that came from space two years ago, people make their own judgment, and it seems like they are connecting these two dots," he said.

"Ok, I agree. These are the instructions to stop the device," and Claire handed Nick a sheet.

"So, then we can trap it? How? Where?" Nick asked.

"No, this just stops the unit. I'll have the rest of the instructions soon," Claire said.

"How can we know we will have the rest of the instructions?"

"You trust in me, and I trust in you. This is the only way we can make it work."

Nick tilted his head a bit and pursed his lips together. He knew he had no other option and that he needed to be fast. Otherwise, there would be no time to set up the device and stop the nuclear scanner.

"I need to go, but I'll be around," he said while taking a picture of the instructions.

"I know," Claire said, opening the door. "Talk to you soon."

CHAPTER 17 – The World Up Side Down

"HI GAVRIEL," CLAIRE SAID, acknowledging his presence and turning her face back toward the table, as she was concentrating on the formula. The conversation between them had naturally diminished because they knew they had to use their time wisely to achieve their goals.

"I'm afraid I can't stay. I need to go to the government building," Gavriel said, slowly floating away from Claire.

"Yup, no problem," she said without even looking at him.

Gavriel flew toward the government building; he needed to find some answers. He got into the building and floated along the hallways to get any sliver of information.

He stopped in front of the security room and tried to make his way through the wall, but he couldn't. When he glanced at the inner walls, everything became black, it seemed as if time stopped, and he froze. He barely made his way back, knowing something had happened that he didn't have control over. There was no time for new experiences.

He moved back and forth along the hallway using the gravity tube's openings to go up and down but found nothing. He made his way out of the building through the front doors when he noticed a jet-Suphcar arriving. He went up to check this unusual landing in an area that was restricted.

He saw four people exiting the car and heading to the top floor entrance. He knew that some authorized users could take the top entry.

A floating red orb guided them toward a meeting room. He followed the group carefully and entered a white room with no windows. In the middle of the room, there was an oval silver table with eight white chairs floating around it. Three other people were there waiting, and they started the meeting without any greetings or introductions.

"I guess everyone is tired," said the bald man who seemed to be the leader. "Some of you have been travelling for six months, and just arrived, so we will have a short time together today.

I requested this emergency meeting because I have some news, and due to its sensitive nature, we cannot discuss this by regular ways of communication. We won't get into details today because of the bulk of information and instructions that need to be addressed before we make any decisions.

"It is so secret that the procedure will be extreme. You'll receive these tubes," said the leader, pointing to the six devices on the table, "containing information written on paper. After reading the report put the material back into the tubes and seal them, and this will activate an automatic process of destroying the contents.

Tomorrow we will gather here at the same time to proceed with any decisions. Any questions?" he asked, handing out the tubes.

"I'm curious to see what is so secret. We have only activated this protocol a few times in our history," said one of the men.

"You are dismissed now," said the leader, ignoring the man who spoke. Everyone stood up, making their way out of the room. Gavriel was by the door just waiting for everyone to get out when one of the attendees looked directly into his eyes, he panicked and awoke.

#

Claire got up and made notes about the formula on paper. She knew she had something, although it was just a fraction of the entire equation. Claire tore the page from the notebook, folded it up, and put it into the pocket of her jeans that were lying beside her bed.

She went to the balcony and looked down toward the street. People were still agitated, but it seemed like the panic was under control.

She came inside and turned on the TV. People were puzzled because the object hovering in space had stopped four hours ago. She grabbed her backpack, a towel, some crackers, and water. She found sunscreen and slathered it on.

Before leaving the apartment, she scribbled *Went to the beach* on a scrap of paper and left it on the table.

She walked about seven blocks and regretted not having fixed the bike. Arriving at the beach, she found a spot by the shore and lay a towel over the sand. She undressed to her bikini, unravelling her beautiful body and laid down. "Now let's just wait, it's going to get hot out here. Let's see how much I can trust Nick."

About two hours later, she felt a shadow covering her face. She peered up and said, "Hi Nick, how do they say it in the movies, what took you so long to get here?"

"Listen," he said, squatting, "I'm sorry, we thought we had everything under control, so we decided to keep going." He paused, but Claire was still mute. "I know we've messed up, I'm really sorry!"

"Let me guess, the permanent nuclear scanner started to move again about two hours ago," she said, sitting and looking at Nick. She now knew he wasn't honest with her.

"I …uh."

"Yes, you did mess up. The problem is that you followed the rules written by bureaucrats and your brain doesn't have room for new ideas. You guys think that you know everything, but right now you are like dogs running after your own tails. You don't know what to do with that thing," she said, pointing her right hand toward the sky where the object was again moving.

"Listen!" Claire said, clearly frustrated. "It seems like we have difficulty to understand each other. I know why and how you got here, but you don't know how to get out of your mess. You got here by checking my apartment and reading the note on the table," she said, looking to the shoreline.

"What you don't know, and that's why you are here, is how to make that beauty over there stop again," Claire said. She knew that the device had started moving again because of the lack of instructions. She knew exactly what had happened, but wasn't going to share that information with Nick just yet.

"Now you have to decide. You play the game by my rules or go back to your mediocre entry-level job," Claire stated firmly, clearly showing Nick, she had the upper hand.

"Wow, you said in your blog that bad feelings and words can kill you or leave scars forever, so are those Claire's words, or did they come from space?" Nick asked, pointing his index finger up.

"You can't blame me for the harsh words, yet you are the one who's jeopardizing the opportunity to make a difference in this world," and Claire calmed down a bit, "Look, I'm sorry if I sound harsh, but there is a lot at stake right now."

"You are right, I'm a newbie in this job, and I have to follow orders. I can't dictate the rules of my work and don't know what to do. It's too complicated for me; I just can't see the big picture."

"If you want to keep going ahead with the plan, you have to keep NASA away from me. My life is balanced, and I'm happy with the way it is right now. Don't you understand that if I mess up my life, I can lose the connection with Novus Mundus?

I don't need the media, and I definitely don't need the government. I just need to finish what I have started. By the way, I'm pretty sure Diane is after me, but I haven't followed up with her. What did you say to her?" Claire said, looking in his eyes.

"I… I'm sorry!" Nick said, his face downcast.

"Ok, now do your homework. Tell your boss that if we want to stop that thing, he needs to use NASA's proper channels of communication. He also needs to assure everyone that everything is under control, and that might bring some peace to the situation.

Can you please contact Diane and keep her up to date? If we have all our ducks in a row by tomorrow morning, we can move on. Otherwise, neither of us will be able to convince people that we have a solution for the environmental problems our planet is facing right now."

"Ok, I'll contact my office and Diane," said Nick as he stood up. "Two things before I leave. You want to play the game with your rules, well keep in mind that life doesn't work that way all the time.

You are very selfish for someone who's eager to save the world. The other thing is, can you please stop this childish hide and seek game? I'm getting a little bit tired of this." he said as he moved away.

"Don't forget to ask them to remove the wires from my apartment," she yelled while he left. She was bluffing. She didn't know if they had wired her dwelling, but she didn't know what to say after his comments on her behaviour.

#

On Novus Mundus, Gavriel was freaking out because of his last visit to the government building.

"I'm telling you, the guy looked right into my eyes. I could feel he was looking right at me!" He said to Lennah and Hallan while sharing a light meal. "What are they up to? It seems critical."

"I'll try to get some information about this visit tomorrow. In the meantime, relax and finish your snack. I think you are just tired. Things will calm down after you guys solve the Earth issue," said Lennah.

"Let's be reasonable here," Hallan said. "I can see only two possible explanations. The guy was looking at something behind you, and you just happened to be standing in front of it. Or, he saw you, but he didn't say anything and didn't sound an alarm, because he doesn't see you as a threat, which is also good. For now, I don't see any reason to panic."

"Yes, you're right. The group is planning to meet again at midnight, so I'll get to sleep and make my way directly to the government building. I need to know what this is all about. See you guys tomorrow," he said, standing up and making his way to the floating car parked outside.

"Hey, you have to finish your snack," Lennah said, but he had left already.

Sleep came as usual, and, from Acqua, Gavriel flew to the government building. He was a little bit disoriented because he didn't know what time it was. There was not a single clock around, so Gavriel had to fly quickly to his house to find out the time. He saw that it was eleven-thirty, so he went back to the building to wait for the group to arrive.

One Suphcar approached the top of the building, and he stood beside the entrance that led to the meeting room. If something went wrong, he had an open area to escape. Three people came out of the vehicle and made their way to the entrance of the building when the door opened automatically. Gavriel followed them until they went into the empty meeting room.

So, these guys are early for the meeting, he thought. He also looked at the wall he was standing in front of last night to see if there was something to look at, like a picture, but there was nothing, so, the guy actually was looking at him, and he was sure of it now.

"Are you sure this room is safe?" asked one of the men.

"Yes, I am, I have access to the recordings, and I'll make sure it is edited," answered the other.

"So, what's your concern about agent P1999?" another one asked.

"Well first, when we were on vacation in the north, he was away from our group for almost the entire time."

"Well, that's not a problem. Although we try to keep ourselves as a family, our privacy should be respected," answered one of the guys who seemed to be the leader.

"I agree, but the situation now is susceptible, according to the documents I read. I also realized that the agent was exhibiting strange behaviour when spending time up north. I was checking his recordings for his time over there, and he seems to disappear, sometimes for days. Also, have you noticed that his votes never follow the team? I mean, I know that we're supposed to have disagreements to fabricate credibility for the Elite-7 group, yet he seems to follow his own rules."

"Well you might have a point, but what's the concern here? The other six of us are well connected, so whatever he decides by himself won't affect our decisions," the leader said.

"Yes, of course, except that P1999 has access to sensitive information, and he oversees Zyon. All this makes me uncomfortable, as now we need to make strategic decisions about that planet. He might form some strategic alliances against our will."

"Ok, I get that, let's talk about this later because the system has just acknowledged his arrival," the leader said, looking at the palm of his hand. "If we find any sign of treason, we can request some security measures over him."

The others agreed and watched the door opening while agent P1999 entered. He sat beside one of the men, facing Gavriel on the other side of the room. He ran his eyes over Gavriel and briefly made eye contact, but then turned his head toward the leader in a sign of readiness. At this point, Gavriel knew that the guy could see him, but Gavriel wasn't afraid.

Three other men arrived, and they started the meeting.

"You are now fully aware how dangerous our situation is. To maintain security, recordings of our meetings will be entirely erased afterward. As you've read, new military computer simulations from two honeycombs revealed a disruption in our local planetary orbit. This means that eventually Novus Mundus and Zyon will collide," the leader explained.

"Yes, and I'm shocked!" one of the men said.

"I'll be concise because we don't have much time for details. The system projected that the collision by itself is going to happen in forty-eight years, but this planetary orbit change will dramatically increase the temperatures before that. In about thirty years, we won't be able to live on the surface of our planet, and we might need to build underground dwellings."

"What are we going to do? What's the plan?" agent P1999 asked.

"Headquarters has projected a dire picture. Saving the entire population of both planets is impossible. The only plausible solution is to relocate just a few thousand to another planet. That's why we are here, we need to choose where we are going to move."

"What about Sion? Are they going to be spared from this catastrophe?" one of the men asked, and the leader just shook his head.

"I know you might have more questions, such as population reaction, the scientific community, etc., and we can talk about it tomorrow. I didn't have time to read my document, which is a detailed version so I can keep you updated as we continue to meet. For now, let's just vote on what we are supposed to vote on today," the leader said and projected some documents in front of the attendees.

"We are welcome to move to another honeycomb, but there is always the cultural adaptation that needs to take place, and it is almost sure that our culture will disappear.

There is a list of elected planets for our colonization, and we can pick one today because the arrangements have to start as soon as possible.

The option suggested by the system is Earth because it complies with all the requirements to sustain a comfortable life for us and should be ready upon our arrival.

My suggestion is to vote on Earth as our option. If we don't reach the majority of votes, we can discuss other options. Those in favour put your right hand over the projected file, those against putting your left hand on it," said the leader.

The seven people put their hands over their files, and the projected images disappeared.

"As per our decision, Earth is chosen to be our new home. The forecasted planetary reaction to the current system deterioration should start soon, and by the time we get there, their civilization will be just a fraction of today's population. Once we get close to Earth, we can start the reboot process even before landing."

"The report says that we will use the military spaceships that will be ready in four years. Is there any change in the vessel construction schedule? With the updates in this report, we might not be able to hide this information from the public any longer. Signs will soon be visible, and the current temperature will increase," one of the men interjected.

"I have no information about changes in the schedule. We will abandon Novus Mundus in four years as planned. Let's leave it to the proper departments to deal with the public issue," the leader said.

"I hope they can deal with that. If people find out that just a few thousand will embark on this forty-year trip, and the rest will perish, nobody would be able to contain them. Not even the army."

"I wish we could have come up with the new spaceship project earlier," another guy said. "It seems like time, which has always been in our favour, is against us now."

"I think we should have a plan 'b' for our own families in case we need an emergency exit. Things might get messy if our population revolts," one of those present suggested.

"We can think of a plan 'b' another time. For now, we have other issues to deal with," the leader said, raising the tone of his voice. "We have received our first load of Zxylon from Zyon, but we need at least one year of regular supply to ensure our needs for the spaceships.

The problem comes from a legal agreement. It states that we need to transfer the low-density gravity technology to them, but we won't do that, of course. Any suggestions on how to handle this issue?" the leader asked.

At this point Gavriel was getting nervous; he knew he needed to keep calm. Otherwise, he would wake up.

"Can we transfer a bogus process? Or something missing in the process?" someone asked.

"In theory, you are right. But Sion knows the process and can help Zyon," the leader said.

"That's true," said another man, "but we can quickly identify if they involve themselves in this. If they interfere, we stop selling food to Sion, and the ones who don't die from starvation will suffer military action."

Another guy who hadn't spoken yet interjected, "If we have the power to subdue them, let's just play the good cop as we always do. Let's ask our engineers to introduce a bug into the process, once they find out that it originated with us, it will be too late."

"It sounds like a logical idea agent A989," the leader said. "Unless anybody has a different suggestion, let's vote on this option now."

Everybody placed their hands on the projected document, and the proposal was accepted. After three hours of deliberations, they finished the meeting and started to leave the building. When passing by Gavriel, agent P1999 opened his left hand showing the words *Follow me.* Instead of heading to his car, he took the gravity-controlled tube and went down to the reception area.

Gavriel followed the agent, who walked for about one hundred and fifty feet, stopping by a tree. He then turned his face to Gavriel and asked intimidatingly, "Who are you, and what are you doing in our meetings?"

Gavriel was surprised by agent P1999's reaction. This man was an inch shorter than Gavriel with shiny brownish-orange skin. Wrinkles in his forehead and smoky-gray hair suggested that he was in his sixties, but the dark circles under his deep nebulous eyes made him look much older.

"Hey, hold on! Why such mean behaviour? Are you afraid of me?"

"Listen, I don't know who you are," the man said, a little bit nervous. "I saw you yesterday, and also noticed that the others didn't acknowledge your presence, so I kept my secret. Now you show up again in our meeting, and yet nobody saw you.

I just noticed that you are not a customized holograph image because of the life present in your eyes. You are definitely some sort of new technology. Anyway, whoever you are, or whatever you are, you don't scare me, and I have nothing to hide," agent P1999 said, and abruptly turned, making his way back toward the building.

"They are setting you up," Gavriel said.

"Who is setting me up?" the agent stopped without turning back.

"Three guys from your team. The ones that were there before your arrival, but I don't know about the others."

"Did you hear something? What is it?" the agent asked, now turning and getting close to Gavriel again.

He listened carefully to what Gavriel had heard, and agent P1999 looked down like he was deep in thought.

"Why are you telling me these things? Who are you?"

"I'm telling you these things because I think that what they are doing is wrong. Although you are part of the team, it seems like you are not entirely on their side. For now, I don't know if I can tell you who I am, although I can try to meet you again. Who are you, agent P1999?" Gavriel asked.

"I'm an agent for planet Zyon."

"So, you are a spy?"

"Technically, no. I'm formally designated to work with the Zyon government as a consultant." Gavriel said, and unexpectedly awoke.

"What the heck? Where are you?" agent P1999 said when Gavriel suddenly disappeared from in front of him.

"What's that guy doing over there? Is he out of his mind? Look, he's talking to himself," one of the security members said to his co-worker while pointing at the projected image showing the outside of the building.

"He's nuts. Just keep an eye on him," the other guy said, while agent P1999 was heading toward the building.

#

Claire awoke with a lot of information about the synthetic fuel in her head. She was worried some of the symbols wouldn't be familiar to scientists on Earth. It would be a whole other task to decipher the entire thing. She made notes in her notebook, turned on the computer, sent an email, and then headed for a shower.

The telephone rang, and she guessed it was Nick, so she took her time. After showering she decided to check the news and, as expected, NASA had released a notice saying that they were aware of the object in the skies, and they would soon stop the device. They assured everyone that everything was under control.

The telephone rang again, and she picked it up.

"Hello?"

"Hi, it's me, Nick. Have you watched the news?"

"Yes, I did. It seems like we are speaking the same language now. Anyway, check your email inbox, you should find the remaining instructions there.

Just make sure you have a site big enough to trap the device and that there is no opening larger than the size of a small van; otherwise, after a few days, the device will try to make its way out. It's a self-protection procedure.

In the email, there are also preliminary instructions about synthetic fuel. I'll be in touch to answer any questions that may arise. For now, you have enough to keep yourself busy for a long time. See you, bye," Claire said.

"Wait, you can't send me the formula by email, it's unsafe!" Gavriel rushed to say.

"C'mon, remember what I said? The formula supposed to be public, so problem if someone intercepts it. Bye," she said and hung up.

Claire prepared her backpack with some clothes and food. She had different plans for the week. She drove to her aunt's home, as she was missing her family, especially her dad.

"Hi Auntie, happy to see you!" she said, hugging her aunt.

"Where have you been my dear? We have been missing you! Your dad has been asking about you. We had faith that you were in good hands, but it's nice to see you in person," aunt Mirna said.

"Yes, it was a little bit crazy, but God is good, and, as you say, I know how to keep the dogs out," she said, and both of them laughed. "I'm missing dad, can I use your phone to contact him?"

"Sure sweetheart," her aunt said, handing her the phone, "take your time."

"Dad? How are you? Oh, dad, I miss you so much!" she said, her voice shaking. She wanted her dad to think that she was strong, but she could barely keep talking.

"Yes, everything is all right. I was able to distance myself from some nasty people. I have had good people around me too, so I am okay," she said while wiping away her tears. "When are you coming to visit us? Please, please.

… I know there is a lot to do over there, but you deserve some time off … Yes, I love you too. Listen, I'll be away for a week, but as soon as I come back, we will buy your ticket, and you are coming to visit us.

… I know, but there are no excuses, ok? All right, hope to see you very soon. I love you, bye." She hung up but looked longingly at the phone for a few moments longer.

"Thanks, aunt, he is stubborn. He should buy a computer so we could video chat, but he doesn't feel comfortable using technology. I came to say hi and ask you for another favour. Can I borrow your cottage in the woods? I know you don't go there this time of the year, and I need to meditate. There is nothing better than a peaceful and quiet place to get in touch with my spiritual side."

"Oh, sure you can," her aunt said, grabbing the key for the cottage. "You'll need to bring along some supplies because there isn't much there."

"Yes, I'm aware of all the things I need to bring with me. Don't worry. I'll just need a quick map because I forget how to get there."

"Sure," aunt Mirna said, drawing her a map.

She said goodbye to everyone and headed toward the cottage. The place was in the countryside, about three hours from Miami.

Before getting there, she bought some food and supplies for the week. She didn't buy much, as she knew she wouldn't need a lot.

After arriving at the cottage, she paused in front of the brown, rustic, wooden building and took a good look around.

She unlocked the front door and started some necessary cleanup to get rid of some uninvited bugs.

She noticed that the propane tank was empty, so she drove to the local shop to buy wood for the wood stove and propane for the oven.

After returning, she enjoyed the sunset by the pond. She was beginning to truly relax, in the quietness of the place. She loved the privacy, and it felt like being in heaven.

Darkness came slowly, and soon the late-night calls of nocturnal creatures replaced the singing of the early birds, and she went into the cabin. She was alone, but she wasn't afraid. She closed the blinds over the windows and took the hunting rifle out from its hiding place, under a floorboard. She would sleep with it as her companion that night, just in case, any unwanted visitors arrived.

The position she fell asleep it was the way she woke up. *Unbelievable*, she thought. She didn't remember a single second of being in a dream, and this was very odd for her. She prepared a cup of coffee and had some bread before heading to the nearest neighbour's cottage.

Mrs. Walton was a lovely lady living by herself after her husband passed away. Claire spent a full hour walking to reach her home. She walked along the three hundred foot long driveway that leads to the house. The German Shepherd announced her arrival with loud barks, as he was very territorial, but calmed down once he realized that she was not a threat.

"Hi, Souvenir, how are you? I missed you!" she said while holding and petting the dog's head. "Where is your mom?" she asked, looking toward the log cottage just in time to see Mrs. Walton popping up behind the front windows.

"Wow, look who is here! My sweet Chilean child, Claire. How are you doing? What a lovely surprise!" Mrs. Walton said, welcoming Claire.

They hugged each other. Claire liked Mrs. Walton. She was very energetic and thin, with short gray hair, and always wore a different cashmere pashmina. This was her one indulgence. If one wanted to please Mrs. Walton, one would get her a pashmina.

They spent the day chatting, drinking tea, baking, and preparing their meals. They were so engrossed in their conversation that Claire didn't notice the night approaching.

"Oh my God, it's already dark. I need to go!" Claire said while looking outside.

"Oh, don't worry sweetheart. Take my car and tomorrow, or whenever you decide, you can bring it back," Mrs. Walton said.

"Oh, no, you might need it. If I leave now, I should be able to make it back."

"Listen, sweetheart, you might be young, but I know you aren't stupid. You know that it's not safe to go by foot, and you are aware that you'll be walking in the dark. Your options are to stay here for the night or take my car. Don't waste my time arguing otherwise."

She was right. Claire accepted the offer and planned on bringing it back the next day. She drove for one mile only to realize that it was low on gas, and went to the gas station to put some fuel in.

She arrived at the cottage and looked at the sky before entering. The stars were shining brightly. Claire thought about Mrs. Walton's simple life and wondered if living in the countryside immersed in Mother Nature was something that helped people to develop deep relationships. She asked herself, if it was being surrounded by all this beauty the reason Mrs. Walton was so joyful and generous. "What a beautiful world we have," and entered the cottage and made her way to bed, counting on another good night of sleep.

In her dream, she found herself alone in Hallan's breakfast cabin. On the table was the same instruction for the synthetic fuel formula. She memorized what was supposed to be the last part of this set. She knew that there was more, but she was feeling uncomfortable not having Gavriel around. The place felt deserted. She flew toward the lake of Acqua, but he wasn't there either, so she decided to go back to the breakfast cabin, and before arriving, she awoke. She opened the notebook and made notes about the formula.

#

Gavriel awoke. He needed to tell someone everything he saw and discovered during his dream. Getting up, skipped breakfast and went straight to the government building. He couldn't just make his way to Theena's department without an invitation because he was technically off duty.

After reporting to the security area, he was authorized to head to Theena's office by following the floating red orb. If he tried to deviate from this course, the luminous sphere would disappear, and the safety team would track him down.

The only way to talk to his grandma was to speak to her face-to-face. He needed to look in her eyes to transmit a signal. Any other communication could be hacked.

"Hi, Theena! How are you doing?"

"I'm fine, how about you?"

"I'm feeling way better. I wonder if you can set my status to 'active' for me to fulfill my duties over here," Gavriel said, looking straight into Theena's eyes.

"Yes, for sure. Let me do it right away. I'm glad you are back, we need help over here," Theena said while proceeding with the activation.

"Thanks! I don't know how to thank you for your patience. Can I buy you a coffee at lunch? Would that work for you?"

"Sure, why not? Come at lunchtime, and you can buy me a coffee."

"Ok, see you at noon," he said, exiting her office and making his way to the work area.

"Hi Zenya, I'm back," Gavriel said, giving Zenya a hug, which made her flush.

"Hi, I heard you were not feeling well," she said, tucking her hair behind her right ear.

"Yeah, you know, I think it's adulthood stress," he said, making Zenya laugh.

"Yeah, I see what you mean, my dad has the same problem."

"Ok, what do you want me to do?"

"Well, right now we are in a waiting mode with planet Earth as you have baptized it," she said, smiling. "While we were waiting, another world came on our radar, the 1H, 14C, 268Y, 18T. Your task is to check the data pattern and find out if there are any discrepancies with our database. Is that clear?" she said.

"Yes, very clear. Can we access information from the extended missions?" Gavriel asked.

"What?" Zenya answered, feeling lost.

"Oh, sorry, my bad. I just recalled some lectures from my UCD classes," Gavriel said, remembering that extended missions were secret. When lunchtime came, Gavriel made his way toward Theena's office. "I'm here," he announced, and she promptly left her chair and followed Gavriel to a coffee shop using her car.

"We can talk here. For some reason this coffee shop is a blind spot, go figure," Theena stated.

"Someone knew about this blind spot and built a coffee shop here. It wasn't by chance, it was planned," he said while ordering two coffees, which came floating to them.

"Ok, first question, why did you come and ask to return to work?" Theena asked.

"Simple. Remember that guy that I said had seen me when I was dreaming? Last night we talked. Also, I was at their night meeting, and something terrible is happening."

"What is going on, and who is the guy you have talked to?" Theena asked.

"Well, I found out that most high hierarchy Novus Mundurians will abandon Novus Mundus, and head to Earth in four years."

"What? Why in the world are they planning to leave Novus Mundus? That's crazy," Theena said, raising her voice, looking around and checking if the tone of her voice attracted anyone's attention.

"Apparently, our system had an abrupt change in its orbit, and this move is putting us on a collision course between Novus Mundus and Zyon in forty-eight years. Also, the North Sun is heading toward our planet, and in thirty years we will be like Sion."

"Oh, my word! I'm shocked! We need to verify this information, and we can't take for granted that such a thing is right."

"They are hiding it from the public. It seems like they will use some military spaceships under construction now to evacuate those they have chosen to escape."

"Yes, there are some humongous ships under development in Acqua, that makes sense, but, wait a minute, who are they?" Theena asked, frowning.

"Apparently, they are part of an Elite-7 group, and they rule what we know as the honeycomb. They are also planning to undermine the agreement you just have reached with Zyon. Apparently, the transfer of technology is against some master policy, so they will actually sabotage the deal."

"Unbelievable, what is wrong with our government or whoever is leading it?" she said, raising her arms in frustration and looking at Gavriel.

"I know. About the guy who saw me during my dream, I don't know him. But his code name is agent P1999. I wonder if you can trace this guy and get more information about him. Apparently, he isn't on their side, but who knows. I don't know who we can trust at this point."

"Ok, things are really dark here, and we can't take any chances. You said that Lennah was flagged, as well as Hallan. There is nothing we can do about Hallan, but I'll suggest to Lennah's supervisor to dismiss her for disorderly conduct. Once she is laid off, the government can't force her to move to another place or planet, and we can spare her from some harmful directives.

I'll try to check who this agent P1999 is. Perhaps we can approach him in real life and see what his reaction is. For now, just go back to work and act normal," she stood and made her way out, without even touching her coffee.

Gavriel was going back to his office, but it seemed like his grandma wouldn't need to search for P1999 because he was walking directly toward Gavriel. The agent looked downcast as he walked by the entrance of the building.

Gavriel followed him from a distance of about eighteen feet until the man went into the gravity-controlled tubes. Once he got in and started to float up, he noticed Gavriel. P1999 put his hands toward the glass, and this automatically stopped the flow. He released his hands, let the flow move up, got out of the tube on the first floor, and then made his way down from another tube.

He came up to Gavriel and looked into his eyes before turning right, and walking away. Gavriel followed him until they reached the same spot, they met the previous night.

"So, you are real, and you have connections with our government. We need to talk, meet me at the Novus Mundus coffee shop at six o'clock," he said, and Gavriel nodded his head. The agent walked past him and went inside the building.

At six o'clock, Gavriel was at the coffee shop waiting. He was drinking juice when the man arrived. The agent bought a coffee from inside the store and sat by Gavriel's table.

"So, at this point, it seems like we don't need further introductions," said Gavriel. "As you can see, we are both real. I'm here, and here you are. Is there something we should talk about or do we just pretend we don't know each other?"

The man put his hands on the table and added some sugar to his coffee. He looked around as if he was checking the perimeter for someone.

"I can see you are both real and unreal. You know my name and who I am. Now what, or who are you?"

"My name is Gavriel, and I work for the government in the Alien Research department. I met you in a dream last night, and I have no idea how you were able to see me."

"You were dreaming, huh? I don't know what you mean by dreaming, because I know I was very awake. One thing I know is that you are not a new high-tech Droid because last night you were as real as you are right now. This freaks me out, but I don't feel threatened by you," agent P1999 said, pointing to Gavriel with his chin.

"How do you know this is a blind spot?" asked Gavriel.

"Because I have access to privileged information. How do you know?" the agent asked, intimidation dripping from his voice.

"I have my sources, but if you know this is a safe spot, why doesn't someone from the government begin to monitor it?"

"It's simple. We are aware of the blind spots, and we want to keep them blind so we can use them for private purposes. This way we make sure nobody is sneaking in on our private conversations as you did," he answered.

"Private conversation? You mean things that you want to keep in secret even from your bosses?" Gavriel asked, trying to give the impression that he knew more than he did.

"Are you threatening me?" the agent asked, looking into Gavriel's eyes. "I think you have no idea who you are talking with." He slowly sipped his coffee. "How did you end up in our meeting?" the agent asked, his voice softening a bit.

"Ok, let's get this straight. I know you are a Zyon agent, but I don't know anything else about you. I have dreams and, in one of my dreams, I ended up in one of your meetings. You don't have to believe me, but it's the truth," Gavriel said, leaning back in his chair and crossing his hands behind his head. After a brief silence, he moved his body toward the table and reached for the straw, to drink some juice.

"I'm as confused as you are," continued Gavriel. "So, if you want to stop right now, we can leave and pretend that we never met. It's that simple, however, how can you hide from the public, for four more years, that everyone is going to be cooked alive on this planet, while you guys are saving your bacon fleeing to another planet? And how can you be sure that there won't be more people dreaming, like me, sneaking into your meetings and discovering everything? How?" Gavriel was now defiant.

"Wait," the agent said, waving his hand slightly up and down and then moving both of his hands from his forehead to the back of his neck. He stood up and walked around some tables, shaking his head and returning a few moments later.

"If neither of us knows how these dreams are happening, we must find someone who does, someone else must know. And if someone does know, they could be monitoring us right now," the agent said, looking around.

"That might be true, but right now, that is the least of my problems. Is there something I can do to make you believe in me?"

"I'll pretend that I believe in you, for now. Besides, I'm sick and tired of those secret meetings, and I don't think I belong to that group. I'm not surprised they are trying to get rid of me. But if you want to set me up, I swear I will make you pay," the agent said, showing some distress.

"Relax, I'm not trying to set you up," Gavriel said, looking firm into agent P1999's eyes.

"Ok, so what do you want from me?" P1999 asked.

"I need to know what organization you serve, and why you guys are hiding this North Sun threat from the public."

"What do I get in return for revealing this information?"

"You are the only one who can see me. I can infiltrate in your group and find out what they are plotting against you. Moreover, I can see other people who dream like me and warn you if you do not see them."

"It sounds reasonable. Well, besides my position on Zyon, I'm also a member of the Elite-7 group, and I'm entitled to vote on 'sensitive' decisions to help the system to remain stable. I mean to keep people thinking that it's stable.

Why are we hiding the Novus Mundus collision from the public? C'mon, don't be stupid. How can we move all these people from their planets? It's impossible! There is no alternative, most people will die, and that's it," agent P1999 said.

"Yeah, very convenient for someone who has an escape plan. What's the rebooting thing you guys mentioned in your meeting?"

"Rebooting means to implement procedures to rebuild a planet, and the process starts before colonization. We need to make sure that the world will be ready for our establishment."

"Why does Novus Mundus have to intervene in another planet's development?"

"Oh, once we detect that civilization is growing in technology and might become a threat to us or our plans, we intervene in its development to keep it under control. We try many options before opting for its annihilation, the more nature-friendly the method, the better because it keeps the planet alive."

"What about the communication threat to our system? It seems like Earth's destruction may affect organic waves, therefore damaging our most important source of alien information."

"Oh, that's true, but we had other planets going through the same process. We realized that there is an interruption of the communication system, but it's only temporary. The connection is re-routed, and everything comes back to normal.

We've been using the threat of organic waves interruption as an excuse to collect the resources we need for military purposes, as the construction of military spaceships. The public always agrees to tax increases when there is a threat involving security."

"You are telling me that people from Earth were set to die, and there was no real threat to our communication system?"

"Yes, but don't be theatrical! That's irrelevant now. Our planet is about to be incinerated, our priority is to save our bacon," the agent said aggressively as he sipped his coffee.

"I got the information that Earth is receiving a kind of signal from outer space. Are you aware of this message?"

"It might be one of our dummy signals. They set up radio transmission devices on remote planets away from our civilization to attract previously undetected civilizations. Once an unknown civilization is able to reach the radio, we know that they have developed high-level technology. We seize their device, identify the source, and head to the planet to track its development. Our policy is to hide, not to expose ourselves."

"I can't believe that all these actions run without any scrutiny. I honestly don't think that anybody with a little bit of knowledge wouldn't search for information like this, connect the dots and figure out what is really going on," Gavriel said, leaning back in his chair and crossing his arms.

"Oh, that's another story!" the agent continued. "There are always people inside the government sneaking into the database, but the Elite-7 group engineered a drink that is sold in all government social gatherings. This drink contains nanocapsules that attach themselves to the internal organs, especially the liver and stomach. These capsules stay there forever. Everyone working for the government has had this stuff.

"There is a particular helicoidally ion gun that catalyzes those capsules to release toxic substances that attack the nervous system. Mild side effects include depression, but it was developed to cause internal organ failure. The Elite-7 group uses these guns to get rid of people that pose a threat to them. You might have heard about people who simply disappear?" the agent said, and paused for a sip of coffee.

"The government creates as many artificial structures as possible, to employ as many people as possible. The bigger they are, the more powerful we become. They give jobs and security in exchange for loyalty, it's all about power."

"Unbelievable! Why did you guys choose Earth out of all the available planets? By the time you get there, you'll be at the end of your lives, if you make it there alive."

"What do you mean by the end of my life? How old do you think I am?"

"Sixty, maybe seventy years old," Gavriel said, looking him over.

"Wrong, I'm 202 years old. We have the means to prolong life up to three hundred, and that's why we are in power. We have no power to control death, but we can make life 'eternal,'" agent P1999 said, making a quotation sign with his fingers.

"Do we have someone around three hundred years old among us? How can it be? The community would know, or at least the system would flag it," Gavriel argued in disbelief.

"When we reach a certain age, we just switch to another place, that's why I'm currently located on Zyon. We are the system, we make it work. By the way, I'm one of the oldest genetically modified human beings. I'm actually the pioneer in this field, and I was responsible for its research and development. I can assure you, we are about to break the current limits and extend our lives up to 340 years."

"That's craziness," Gavriel said, shaking his head.

"Back to the Earth subject," P1999 continued. "Before our arrival on that planet, we will deploy robots to check if its atmosphere can sustain life at minimum levels. The robots will also sow Earth with seeds from our genetic storage. They will reintroduce animal life for reproduction, and everything will be genetically developed and controlled. Once Mother Nature is stable and has passed some preliminary tests, it will be ready for our arrival."

"It seems like we, ordinary people, are living a lie. We are like rats in a universal social experiment, this is sick. Ordinary citizens are taught to believe in the government since the day they are born, and the ones who dare to challenge the system are eliminated, unbelievable," Gavriel said.

"You are right, this is craziness, and now you have just a glimpse of what I'm living through. It's my daily burden. I feel the weight of this night and day, and what I have just shared with you is a fraction of the level of corruption we live in. The system is rotten from deep inside," agent P1999 stopped for a moment and showed the palm of his hand in a sign that he had more to say.

"There are some side effects in this extended life achievement. The genetic manipulation increases the levels of anxiety, leading to extending periods of depression that seem to grow exponentially. The benefits of an artificially extended life don't include life-long happiness. It's just an illusion, and it seems to me that you have more life in your dreams than I have in my unfortunate reality."

"I don't know what to say. I don't know what to do. I wonder if it was better for me not to know what I know now." *Do you understand that having access to some information can hurt you or cause your death?* Hallan's words came back to his mind.

"Gavriel are you there?" the agent asked, snapping his fingers in front of his eyes.

"Yes, I'm here, although I wish to be somewhere else," he said, looking down.

"I'm also concerned that seeing you when you were dreaming is another side effect. I'm aware that I see some people that aren't real, or alive. A couple of time,s I've found myself talking to people, just to realize later that I was the only one noticing them. When I have checked the recordings, they weren't there," P1999 said, looking nowhere.

"I'm aware that the government can edit your life, maybe someone is editing your," Gavriel was saying but was cut off by agent P1999.

"Gavriel, don't be naive, I have powers over the governments. I'd know if someone was editing my life. Listen I have to go," P1999 said while standing up. "I don't know why, but I want to say thanks. I feel lighter now that I shared this with you. Whether you like it or not, now you know about good and evil, and there is a price for this knowledge, enjoy it," the agent said sarcastically, walking away.

#

Claire was getting anxious because three nights had passed, and she hadn't met Gavriel, and there were no further instructions on the table. She made her way toward Acqua, to find him walking by the lakeshore.

"Hey, look who's here!" she said, smiling, but noticing the sadness in his face.

"Hi, Claire, yes, it's been a while. I was dealing with some issues in my life that I couldn't postpone. I'm sorry if I disappointed you."

"No worries, you look tired. Is there anything I can help with?"

"No, I don't think you can help. It has to do with our daily life on Novus Mundus," he said with a nervous smile.

"What's wrong? I can feel something different in you," she said.

"Nothing, really nothing. I'm feeling tired," Gavriel said, avoiding eye contact. He couldn't tell Claire about what he had discovered. It wouldn't help her save Earth, and getting her discouraged now was pointless. He had to hide his emotions at any cost.

"Ok, so what's up next? I've finished transferring the first set of instructions, and I need that paper to be replaced. Can you take care of it?" she asked, smiling at him.

"Oh, for sure. Is there anything else I'm forgetting?"

"No, you did not forget anything else. Once we release the formula to the public, we should explain where it comes from. We should tell people what kind of structure you guys live in. Perhaps it will encourage people on Earth to pursue values that can lead us into a better society. That's my goal. I wonder if you can tell me more about your way of life," she said.

"Yeah, I understand what you're saying, that's precisely the problem. I don't know if the way we organize our society should be a role model for any civilization. Recently, I came across so many bad things about our system, that it looks like we aren't better than you guys."

"Uh, I'm sorry you came across this, but you have to understand that you can make choices. So, will you make a decision to fight for what brings life or will you just surrender to what brings death?"

"Well, it doesn't work that way, and it's hard when the entire universe seems to conspire against you," Gavriel said.

"Well, that's very true. It seems to conspire, which means that 'it gives the impression,' so it doesn't reflect the reality; it's just to make you feel down. Don't you realize that you are part of a bigger plan, and you have been invited to be part of this creation? Can't you see that or is it just me?" Claire asked.

"Well, you are right, doing nothing is the worst option, but regarding development, our societies are light years apart. As you said to me, the level of life degradation on your planet is so intense that it seems like your people got used to it, and the abnormal became the new standard. Poverty, greed, and wars, which are not even supposed to exist, are thriving on the surface of your society.

There is a need for changing in people's hearts," he said increasing the tone of his voice, and then continued with weariness, "right now, I hope the synthetic fuel formula will help your society to turn back the path of destruction against the planet. Earth is a living body, and you are the guests, and the guests are killing the host. It's ludicrous," he said roughly.

Claire was just mute; she was hoping to hear something practical to help her in her mission, and Gavriel's answer sounded more like frustration.

"Apparently, our system has been working well for thousands of years, now it seems that it's rotten too," Gavriel said in a lower voice, "our families are fragmented, authentic friendship doesn't exist, spiritual life is dead, and we have become selfish.

People's relationships are septic, and it seems like our leadership is entirely corrupted. I think there is a lot to be done on both of our planets," Gavriel finished.

"Ok, I think I understand what you are trying to say. We need to find our own way, and nothing is going to work if we don't change our hearts and minds first," she said with some weariness in her voice.

"I'll post the rest of the formula on the table so you can start to transfer new information. I need to go now because I need to double check some information at the government building," Gavriel said, hugging Claire and making his way out.

#

Claire awoke, lay back on the bed and looked pensively at the ceiling. *I know Gavriel wasn't lying to me, yet something was different about him. He was there in the dream, but his eyes were somewhere else, I could feel the heaviness in his spirit.* She started to weep, and after what seemed to be ten minutes, she wiped her tears and said to herself: "Move Claire," and got out of the bed, heading for a shower. She finished her shower, grabbed fruit from the kitchen table, and made her way to Mrs. Walton's house to return her car.

"Good morning sweetheart," Mrs. Walton said, opening the door, "come on in, the water is ready for your tea."

"Oh no, Mrs. Walton, thanks, but you don't need," Claire was saying, but she was cut off.

"I don't need to, but I want to make you tea, and besides, you are here to rest, so, no rush. What can be better than a cup of tea in this crazy world, huh? Now, as if we humans are not bad enough, we have aliens coming to join our stupidity. What else can go wrong?" Mrs. Walton said.

"Yeah, don't worry Mrs. Walton, I've heard that the thing crossing the skies is an experiment from NASA, and they have probably dealt with it at this point."

"Oh no sweetheart, that is old news. I'm talking about the spaceship that is stationary in the Earth's orbit right now. Now we have a traffic jam in space, Good Lord!" she said, laughing.

"What do you mean by spaceship?" Claire asked, pretty sure that Mrs. Walton was confused.

"Oh, you might not have a TV in your cottage. Here, check the news, it's everywhere," Mrs. Walton said, turning up the volume.

"The Russians claim they are in touch with the alien spaceship, but nothing has been confirmed yet."

Claire took the remote and clicked to another channel.

"These are the images we have so far. United States satellites took the pictures, and we are aware that there are, so far, five countries positioning their satellites near the spaceship. No contact has been made… wait," said the reporter, "we have news that the Vatican just released a document stating that they are aware of the arrival of the spaceship. Apparently, the ship has come in peace, and no military action should be used against it, so a lot of confusion in what seems to be an unprecedented event in our history."

"What the heck, what is that?" Claire said, pointing at the screen, "and who are they?"

"That's exactly my question sweetheart, but sooner or later we will have the answers. Don't worry, this is not the end of the world," Mrs. Walton smiled.

"Thanks, Mrs. Walton, but I need to go," Claire said, making her way to the door.

"Oh dear, wait, if you are not staying for some cookies, at least take some with you," she said, handing a little basket to Claire.

"Thanks, Mrs. Walton," she said, taking the cookies and leaving in a rush.

"Oh dear, these young people, always in a hurry," Mrs. Walton said while watching Claire make her way through the front yard.

She started to run, but the basket was not helping, so she put the cookies into the pockets of her vest and placed the basket on the top of a mailbox. She was running at a good pace, but she knew she couldn't maintain it, so she slowed down. A car approached her then slowed its speed. The window opened, and Nick showed his face.

"It would take a week to reach Miami at your speed, do you want a ride?" he said, with a mocking smile on his face.

She got into the car and closed the door.

"What is going on?" she hissed.

"What's going on? Is this the new way to say hi?" Nick frowned.

"I'm sorry," she said, acknowledging her poor behaviour.

"Ok, so if you have no clue what is going on, we are lost because I don't know either. We just noticed this thing last night. It was caught by our satellites. We have a recording of its presence, but we couldn't detect its coming," and he looked at her like he was waiting for answers.

"Ok, slow down, take this way, I'm staying in that cottage," she said, pointing to the wooden building on their left side.

"I knew you were here because I got the information from your aunt. I was going back to KSC when my boss pushed me to find you. My team asked me to ask you that stuff, and I was pretty confident that you had the answer, now I'm stuck," he said, stopping and getting out of the car.

"Wow, this is what I call a real cottage. I like it, I really do," Nick said.

"Let's go in," she said, opening the door while speaking. "Are you sure NASA is taking me seriously? Are you sure they aren't hiding anything from you?"

Nick stopped for a moment, looked at her, but said nothing.

"I've heard the Russians are aware of the spaceship, even the Vatican, or whatever it has left in its ranks, said so. How can it be?"

Claire asked, sitting on one of the worn fabric couches at the right of the main entrance, while Nick sat on the one in front of her.

"You know the media better than I do, and they say what they want to say. Personally, I doubt that the Russians know about it. I think they are scared, and they are pretending they know what's going on, especially because we control the plasma nuclear scanner."

"Yes, but what about the Vatican? Why are they making statements on the subject?"

"They might be trying to show off power, but if both can prove what they are saying, we are in trouble because we have no clue about it. I guess you can get some information for us, with your friends out there," Nick said, suggesting her contact in Novus Mundus.

"I can ask, although I'm sure he would have already told me if he knew something," Claire said.

"Are you coming with me? We can check after you sleep tonight," Nick said.

"I'm afraid I can't go with you. It took me three days to be in touch with them through my dreams after arriving here. I don't control it, and for some reason, these moves affect the dynamic of the dreams, especially during the first days. The best thing right now is to stay put. You can come back tomorrow, and I can update you."

"If you don't mind, can you call me? No, it's not a cell phone, I know you don't like them, wait a minute," Nick got up and went outside. He came back minutes later with two devices.

"These are my military radios, and we can talk through them because there are many repeaters between us, so there will be no problem. Both devices are locked into the same frequency, so you just need to press this button here," Nick said, showing her the button. "Press the button, speak, release, and wait for the answer. Do you understand?" Nick asked.

"Come on, I'm not stupid," Claire said and stood up.

"Ok, are we cool? You have to understand that it takes me six hours to get back and forth. If you have something, just call me, and I'll come right away, ok?" he asked, looking into her eyes.

"Ok, deal."

"Meanwhile, keep watching the news. Maybe we will find out something from the media," he said sarcastically as he made his way out.

Thirty seconds later he came back with something in his hands. "I almost forgot. This is the charger for the radio. It has an adaptor to connect to the car lighter outlet," he said, dropping off the devices on a small table between the couches.

"Also, I'm going to Miami for a week, so if you need something from there, let me know," with that, he left.

Claire spent the day walking around the property, exploring some trails and sitting around the pond, just meditating. As the dusk came down, she went to the door and realized it was eerily quiet outside; there wasn't a single chirp in the air. *Weird,* she thought.

Before going to bed, she went to the car and turned on the radio, hopingg to catch some news. She turned the dial back and forth until she got something.

"And the official spokesperson for the government just released new information. They are answering questions right now. A quick recap for those just joining us: yesterday, on the Norwegian island of Spitsbergen, there was a robbery of the Svalbard Global Seed Vault. Thieves stole almost a million seed samples stored in the vaults. So far government officials have been scrambling to find out who is responsible and why someone would want these seeds."

"When did you notice the break in? Why didn't the alarm systems work?" a reporter questioned the spokesperson.

"We saw that the vault had been broken into this morning. There were no incident reports, and we don't know why the security systems in place didn't work. We are checking into it, but it will take a few days before we have anything conclusive," the spokesperson answered.

"How much did they steal from the vault?" another reporter asked.

"Everything, just everything," the man answered.

"Why doesn't Norway want help from other countries? What are you hiding?" The reporters kept peppering him with questions.

"We are not refusing help or hiding anything. We just need to do our work, and then we can open the investigation up to nations who have been affected by this."

"I've heard the doors were cut as if they were literally butter. What can you tell us about this?" the first reporter asked.

"I have no such information, and, anything beyond our official statement is simply speculation. We will keep you posted on our investigations, but that's all I have, for now, have a good day," the man said.

"That's it," the radio station reporter continued, "that was the official spokesperson from the Norway Public Affairs office. We will keep you updated as we learn more, back to you, Nathan."

"Thanks, Martin. Now, the…" the DJ continued, but Claire turned off the radio.

"That's weird, why would someone steal seeds?" she said, going back to the cottage and locking the door behind her. She made a cup of tea before going to bed.

Sleep came fast, and soon she was by the lake, but Gavriel was nowhere to be seen. Reaching Hallan's place, she found new instructions on the table. She wished Gavriel would come quickly, as she needed to know about the spaceship above Earth. Claire remembered that he was planning to sneak into the government building, and flew over there. She found the glass doors closed and passed through them. She floated back and forth, up and down, but couldn't see him. She flew around and finally found him as she flew to the top.

"Hi Gavriel," she said.

"Oh, hi, you found me here. You are getting good at this," Gavriel said, surprised at her.

"Is this the place you are trying to access?"

"Yes, this is the place people are using for some secret meetings. I was trying to get in, but I can't. Unless someone pops up to open the door, there is nothing I can do."

"I see, do you mind if we talk a little bit while waiting?"

"No, I don't mind, what is bugging you?"

"Are you aware one of your spaceships has arrived on Earth?"

"A spaceship? No, I just know of the scheduled nuclear scanner. I mean, it could be one of that plasma screener on an extended mission," he said.

"Well, it isn't a plasma screener, it's a real spaceship. It looks like a big tube," she said, but it seemed that Gavriel was distracted with something else.

"Should I be scared?" Claire asked, noticing his distracted behaviour.

"I don't think so… it might be something from another department or maybe another honeycomb," he said, trying to ease the pressure she was showing.

"What do you mean another honeycomb? I can feel something is wrong. You're scaring me!" she said, feeling anguish building up inside her. "Is there any way to get more information from the organic waves?"

"Hey calm down, it's just a guess, relax," he said, placing his hands on her shoulders.

"Let's check the organic waves. If something is happening with the planet, the system will show it to us," Gavriel said, floating inside his department. He stopped in front of one of the many projections over the wall, as he needed to appease Claire's worries, or the stress might wake them up, and he would miss the Elite-7 meeting.

"Although organic waves detect threats or anomalies over the planet, it won't give us any sign about a spaceship orbiting the body."

"Listen, Gavriel," Claire said, "this is important for me because we are in the middle of something that might change the future of my planet. I don't want to be caught in something that could derail what we are doing.

Someone just stole an entire vault of seed samples from one of our storage facilities. There are enough seeds to build a new world. Something strange is happening, and neither of us knows what is going on, and that scares me. Can you please check to see if there is anything unusual happening?" Claire asked, almost begging.

"I can look into it tomorrow," he began but was cut off by Claire.

"Not tomorrow, tonight, now. Please?" She looked into his eyes, and Gavriel could see she was trying to hold back tears.

The pressure inside him was unbearable, and He could share Claire's anguish, and there was no way to avoid it. He had to help her, even though it was probably too late to make much difference.

"The only thing I can do is wake up and enter the building. I can check the programs and see if I can get any further information. I have access to the system now. The problem is, I don't know how to wake up right now," Gavriel said.

"Remember the times you awoke before? Usually, they were times of distress or panic. What if you try something that triggers some fear?" she asked.

"We both know that might not work."

"Yes, but if it doesn't work you will still be dreaming," she reasoned.

"Ok, let's go home. I'll try to cross a wall, and, hopefully, I'll wake up if everything goes as planned," Gavriel said, without much conviction.

She agreed, and they both flew to his home. He was sleeping, and before doing anything else, he said: "I have another idea. When

I'm trying to cross a wall, I fear that I'll be trapped inside the wall. You know what, I'll try to cross my own body. If I get stuck, at least it's going to be inside my own body, not somewhere else," he said.

"I think it's a stupid idea, but I'm fine with it, as long as you are not trapped inside my body," she said, and they both laughed nervously.

Gavriel approached his sleeping body and soon disappeared in front of Claire's eyes. Strangely enough, nothing else happened.

Now she was panicking, but knew that she needed to control herself; otherwise, she would wake up.

She started to call out, "Gavriel! Gavriel! Are you there? It's me, Claire. Gavriel! Wake up, Gavriel wake up," she wanted to shake him, but she knew it was impossible.

Someone turned on the lights and startled Claire. She turned her head toward the door and saw Hallan coming toward Gavriel's bed.

"Gavriel…" he said calmly, trying to wake him up. He wasn't aware that Claire was in the room.

Claire tried to talk to Hallan, but he wasn't listening.

"Gavriel, wake up! It's me, Hallan," he was puzzled as to why Gavriel wasn't waking up, "Gavriel!" he said louder, shaking Gavriel's shoulder.

Gavriel awoke abruptly, panting and sweating as if he had been having a nightmare. He rubbed his eyes and saw Hallan.

"Hallan, is that you? What are you doing in my dream?" he asked, looking around.

"Unfortunately, you are not dreaming. I received a call from the hospital. Your grandmother has been hospitalized, and her condition is critical. Her personal emergency transponder sent signs of physical distress, and she was found unconscious and bleeding from her nose. I came here to take you with me to the hospital," Hallan said.

"I was with Claire, and I'm supposed to do something," he said, trying to synchronize his thoughts. "Yes, I remember now, I am expected to check Earth's vital signs from the organic waves, what do I do?" he said, looking confused.

"Do, what you feel you need to do. I'm going to the hospital, and I'll wait for you over there. For now, get your thoughts together, you look disoriented," Hallan said, making his way out. Gavriel checked the time, it was three in the morning, so he missed the Elite-7 meeting already.

"Wow," he said, shaking his head and trying to wake up, "what happened?"

He tried to remember something from his dream, and he recalled his conversation with Claire. Based on the time, she must still be dreaming and in his room as they planned.

"I don't know what has happened. I guess I'll only understand in our next dream Claire," he felt that she might be in the room, but it was just a feeling. He decided to go to the government building to detect something from organic waves and give some perspective to Claire. He was torn though because Theena needed him more than Claire right now, so he needed to move fast.

He quickly got dressed. "Anyway," he said, guessing that Claire might still be around, "just for the record, whatever we did to wake up, it was a stupid idea. Never do that to yourself. You probably heard about my grandma at the hospital. I'll try to get some information for you from organic waves, but I won't have much time," he said while heading to his Suphcar.

The trip was fast, and soon he was at the building.

"Ok, here we go," he said, entering in his working room. All the projections were on, so he needed just to introduce some commands. He didn't know what to look for, so he decided to quickly scan the data from Earth, and then make his way to the hospital.

"Beta, planet Earth, vital signals," he said to the computer. Images spewed onto the screen.

"Beta, anomalies on Earth, last twenty-four hours," he said, but the images didn't change.

"Beta, alien devices, last twenty-four hours," a screen flashed and Gavriel read it. "There is nothing wrong. It's just our permanent nuclear scanner, probably still active."

"Beta, any signal out of the pattern in the last twenty-four hours?" The system halted for a bit and took a while to send an update. Suddenly an image flashed red on the screen, and an alarm sounded. Gavriel was still reading the information.

"Claire, listen to me carefully. You have to get up and go somewhere safe. Stockpile food and water and protect yourself. The planet is showing two large open wounds, and they're starting to spill ashes into the atmosphere. It is happening right now, and you have a short time. The signal is showing four more points of stress, and they probably will be activated in a short period. They are huge, and parts of the planet will soon be covered by ashes.

Go! You don't have a lot of time, and I have to go to the hospital to see Theena." He stood from his chair and made his way out of the room, but not before saying, "don't forget, I'll always wait for you at the lake."

He got into his Suphcar and travelled about four miles when he saw a bright light coming from behind, and about twenty seconds later, his car shook violently due to the shock wave. He stopped and turned his face to the direction of the explosion. His jaw dropped; the entire government building looked a giant ball of flames. He looked confused, nevertheless his heart was focused on grandma's health, so he rushed to the hospital.

CHAPTER 18 – A Hundred Years of Solitude

"DON'T FORGET, I'LL ALWAYS…," were the last words she heard from Gavriel. She was panicking when she awoke.

"Oh my God; dad, aunt Mirna, NASA, they need to know! They need to protect themselves," she said, while quickly dressing up. She grabbed the radio and raced to her car. She tried to call Nick using the radio, but it was four in the morning. He was probably still asleep.

She drove toward Miami. Hopefully, people would have time to prepare themselves, but she knew it was going to be bad. Her car radio had AM waves, and she tried to hear some news about the events. She went up and down on the dial, but the only story was about the spaceship.

She looked at the passenger seat and saw the military radio communication, so she stopped the car and turned the device on. She could see the transmission and reception frequencies, so she made a note of both frequencies before making any change. She started to drive again while changing the channel reception one by one. She had both the AM radio and the radio communication on, and later on, she heard something over the military communicator.

"It's huge, it's a massive explosion, and it's starting to spill lava now, over."

"Yes, we are heading there to help the evacuation, over."

"I don't know, for now, it seems like just one of the Hawaiian volcanos is active. We need to check later on about the others, over."

"Yes. I agree. We have to be fast to evacuate the people close to its base, but I can tell you right now, the place is covered by ashes already, it won't be easy, over."

"Ok, copy that, talk to you later."

"That's it! It's the first one. Another one is probably active somewhere else, so let's keep trying," she said while switching the car radio station.

She arrived before seven o'clock at her aunt's house. She still had the house keys, although it was wise to ring the bell before entering. Her aunt had guns, and it wouldn't be safe to open the door unexpectedly.

"Claire, what are you doing here so early?" she said, still in her pajamas.

"Auntie, listen. You have to come with me," Claire said, quickly entering the house. "We are all going to the cottage. There will be some events happening that will be life threatening to us, and the best way to survive is to be away from the cities. Pack your things fast, we have to go," she continued while heading to her room.

"What you mean, some events happening?" asked her aunt, while following her.

"Right now, there is a volcano in Hawaii that just became active; there will probably be others. This is going to be catastrophic, and our lives are in danger. We need to leave now. Can I use the phone? I need to contact dad right now," she asked, reaching for the phone.

"Of course, you can. This thing about leaving right now is not right. Volcanoes erupt every day." She stopped as she noticed Claire talking to someone on the other end in Spanish, and then hanging up the phone.

"See what I was just telling you? Another volcano has erupted in Chile, close to where dad is working. They are evacuating the area and moving people to a safer place. Something is going on, aunt Mirna, you need to believe me. It's going to be bad," she said, packing some extra clothes in a bag.

"Listen, Claire," her aunt said, "I understand that you've been under stress, and I believe you, but this is my home, and moving to a cottage won't save my life any more than being here will. Besides, I have a haircut appointment today, and there is no way I'll miss that," she said like she was joking. "You go, I love you, but I'll stay. Ask your other aunt if she wants to come with you, but I doubt it. She found a boyfriend and they are spending the night together. I think the end of the world will have to wait for now, especially for someone in love," she said.

"Oh, I don't understand your point, but I can't stay longer to convince you. I love you too if you change your mind just head to the cottage," Claire said, hugging her aunt and making her way out.

"I'll keep your room vacant so you can come back after the end of the world," her aunt yelled after her.

Claire turned on the military radio.

"Nick, this is Claire, do you copy?" she waited.

"Nick, this is Claire, do you copy?" she tried again.

"Do you copy, you said? Very good for someone who doesn't like technology. It's Nick, over."

"I never said that I don't like technology. I just don't use technology to waste my time or make my life miserable, and right now, I love it, over."

"Ok, ok, this is a military channel so how can I help you?"

"You don't use technology wisely because you are supposed to know the news before me," Claire said.

"Ok, again, this is a military channel, let's keep the conversation straight forward. What do you mean, knowing the news?"

"The volcano on Hawaii."

"Wait a second…" he said. "Yes, I can see it on the news, and there's another one in Africa."

"Well, I'm still winning; there is another one in Chile," Claire said.

"How can you know that from your place?"

"I'm in Miami right now. Can you meet me at my apartment in half an hour?"

"Yes, I think I can make it," Nick said.

She arrived at her garage, placed the keys inside the ashtray, and headed to the apartment. She got in and heard the blip of messages on the answering machine.

"Hi Claire, it's Rachel, we are returning to the USA sooner than we thought. My fiancé received a text from his boss asking him to go back to his work, so we're supposed to arrive Saturday around noon. As I said, you can stay in the apartment, so no worries. I will need the car, though. Talk to you later!"

"Great timing," she said. She wrote a note explaining the situation to Rachel and drawing a map to where she was going.

I know you might not take it seriously, and I don't blame you, but if you feel your life is in danger, you are welcome to come to the cottage. Please keep it secret because it's a small place and we won't be able to hold more than three or four people. I love you! God bless you! Bye.

The bell rang, and she opened the door for Nick.

"Listen, I don't have much time. I need one favour from you, so if you can help me, I'd much appreciate," Claire said, packing her bag full of food and other essentials.

"Sure, what is this particular favour?"

"We need to go shopping."

"Yikes, you know that I hate shopping. Is this just to torture me?"

"No, it's grocery shopping, and it's not the end of the world, that comes after shopping." Claire said, "Also, can you give me a ride to the cottage? I'm "carless" now, and I can update you as we travel."

"Ok, you're the boss. I've noticed that my choices are always limited. Let's go," Nick said as they left the apartment.

"Wait for a second," he said as she headed to the door, leaving and returning a few minutes later.

"I had to leave the apartment keys in Rachel's car. This is what I know ... "and told Nick her dream from the night before.

"Can I use your cell phone?" Claire asked, after finishing her story, and Nick gave it to her.

"Hi Diane, this is Claire Luan. I'm sorry to take so long to get back to you. Things are crazy as you can see. I've asked Nick to keep you posted about the plasma permanent nuclear scanner and the other developments..." she said when Nick started to make some gestures to catch her attention, but she ignored and continued her phone call with Diane. "Sorry for the interruption. I'll briefly tell you about the volcanoes that are now erupting, so you can listen and make your judgments. The first part of the synthetic fuel formula is hidden inside a blue jar above the china cabinet at my friend's apartment," and she gave the address to Diane.

Her name is Rachel. I left a message in the answering machine, asking her to give you the notes. You can ask NASA to take pictures of the permanent nuclear scanner, so people will believe what you say," she took a breath and continued, "and this is the thing about the volcanoes," after ten minutes she finished her report.

Diana replied, "I'm afraid we won't have a significant audience because people are looking for something spectacular and right now the spaceship is magnificent. We've already said that NASA was behind the permanent nuclear scanner, and if we assume that the scanner is from another planet, and it could actually harm NASA's reputation.

We could concentrate on these volcanoes erupting, but people don't give a shit about natural disasters anymore. We've had so many of these events lately that it seems like people are desensitized to natural disasters the way they are with poverty. Besides, it looks like most people feel distant from events like erupting volcanos, and don't see it as a personal threat..." she paused.

"Besides, we still don't have the synthetic fuel formula, so we have nothing to prove our story. I'm afraid we need to wait for consistent information and the results from NASA studies on the nuclear scanner, so then we can have something credible," she finished.

"Ok. We will be in touch, bye," Claire said and hung up the phone.

"What? What were you trying to tell me?" Claire asked Nick.

"It's not important now," he said, avoiding eye contact.

"Let's stop here for groceries," he said, entering a supermarket parking lot.

"I understand what she said about people wanting something spectacular, but the reality is right before our eyes and individuals don't see," she said, walking into the store.

"I might be wrong, but it seems like people can't see, and It's not that they don't want to see. We have been through so many things lately. A lot of catastrophes, a lot of nasty human behaviour, and what is supposed to be right is now wrong, and vice versa. Beautiful became ugly, and horror is a new beauty. We love to hate, and we hate to love. It isn't about you, and it isn't about failing to accomplish your mission; this is about human beings and the poor choices that we've been making," he said.

"Wow, you totally comforted me in my sadness. I feel so encouraged by your low view of humanity," Claire said sarcastically.

"One thing." He stopped walking and turned to her.

"Yes?"

"Can I come with you? I believe what you are saying, and I don't want to be caught in the middle of all of this," he said as he started to walk again.

"Yes, you can, although, what made you make this sudden decision?" she asked.

"Rationality!" he replied.

"What's the rationality in following a dreamer like me?"

"There is a chance that you may be right. If I believe you, I have the opportunity to save my life, but not thinking about this, might jeopardize my future," he answered.

"What if I'm wrong?"

"Well, I'll still have my life. There is another reason, I was dismissed from this case, and I'm waiting to be transferred."

"What? What do you mean dismissed from this case? What reason did they give you?"

"I have no clue, but I guess it is because the nuclear scanner disappeared, it's gone. That's what I was trying to tell you when you were talking to Diane."

"Oh my God, I'm glad Diane decided not to go on with this nuclear scanner thing. I'd feel embarrassed to say that not even the scanner is available now. What happened? I will be furious if Gavriel knows something about this."

"Oh, don't worry. I guess you are not the only one being fooled. I believe that NASA had previous knowledge about the nuclear scanner because they didn't show much excitement about it when I brought it to the surface. But this is another story, right now my heart is telling me to follow you," he said, and stopped filling up the shopping cart, as he turned his head and looked deep into her eyes.

She looked confused and didn't know how long they stood there until someone behind them asked them to move. Nick bought some clothes as well, and they loaded the truck with everything they needed and headed to the cottage.

By the end of the afternoon, they arrived at their destination. After unloading the truck, Nick realized that they needed more firewood.

"Let's go to a nearby store to buy more wood, and maybe withdraw some cash from ATM," he called out.

"The road seems busier than the usual now, what's happening," she noticed, looking at the cars in front of them.

"Darn, we forgot to turn on the radio," she said, pushing the radio button.

'...so, what now? Where is this thing? It seems like nobody knows what is going on. The scarce information we have says that the spaceship just disappeared. It isn't there anymore. Vanished, there is no trace of it,' they just heard on the radio.

Nick immediately turned off the radio, grabbed the military radio, and turned it on. He managed to park on a secondary road while trying to make contact.

"KSC, this is Nick M, can you read me? …. KSC, this is Nick M, can you read me?"

"Yes, we can hear you, Nick, where are you? Things are getting nasty out there," a voice answered.

"I'm stuck in traffic away from Miami. What's happening with the spaceship?"

"It totally disappeared, and nobody knows where it is, not the Russians, the Chinese, or the Vatican," he chuckled.

"Do you have something for me right now? Over."

"We don't need you here. We have warnings that roads are clogged so if you're outside of Miami, you won't be able to get in, and people inside the city aren't able to get out.

We are turning our eyes to the west coast. There is a wall of ashes that we assume is the Hawaiian volcano which is approaching the continent and suppose to reach crowded cities tomorrow at noon. Similar occurrences are happening in Africa, South America, and Europe. The erupting volcanoes are pouring ashes everywhere."

"Do you know anything about the impact of the ashes on the Hawaiian population?"

"This is something we can't confirm over the radio. NASA can't connect with the islands at this point. Communication with the island is down, and we are relying on pieces of information coming to us via the military network."

"Should I be concerned?" Nick asked.

"What I can tell you is that this is serious. Emergency services are almost impossible to deploy, and the few ones that can partially operate are saying that whoever was found in open spaces or inside their cars are dead … we don't know all that is going on. If I were you, I'd stay put until everything cools down, if it will, over?"

"Yes, thanks, I'll take your advice. Take care of yourselves guys, good luck."

Nick started to drive. At the entrance of the nearest small town, they faced some car congestion, and people walking in a rush on the sidewalks, something unusual for a little place like that.

He entered on a secondary road, stopped, and looked at Claire. "Let's keep going on foot. We won't be able to get anywhere by car." He parked, locked the car, and they started to walk.

After three blocks, they reached a gas station with a small store. Inside, it was clear that people were beginning to become agitated, and some were starting to push others to grab items from shelves almost empty.

"Your attention please," the manager announced from the front desk, "We are bringing more supplies. However, because we had to get them rushed here, they have cost us double the price. We will need to charge double the listed price for whatever you want to buy, I'm sorry."

They headed to the ATM located in the corner of the room, but there were two people in line before them, and no signs that the first person was having success withdrawing money.

At the cashier line, a troubled man started an argument with the clerk. "What do you mean no credit cards? You're supposed to have cash in your ATM, and you don't have that either! How am I expected to pay?" the guy argued.

"I'm sorry, but the system is down so I can't make the transaction go through. We have to wait for the system to be restored. Right now, I can just accept cash," The cashier replied.

The quarrel became more intense, so Nick and Claire decided to get out of there as quickly as possible. A few moments after leaving the building, they could hear people smashing the store windows, so they ran toward their car. Thirty feet away from it, they witnessed someone breaking the passenger window.

"Hey!" Nick yelled. The guy jumped back and ran away.

They got into the car, but Claire's seat was full of glass, and she had to sit in the child's chair located between the driver and passenger seats. He started the car and made his way out, using the ditch as a road.

"What was he looking for?"

"Probably the military radio communicator. We were lucky to get there before the thief got his hands on it."

They drove back home, and Nick cleaned up the shattered glass. He closed the window opening with duct tape and some plastic bags as Claire got in.

They didn't have the internet or a TV, so they turned on the portable radio and the military radio communicator to hear the news. As they listened to the story, they used tape to seal the gaps around the door that could allow the toxic ashes inside.

From the radio, they could hear sporadic updates: *'There are so many things happening and little information coming from the official channels of communication that people are panicking everywhere. Chaos seems to reign in the United States and on Canada's west coast.*

We don't have detailed information about the situation in Hawaii because the ashes have cut out almost all communications, and here, in our LA studio, the internet is down. It feels like the ashes can move us toward the Stone Age.

We received some news from the remaining channels of communication still operating in our globe. The ashes from other erupting volcanos are now travelling everywhere, and, due to the jet streams, it's just a matter of time before the entire world will be engulfed by the darkness... this isn't ending well.

Our team is now evacuating the studio as well. If we get the internet connection back, I'll bring you news from my virtual studio at home. Good luck to everyone," the radio anchor said soberly as static filled the airwaves.

They turned off the radio, sat by the small table face-to-face and looked at each other in silence. Outside, the wind began to blow. Claire crossed her arms over the table, laid her head on them, and closed her eyes. She heard the wind fading into the distance as if she was leaving Earth until the sound disappeared, and Claire knew she was no longer in the cabin.

#

Gavriel arrived at the hospital and made his way to the reception. He saw Hallan walking toward him at a slow pace. Hallan looked into his eyes and shook his head as his head hung down.

"What? What happened?" Gavriel asked. But Hallan was silent, and his eyes were wet. Gavriel tried to move around him to make his way to where his grandmother might be, but he was blocked by Hallan, who grabbed his shoulders.

"Don't! She is unrecognizable. Besides, they removed her body from the room already because they don't know the cause. Safety precautions, they said."

"It can't be!" He was agitated, and tears started to come down. Unable to control his emotions, he began to cry. It was the first time he'd had a breakdown like this. He kept crying for some time on Hallan's shoulder.

"What happened?" he asked.

"Doctors don't know why, but all her internal organs melted."

"It's the drink she brought from Zyon. I'm sure of it!"

"Yes, it was. The Novus Mundurian defence system detected our moves into the planet and activated countermeasures. Some people who had been flagged by the system were targeted, and your grandma was one of the targets," Hallan said, looking beyond Gavriel's eyes as if something else had caught his attention.

"What do you mean our moves into the planet? What do you know about the drink?" Gavriel said, confused. Hallan directed his gaze toward the end of the building. He was pointing something out to Gavriel.

Gavriel turned back and saw a large door open in the air, right by the end of the building top, as if there was a portal connecting two worlds. Soldiers carrying laser guns came through the door.

"This is what I mean by detected our moves into the planet. This is the military intervention I have told you about," Hallan said, grabbing Gavriel by his arm, and dragging him toward the door.

"Military intervention, how come? he asked Hallan. "What's going on here?" he challenged soldier coming toward him, but the soldier shoved him aside and moved on.

Another soldier with a gun strapped to his shoulder came near them and demanded that they raise their hands and identify themselves. He used a device to read the rings on their fingers for identification.

The soldier made a military salute to Hallan. "Thanks for your cooperation Captain. Is this man with you?" he said, now looking at Gavriel.

"Yes, he is," Hallan said, holding Gavriel by his arm.

"Thanks again, Captain," and the soldier made his way toward the hospital.

"What's going on here? Why don't you tell me?" he kept asking Hallan while they were approaching the large open door in the air. Hallan stopped and looked at another soldier by the door.

"Noah, is that you?" Gavriel said, watching the soldier whose arms were crossed behind his back, and was looking at the main entrance of the building, overseeing the operation.

"Gavriel? I'm happy to see you, my friend!" he said with a broad smile.

"Hallan can explain everything to you while we proceed with our operation. All I can say now is that there's a revolution happening, and we came here to get medical supplies."

"Are you nuts? You guys don't have a chance against the army!"

"We know what we are doing. Now, for the sake of our friendship, get inside the spaceship, we can talk later!" Noah said, turning his back and moving away. On his way, he stopped to speak to some soldiers who were coming in his direction, and the three of them ran into the hospital.

"Let's get in, this is not the time to discuss academic war strategies," Hallan said, taking Gavriel by his arm and getting into what seemed like a spaceship. They found a place to sit while other people were boarding the vessel.

"As Noah said, we can explain the details later. For now, I'll give you the big picture. You don't need to come with us and are free to go anytime. However, you are an essential part of our mission. Right now, we are picking up some people on this planet, some medical supplies, and equipment. Afterward, we are heading to Earth as fast as we can go."

"Are we leaving? What about Mom? What about Lennah? If grandma was killed, Lennah might be in danger too, because she drank the golden drink as well."

"Your mom is safe. There is another vessel like this gathering people on the north resort, your mom is one of them, and they will join us later on. I'll ask someone to pick up Lennah while we wait here," Hallan said and went to talk to a soldier by the control center door. He came back and said, "They are sending a unit to her address right now."

"Ok, you said that our life is about decisions, and I can make one about this, operation, or whatever it is. Can you please tell me what is going on and how do you know Noah?" he said, looking into Hallan's eyes.

"I made the arrangements for Noah to receive military training on Acqua. I'm his dad's friend and," Hallan stopped talking when he saw a man escorted by two soldiers coming into the vessel.

Gavriel looked toward the door and saw agent P1999 getting into the spaceship.

"We need him too. I was warned by Theena that he knows way more than what he has said to you. Anyway, we've been trying to convince Novus Mundus to accept immigrants from our planet and save our population. Two years ago, we detected that something was changing in our star system that could speed up Sion's destruction, but last month we hacked communication among honeycombs and found out that a collision between Novus Mundus and Zyon is on course right now, so we had to change plans. Our army is seizing one of those spaceships under construction, and we a heading to Earth. That was the Elite-7 group plan, we are just taking ownership of it."

"That doesn't solve the problem for the population or for Novus Mundus and the Peer planets. You are just replacing the passengers," Gavriel said, mocking Hallan.

"No, we have a plan to rescue a third of the population by relocating them to a nearby planet temporarily. It's a rough world, but Sion has the technology to keep people alive until we move to a better body."

"You are saying that two-thirds will perish?"

"Unless there is a miracle, yes, two-thirds will die. But our options are limited now, and this is better than only saving two thousand people, as per the Elite-7 plan."

Lennah entered the ship, supported by her parents. A man dressed as a doctor took her in his arms and went to another room, followed by Lennah's mom, while her dad came to talk to Gavriel.

"She was throwing up at home, but she is better now. The vital signs are okay. What's going on here?" he asked.

"Gavriel can talk to you about this later," Hallan answered when the doors were closed, and the spaceship started to move. He continued, "For now just make sure Lennah receives attention," and the man moved away.

"You have two major problems right now; "Gavriel said, "Firstly, you can't fight against Novus Mundus's army, it is too risky. Secondly, those spaceships on the micro planet aren't ready. They need Zxylon and other parts."

"We know we can't fight against Novus Mundus, we aren't stupid, and we just want to run away from them. We developed a technology to make space vessels invisible, and that's how we invaded Novus Mundus under the radar. Our team of engineers and workers who helped to build those spaceships on Acqua had prepared everything in advance. They have commandeered one vessel and are heading to Zyon to load Zxylon, and then they are heading to Earth."

"But how are you guys planning to run away from Novus Mundus's army and keep your population safe?"

"They won't be able to track us down, and locally our soldiers are prepared to protect both Zyon and Sion. You might be aware that we destroyed the main center of operations to shut down the organic waves communication, so Novus Mundus is vulnerable, and they won't take risks before the connection has been restored."

"So, you knew about everything. I could have died at the government building explosion," Gavriel said upset.

"No, we waited for you to leave the building. We also will spread the news about the collision of the planets among the Novus Mundurians population. Novus Mundus army will have enough local problems to deal with, before thinking about fighting on another planet. Are you coming or not?" Hallan asked with signs of rush in his voice.

"I don't know, I wish I were dreaming," Gavriel said, putting his right hand on his forehead.

"We are pretty sure your dreams use the structure of the organic wave, so we need you to help us decode it. We will have help from our scientists, and others we are 'borrowing' from Novus Mundus. We hope to decipher it during our voyage. The other idea is to use genetically modified genes to increase our life to three hundred years so we would be able to live on Earth for real, not just in dreams," Hallan said, smiling at Gavriel.

"There is no point in staying, I'm in," Gavriel said, looking into Hallan's' eyes.

"You made the right choice. We can talk about the details later. Right now, I need to go to the control center, and later on, I'll introduce you to the crew members, enjoy the trip."

Gavriel looked sad and lost in his thoughts. Everything was happening so fast that he wondered about what was real. The loss of grandma was weighing on his soul, and now Gavriel was leaving everything behind. He felt losing his sense of belonging, and Claire came to his mind.

'*What an irony, Earth, a planet that I despised as a place to live just two nights ago now is set to save my life. Maybe this is all an illusion. Maybe one day I will wake up and realize that it was all a big dream. A dream where we were supposed to learn and be refined, so we can fit into the masterpiece of the universe,*' he thought.

Suddenly something sparked in his mind. He stood up quickly and went to talk to agent P1999, who was seated in a cocoon chair in the back of the room.

"It seems like destiny has planned to keep us connected," Gavriel said, squatting by agent P1999's chair.

"Whatever it is, it looks like fate in your hands, for now," agent P1999 said, without significant interest in the conversation.

"I'm as powerless as you, and had no idea about this coup, but that's a discussion for another time. For now, I'd like to have just one answer from you, and I'd appreciate it if you would tell me the truth. Is it possible to implement the extended life technology on Earth's people remotely, I mean just by giving them instructions?" Gavriel asked, looking deep into P1999's eyes.

"Of course it is, they are human like us."

"Maybe I wasn't clear. Is it possible to use this technology now if we were able to have real-time communication?"

"If they have the technology to manipulate DNA, yes it's feasible," agent P1999 said. "But you won't get anything from me, not for free."

"Thanks," Gavriel said, standing up and asking the soldier seated beside agent P1999 chair, "is there a place where I can rest?"

"Yes, upstairs there is a cupola with some reclining chairs, where you can also have an OutSpace view," answered the soldier, pointing to an opening in the corner of the room.

"Thanks," Gavriel said, heading toward a floating tube. At the cupola, he lay down on a recliner, facing the stars, holding a broad smile on his face.

His eyes stared into the distance, and slowly shut. The surrounding sounds faded until a warm silence filled his mind. He found himself facing a long gravel road, with thousands of small daisies on either side under a sunny day. The warm sunlight filling the atmosphere, and the sweet fragrance coming from the fields told him that it was Earth. He couldn't see the end of the road, but he knew it was a journey of a hundred years of solitude, nevertheless, at the end of it, someone was waiting for him.

CHAPTER 19– *To Dream and to Live Again*

CLAIRE FELT HER EYES OPENING, but a glowing light makes her blink a few times, yet the brilliance lingered. She squeezed her eyelids in an attempt to block out the light as a sharp sound invaded the room and remained for a long time, pausing only for a few seconds, until the sound of a door-knob opening was heard.

The light over her eyes disappeared, and she felt someone lifting her eyelids and dripping a liquid. A slight initial pain was replaced by a numbness in the area.

"Call Dr. Jenkins and tell him that the eyelid motion detector alarm went off," she heard a firm, but a low-pitched female voice.

"Good morning, Dr. Jenkins. It's the nurse from ward 21B, the alarm from Claire Luan's intensive care unit fired ... Ok, Thanks." He's on the hospital premises and will be here in five minutes," said another female voice.

"It's incredible! She was pronounced dead long ago and now came back to life," Claire heard followed by a sound of "Shh."

She felt herself waking up from a long night's sleep. Her eyelids trembled again, and she felt a warm, soft light slapping her cheek on the right side, so she turned her head slightly to the opposite side. A warm scented breeze invaded her nostrils, suggesting she was inside a room with open windows and felt herself floating in a mystical place.

The intimate moment was interrupted by the sound of rubber soles walking on a polished floor and stopping beside her. An inconvenient shadow blocked the heat of the sunlight, which caused her to turn her head toward the shadow as she tried to open her eyes. The blurred vision slowly revealed the shape of a person in front of her, and she found herself lying on a half-tilted bed. After a moment, she clearly identified a man dressed in a gray apron, standing at the side of the bed.

Claire tried to lift her body a little more but found no strength to do so. The man by the bed seemed to be in his sixties, but the thin silhouette, gray hair and rare white beard on black skin, might underestimate his supposition, yet she did not recognize him.

"Good morning Claire, it looks like you had a good night," the man said, moving away from the bed to pick up a pen from a small table in the corner of the room.

"Hi, good morning, what am I doing here, the ashes covered the planet? I was affected, and I'm in a hospital? Who are you?" She asked, blocking the sunlight with her hand, as she tried to keep her eyes open.

"Let's break it down, I'm Dr. Jenkins, Steve Jenkins and I've been one of your doctors for the last three years," he said, going to the window and closing the horizontal blinds a bit to keep the sunlight away from Claire's eyes.

"What you mean, taking care of me three for three years? I've been here for three years, are you sure?" She asked, feeling the room roll.

"Absolutely sure, Dr. Jenkins quietly said as she bent a little to look into Claire's eyes with a medical pen," and your eyes are perfect, with no side effects due to the micro-electronic screen," he said.

"Micro-electronic screen, what do you mean?" Claire asked, blinking after the medical examination.

"It's a new device we use in your treatment. Tell me what you remember," Dr. Jenkins asked, putting his left arm over the metal headboard while frantically rubbing the pen with his right thumb.

"I remember... living in Miami and having lots of dreams," she said confused.

"What about Chile, what do you remember?" Asked Dr. Jenkins

"I left Chile two years ago after an earthquake, and I don't understand why you said that you are taking care of me for three years.

"Very well," said Dr. Jenkins, without expressing any emotion. "You said you had many dreams; can you summarize them for me?

"Yes, I can, but you need to hear the details if you want to find some meaning in them, and it will take a long time."

"Just give me a summary, and I'll ask for more details if necessary," and he took a small paper notebook in the pocket of his apron, indicating he would take notes.

"Okay, I had a lot of dreams about earthquakes and an alien civilization as well. Apparently, the aliens were aware of many problems on our planet, and they warned us that the system that supports our society was about to collapse, I was engaged in a mission to help our society avoid a catastrophe, and I woke up in this room, "Claire finished and looked at Dr. Jenkins.

"Hum, I can tell you that in your real life you met Johanna, the psychologist, Nick from NASA, your aunt Mirna, and many others," Dr. Jenkins said with a small smile, "but we need to talk more about these aliens, I'm curious about it. "

"How do you know these people?" She asked, raising her eyebrows.

"I know almost everything about your life after the earthquake in Chile because we actually artificially built most of the events," Dr. Jenkins said and noticed the change in Claire's expression.

Jaw dropped, she raised her hand, as if she was asking for a pause in what he was saying. At this moment, she realized that there was a large scar on the palm of her hand, and fixed her eyes on it.

"I have good news for you, but you need to be patient, listen quietly to digest what I am about to say. Can you do that?" Dr. Jenkins asked.

"I think so, but artificial construction of my life is a bit strange. This is not another dream, and I'm awake, right? "She asked raising her eyebrows and looking around.

"You are well, and this is real life, only the reality you experienced in the last three years is not quite real. You had an accident during an earthquake in Chile years ago, and the scar in your hand is the result of that accident.

In fact, this is the first time you are awake. Most of the memories of your life, after the accident were fabricated and implanted in your mind using artificial intelligence technology, "Dr. Jenkins said in a calm voice, but frantically rubbing the pen between his fingers.

Claire stretched her arms out to her sides and touched the bed with her hands. She looked around with slow movements of her upper body as if trying to gauge the reality in which she was.

"So, my life was not real?" Gavriel was not real? "She asked looking at him in a fragile voice," Listen, doctor, I had so many strange dreams, and many challenges, that I do not believe this was artificial. Are you saying it was all a lie? I want to talk to my aunts and my father, "she said shakily and her eyes watered, suggesting she was about to burst into tears.

"The life you had in Miami was all fabricated, your father died during the earthquake in Chile, and I'm sorry for that, but you're alive, and that's what matters now. Trust me, everything will be fine," he said in a soft voice, leaning her body toward her and lightly touching her hand.

"How can I believe you?" "I do not even know you. Where are my relatives?" She challenged him, pulling her hand away from his touch, tears rolling down her face.

"I understand if you do not trust me now, time will show you the truth," he said, withdrawing his hand.

"If you said that my life was really something implanted in my mind, it was not my life, isn't it? "She challenged as she wiped the tears with her hands.

"Not quite. We implanted some information into your mind, but eventually, you took control of the story. We've also never given you information about another planet or civilization, and that's intriguing me, but this is a subject we'll discuss later, now you have to rest, "he said looking into her eyes.

"No, there's something wrong, I want to get out of here right now," she said trying to move, but could not, because there was a tube of serum attached to her arm.

"Calm down Claire, you need to avoid stress," Dr. Jenkins put his hand on her shoulder.

"So, the alien environment and its characters were not created by you? What really happened?" Claire said in a hoarse voice.

"Artificial intelligence, known as AI, has evolved over the past three years at a pace that no one could imagine. Many projects are using this technology all over the world, and this is one of them. "

"But how did I come to terms with this project?" She asked, her voice cracking and tears rolling down her face again.

"The prospect of you being alive today was remote, using conventional medical resources," Dr. Jenkins said firmly.

"What do you mean? Sorry, I do not know why I cannot stop crying," she said as Dr. Jenkins took some tissue from the bedside table and gave it to her.

"Do not worry about tears, it's a natural reaction of your body after a long period of stress. Either way, your comatose was a persistent vegetative state with some brain damage, which means complete recovery was impossible using known medical procedures."

"But how did I get here?" Claire asked, sobbing.

"I went to Chile as a humanitarian aid right after the earthquake. I found you in a coma in a hospital and asked permission from your relatives in Miami to apply a new procedure based on a theory I developed."

"Ah, a guinea pig, you mean?" She said still emotional.

"Not exactly, if I were wrong, nothing would change for you. At best, you would wake up with permanent brain damage, and in the worst of scenarios, you would be in a coma forever. But I was right, and you're awake, no brain damage and totally conscious," the Doctor said and smiled.

"In my project, we created a complete connection between a computer and your brain to regenerate the affected areas. It worked magnificently, as you can see, "Dr. Jenkins said, smiling again.

"During that time," continued the doctor, "it seems that you have improved your English skills because sometimes you used to speak loudly as if you were asleep. Sometimes it felt like you were having a normal conversation with someone else, even though the room was empty, we recorded everything. "

"Having a normal conversation, with whom?" She asked curiously.

"We do not know, you have to tell us. However, I think you were talking to characters we created for your virtual world, like Nick Martins, your aunt Mirna, and a psychologist named Johanna Smith."

"What happens now? I'm an android? Am I going to have a normal life again?" She asked, eyebrows drawn, her nose wrinkled and lips pursed as if to control her emotions.

"This is something we have to learn together. We will monitor your recovery to see if your brain has been able to create something totally new and embedded in the artificial world we have created. Right now, your mind is under your control, and I believe it will be so without any side effect caused by the artificial world we have created."

"So, I'm going home? Do I have a house?"

"You'll be going home soon. You can stay with your aunt if you want, and she will be happy to receive you. The hospital will contact her and schedule a visit for tomorrow. Today you have to rest.

"It looks good, and at the same time strange. I'm feeling a bit confused, "Claire said in a low voice, shaking her head, as she stared at the foot of the bed and wiped her eyes.

"Do not worry, this is normal. I did not expect to see you awake and jumping up and down. You're three years behind your real life so it will take a while to get your thoughts cleared up, but it will be worth it. Do you believe me? "He asked, raising his eyebrows.

"Do I have options?" she said, voice still trapped.

"I'm sorry for all that I had to pass you on, but this shock was necessary to determine if you'd be in full possession of your faculties. I can foresee many people coming to visit you, including the media, so you need to be prepared. I need to go now, and I'll be back tomorrow to discuss the next steps of your recovery.

The nurse is coming to remove some medical devices from your body so you can eat from your mouth. We will also continue the physiotherapy sessions to return to your regular movements. Any question?"

"I think I'm fine for now," I said looking at Dr. Jenkins.

"Okay, this is an emergency switch," Dr. Jenkins said pointing to a small metal rope on the headboard just above Claire's head "and this is the television remote if you want to update on your new world, "he said, handing Claire an electronic device and left the room, saying goodbye.

Moments later, a nurse came to remove the needle from the serum and the tubes from her body. She was able to take a few sips of water, something she had wanted since she woke up.

"You look the same from the first day you came to the hospital, you just need a sunbath to regain your natural tan colour. You also gained some stature, the last time we measured, you were 70 inches, a bit taller than when you came to the hospital. "

"Taller? Wow, it's not all bad," she said.

"See, just good news from now on. I'll bring something light for dinner in about three hours. Now you must rest for a faster recovery, "said the nurse, and left the room.

"Yes, thank you," she said, watching the nurse leave.

Claire used the remote control and turned on the TV. He looked at the screen showing images of a large luminous object that circled the planet's skies every hour, and panic set on the streets.

"What?" She said confused.

The report was interrupted by breaking news.

'Direct from the Kremlin is speaking the President of Russia on this object that also crosses the skies of that country. If this object is really an American artifact, the risk of a nuclear confrontation between the two countries is very high, as both have escalated their threat of confrontation lately,' the reporter said, releasing the Russian president's speech.

"The Russian people will not be intimidated by this new American threat and demand explanations of what it considers to be a new weapon of mass destruction. If there is no demonstration in the next twenty-four hours, the country does not rule out the possibility of launching preemptive nuclear attacks against the United States, and this country will be reduced to ashes." Concluded the Russian president, when the images turned to the luminous object, now motionless in the sky.

"Ashes," she whispered, eyes wide opened, and staring at the TV screen.

THE END